Praise for
Can't Say it Went to Plan

'Gabrielle Tozer has done it again! Carving out a story about the precious and precarious in-between times for teens, on the cusp of so much and filled with all the joy and terror that brings! In *Can't Say it Went to Plan*, she's taking rites of passage in teenagerdom and giving them a hilarious and honest platform, and there's something here for everyone. It is tender, true and wonderful – as all of Tozer's coming-of-age stories are.'

Danielle Binks, author of *The Year the Maps Changed*
and editor and contributor to *Begin, End, Begin*

'A delightful romp with such relatable and poignant characters. I had a blast spending the week with Zoë, Samira and Dahlia.'

Wai Chim, author of *The Surprising Power
of a Good Dumpling*

'Gabrielle has written a story with so much joy, humour and heart. It was a holiday in the very best way, and I found myself cheering for Zoë, Samira and Dahlia. I loved the ensemble of support characters – they were real and funny; the sort of friends who will help readers discern and aim for real friendship in their own lives. So! In the spirit of the novel …

5 Things I Loved About This Story
Its glorious energy
Fast, furious, funny dialogue
Characters who make mistakes
The Peachies!
The joy at its beating heart.'

Kirsty Eagar, author of *Summer Skin*

'Gabrielle Tozer vividly brings to life the magic and madcap mishaps of the infamous rite-of-passage that is Schoolies. Foam parties, friendship breakdowns, famous pop stars, and unforgettable moments collide in this truly contemporary coming-of-age novel, led by three fabulous female protagonists.'

Tara Eglington, author of *My Best Friend is a Goddess*
and *The Long Distance Playlist*

'An ode to Schoolies with a great big heart. I loved it. Absolutely nails the rollercoaster of emotions that is being eighteen.'

Jenna Guillaume, author of *What I Like About Me*
and *You Were Made for Me*

'Nobody captures what it's like to stand on the edge of the rest of your life quite like Gabrielle Tozer. *Can't Say it Went to Plan* is honest and affirming, and an absolute joy to read.'

Will Kostakis, award-winning author of
The Sidekicks and *Monuments*

'Tozer rejects the moral panic surrounding Schoolies. Instead, this novel serves up a heart-warming celebration of the power of sisterhood and chosen family. Rather than presenting teens as either trouble, or troubled, she also explores the bravery they demonstrate as they leave the structure and stability of school and dive headfirst into adulthood.'

Dannielle Miller, CEO Enlighten Education,
parenting author and columnist

'Life is full of transitions, but the end of school has to be one of the most significant. This book perfectly captures the momentousness of finishing high school – the love, grief, fear and giddy joy of it all. It's Gabrielle Tozer at her finest, deftly painting complex characters and tugging on heartstrings. I loved every moment.'

Lili Wilkinson, author of *After the Lights Go Out*
and *The Erasure Initiative*

can't say it went to plan

gabrielle tozer

Angus&Robertson
An imprint of HarperCollins*Children'sBooks*

Angus&Robertson

An imprint of HarperCollins*Publishers*, Australia

HarperCollins*Publishers*

Australia • Brazil • Canada • France • Germany • Holland • Hungary
India • Italy • Japan • Mexico • New Zealand • Poland • Spain • Sweden
Switzerland • United Kingdom • United States of America

First published in Australia in 2021
by HarperCollins*Publishers* Australia Pty Limited
ABN 36 009 913 517
harpercollins.com.au

A catalogue record for this book is available
from the National Library of Australia

ISBN 978 1 4607 6063 5 (paperback)

Cover design and illustration by Holly Ovenden
Author photograph by Tayla Martin
Typeset in Sabon LT Std by Kirby Jones

For my KHS and UC favourites,
thank you for all the adventures

And for Mum and Dad,
who couldn't sleep for the seventeen days
I was at Schoolies

A note from the publisher

'Schoolies' or 'Schoolies Week' refers to the Australian tradition of high-school graduates having a week-long summer vacation following the end of their final exams in late November and early December. Schoolies often takes place at the coast and is filled with lots of partying and fun. It is considered a rite of passage by many students and is often months in the planning.

A note from the author

The final year of school is often filled with the highest highs and lowest lows, and, for many students, can feel like a pressure cooker.

It did for me.

Can't Say it Went to Plan is a love letter to those who make mistakes and dream big, even though it feels like nothing is going to plan and their inner monologue is raging at them to give up.

Keep going.

School's out.
No parents.
No curfews.
No rules.

Day 1

Zoë

Zoë is still haunted by the final exam. Sweaty palms. Ticking clock. The extra page she didn't see until there was only three minutes to go. She remembers her frozen brain, like she was stuck on pause while everyone else was on fast-forward, and the page filled with nothing but abstract doodling in the top-right corner. How the other students in her biology class exhaled with relief when they put down their pens, but she ran out and sobbed in a bathroom stall.

She takes a deep breath, shaking off the memory. 'I'm heading off,' she calls into the belly of the house. 'First stop Luca's, next stop paradise!'

'Zoë Russo, wait, please!'

She turns, suitcase in hand, to see her father leaning against the living room doorframe. 'That's Dr Zoë Russo to you,' she says with a smile.

'Not yet.' He grins back. 'Only a million years of studying medicine to complete first. Any early acceptance news yet, Chickpea?'

'Maybe this week,' she says, tired eyes blinking behind her cat-eye prescription glasses.

Her father pats her gently on the shoulder. 'You'll hear soon enough. Now, Mum wants to see you. It's important so I'll fix you some breakfast.'

'Dad, she's already lectured me about reapplying sunscreen every few hours. Message received. Besides, I'm eating at Luca's. Aunty Elena always serves an out-of-this-world feast, even better than Aunty Caro's, so I better go before Violet eats all the pastries.'

'Come on,' her father says, and guides her into the living room where her mother is perched on the couch watching the morning news. She's nibbling her thumbnail and curled in on herself.

'Sit, please, Zoë.' She doesn't stop staring at the television.

Zoë follows her gaze. The news segment has *Teens gone wild* running along the banner at the bottom of the screen, paired with footage of young people with fiery red sunburn wearing skimpy bikinis and board shorts. They're in nightclubs, at beaches, in enormous resort pools, at glowstick-packed raves. They're kissing, they're poking out their tongues at the camera, they're licking salt out of bellybuttons before dunking shots. It's obvious they're drunk and there's nothing Zoë can say to disguise it.

'This is the week you and your cousins want to attend?' her mother mutters. '*This*?'

'Yes, technically,' Zoë says, cringing as a group of boys moon the TV camera. 'Luca, Violet and I will stick together, and Prakash and Akito from school are staying at the same resort.'

'Why would a good boy like Prakash want to attend this?' Mrs Russo asks. 'The Patels would never allow it.'

'Not everyone is as strict as the Russos,' Zoë blurts out.

Mr Russo scoffs. 'We're not strict.'

'I'll never look at the Patels the same way,' Mrs Russo says, shaking her head. 'Outrageous.'

Zoë steps forward. 'Don't judge them. Prakash has worked hard all year — all his life! We all have.' She sighs. 'He's already got early acceptance into media studies in the city.'

'And you haven't heard anything yet,' Mrs Russo reminds her. 'Nothing is certain. Who knows what you'll do or where you'll be?'

Zoë's jaw hardens. Her first university preference — nicknamed Number One — is all the way across the country and its faraway location is a sore point with her family. But it boasts some of the highest-performing graduates among its alumni, which makes it Zoë's coveted top spot. Number Two and Number Three are also prestigious institutions but their campuses are closer to home with slightly more modest reputations.

'Mum, I'll hear soon. What else do you want from me? I did my best.'

'That's why I cannot believe you want to flush your life away on partying and public nudity,' Mrs Russo snaps.

'*What?* Why would you even think we'd be naked?' Zoë asks, then glances at the television. A group of girls are baring their pixelated chests to the camera.

Mrs Russo purses her lips. 'No. No. That's it. Not happening.'

Zoë's grip tightens on her suitcase handle. 'What do you mean?'

'I was uncomfortable when I thought it was a small trip away with your cousins — but this ... *No.* Your aunties might be okay with it, but I won't let you.'

Zoë and her two cousins were born within four months of each other, making them as close as siblings, but their parents' views on the world have differed since day one.

'Everything's booked, it has been for ages,' Zoë says, standing her ground. 'You said I could go.'

Mrs Russo sighs. 'It may have been what we discussed but—'

'No, it's what we agreed on! I've paid for everything — it's non-refundable.' Zoë's eyes well up. 'Dad? Say something!'

'I'm sorry, Chickpea. You heard your mum.'

Zoë's ponytail whips behind her as she storms over to the display cabinet crammed with her and her older sister Greta's trophies and certificates. Greta hasn't lived at home for five years — she's away completing a degree in advanced astronomy and astrophysics — but her awards still have pride of place.

Zoë pulls out her chemistry trophy from the back of the cabinet. 'I topped that class!' she says. 'And that one, and that one, and that one,' as she tosses more awards onto the couch next to her mother. 'I was school captain, on the football team, in the musical … and I got the highest marks! Maybe even in the state. Sure, I didn't get into the Gifted and Talented Program like your beloved Greta, but I—'

'Your sister has nothing to do with this,' Mr Russo says. 'Calm down.'

'Don't tell me to calm down!' Zoë rages. 'You have no idea what I've been through this year! I did everything you expected. I studied so hard that my eyes felt like they were going to fall out of my head. I even did extra shifts at the supermarket to pay for this trip so it doesn't add any strain on you. And I didn't complain once! Aunty Elena and Aunty Caro have covered every cent for Luca and Violet, did you know that?'

Mrs Russo switches off the news. 'What your father's sisters choose to do with their children has no standing in this house. My word is final. I'm sorry if you're upset, Zoë.'

Zoë's cheeks burn with anger. 'This was my one thing. Dad!'

'Why don't we arrange a night away with the younger cousins to the lake this week?' Mr Russo suggests. 'That might be fun.'

Zoë groans. 'They're seven and nine. Yes, Dad, while my best friends go on a holiday without me, babysitting the kids by a puddle of brown water sounds like heaven.'

Mrs Russo's lips are pursed into a thin line. 'Unpack your bag and let's have some breakfast,' she says quietly. 'There'll be more opportunities to see everyone.'

'Dad?' Zoë tries again. 'Dad … please?'

He lowers his head, unable to make eye contact.

'I hate you!'

Zoë storms into her bedroom, slamming the door behind her. She hurls her suitcase into the corner, swipes her textbooks off the desk and climbs into bed without taking off her ballet flats. She burrows down into the soft mattress, dragging pillows beneath the doona to curl her body around, and tries to shut out the sound of her parents arguing.

She opens up the group chat. It's got the five of them through exams, and long stretches of holidays stuck with the family, and sick days, and mind-numbing history lessons, and Saturday nights at home with nothing to do.

The messages flood in.

WHAT DO YOU MEAN YOU'RE NOT COMING????

Aunty Rosette has lost her mind!

r u serious?!

i'll send mum over to talk to your dad. This is not ok

It won't work, Luca — he's on her side

Are you trying to prank us?

No, P, I wish, RIP social life

i'll smuggle you to the beach in my suitcase k?

thanks Akito

(Might take you up on that actually)

Zo, this can't be happening

I KNOW

We love you

Love you too x

* * *

Five minutes later, Zoë's mother leads her out of the bedroom and into the kitchen. She places a bowl of muesli, fresh fruit and yoghurt in front of Zoë, who just stares at it.

'It's better this way,' Mrs Russo says. 'You'll understand when you have children of your own.'

'When I ... Mum!' Zoë rolls her eyes. 'I don't want kids. What I want is to go away with my friends.'

'We can't always get what we want,' Mr Russo says. 'And look, your mother and I have work today but maybe we can take a few days off later in the week. Have a fun time as a family. You'll see, Chickpea, you'll forget all about this.'

Zoë sits at the table until breakfast is finished, cringing at her father's loud chewing and her mother's scraping of her spoon against the ceramic bowl. Once it's over, she returns to her bedroom. Too upset to do anything else, she curls up under the sheet and falls into a restless sleep.

When she wakes up, the house is still. She checks her phone. Her parents would've already left for work.

She turns over to lie on her back, her side, her front. She tries the warm side of the pillow, then the cool side. Nothing feels right, so she gets out of bed and massages the kinks in her neck and the tightness in her arms.

As she rests her leg across the desk to stretch her hamstrings, like a ballerina at the barre, she spots her luggage in the corner. Her chest tightens at the thought of unpacking it. She'll be folding her sundresses back into drawers while her cousins argue over which music playlist to listen to in the car.

Zoë swears under her breath, even though her parents aren't even at home. Her mind jumps a week into the future when everyone will be returning from the trip, relaxed, recharged and even more bronzed.

She reaches for her phone.

Left yet, Luca?

She traces over the frames of her glasses as she wills him to reply. But there's nothing. Not even the teasing three dots.

She swears again, louder this time. Then, body surging with adrenaline, she grabs her suitcase and strides through the house.

She pauses in the hallway to look at the framed photos on the wall. There's a shot from when the family visited Zoë's great-uncle in Cefalù, Sicily: she's a baby strapped to her mother's chest, her dark tufts of hair poking out the top of the carrier, while a young Greta plays in the golden sand with their father, and fishing boats bob in the nearby port. Beside it is a snap from Greta's high school graduation five years earlier. Mrs Russo is beaming and her hand rests on Greta's shoulder. Their shiny brown hair and glittering eyes are mirror images of each other.

'Sorry,' Zoë mutters, before slipping out the side door.

Nothing matters except the sound of her feet and suitcase thumping against the uneven footpath. Nothing matters except getting to Luca's in time.

Samira

Day 1: 8.49am

Magic is in the air. It hits Samira the second she walks into the train station. Groups of students hang out on every platform, their laughter and singing echoing around the concourse. She strides on, dragging her father's old suitcase with one hand while keeping her oversized handbag pressed to her hip with the other. Her mum and grandmother struggle to keep up behind her.

Samira checks her itinerary for the fourth time since leaving the car. It's colour-coded with a daily theme and matching stickers. Horse-riding, ziplining, snorkelling, manicures, island-hopping, clubbing, foam parties, beach parties. Parties, parties, parties.

She turns on her heel to rush back and embrace her grandmother's shoulders. 'This is going to be *amazing*, my Teta! I told you about the horse-riding, didn't I? I haven't done it since I was a kid.'

'Your great-grandmother Nafisa broke both her legs riding a horse,' her mum chimes in. 'That's all I'll say.'

'Bones everywhere,' Teta adds.

'That is gross and ... wait!' Samira swears. Her mum purses her lips in disapproval. 'The party passes! Where are they?' She rifles through her handbag. 'They're not here!'

She drops to her knees, sweeping her long mahogany waves over one shoulder as she tips out the contents of her handbag. Cocktail umbrellas, a small portable speaker, three types of chips, an eye mask and a paper printout confirming a hotel booking for her birthday spill onto the tiles.

'What's wrong, my girl?' Teta asks.

Samira doesn't need a mirror to know her cheeks are stained red. 'The party passes! Where are they?'

'Breathe, Sammy,' her mum says.

Samira leaps to her feet. 'But the passes are the key to this week being perfect.'

'Saint Anthony, Saint Anthony, please look around,' Teta murmurs. 'Samira's passes are lost and they cannot be found.'

Her mum sighs. 'Spare us the dramatics, you two. Sammy, by "passes" do you mean *these*?' She flicks the laminated cards swinging from lanyards around Samira's neck.

Samira beams. 'Thank you! These passes are like gold.' She waves the itinerary in her mother's face. 'Anoush wanted a snorkelling trip so we're going on a snorkelling trip. Zain wanted a foam party so we're going to a foam party.'

'How I wish you were this enthusiastic about your studies and future,' her mum says. She does an amusingly accurate impersonation: *'I'm Sammy Makhlouf and I've spent months planning every detail!* It's always friends, and Zain, and parties. What about school? What about work?'

Samira rolls her eyes. 'Mum, you and the bakery will have my undivided attention when this week is over. You can give me *all* the shifts.'

Her mother manages a little Lebanese bakery nestled on a leafy green street off the main drag. Business has picked up since they moved to the city eleven months earlier, so Samira helps out on weekend mornings and after school, cleaning and prepping the bakery for the following day's trade.

'I know,' her mother says. 'And I do want you to have a good time this week, I do. I just …'

'Wish I was having a good time here with you?' Samira finishes.

That gets a smile. 'Exactly.' Her mother sighs. 'And I barely know these new friends. They could be serial killers.'

'You love Anoush.'

Her mother sniffs. 'I like her.'

'*Mum.*'

Anoush had been assigned to show Samira around the school campus when she'd transferred at the start of the year. Since then, Samira has been glued to Anoush and absorbed into her circle of friends. Anoush was moving away to study industrial design after school, but Samira knew they'd talk every day.

Her mum clears her throat, jolting Samira back to the present. 'Speaking of love ... you've been with Zain for nine months and I still haven't met his mother.'

'No-one does that here,' Samira says. 'And it's nearly *ten* months.' She smiles. 'Now I'd love to spend another eight hundred hours convincing you I'm fine, but everyone's waiting for me.'

Her mum pulls her in for a hug, and Teta envelops them both.

'How did you grow up so fast?' Samira's mum murmurs. 'I swear you were a toddler staggering around on beautiful, squishy legs just yesterday.'

'It's only seven days, and I still have beautiful, squishy legs,' Samira says with a wink. She pecks them both on the cheek. 'Things don't change that much. Although I will be another year older when you see me next. Probably not wiser.'

Her mum cups her face. 'Make good choices.'

'Go quickly before she changes her mind,' says Teta, squeezing Samira's hands. 'I never let her do anything this exciting.'

Samira walks towards the ticket gates and blows them a kiss over her shoulder. Her mum dabs at her eyes but waves her on.

'Love love love you! Best week ever!' Samira calls out, before barrelling through the gate into the maze of platforms.

A crowd of people with leis looped around their necks stride past. Samira's mouth cracks into a grin so wide it hurts a little. The mood is electric. In less than a minute she'll be with her people and, suddenly, anything feels possible.

* * *

She checks her ticket against the rolling information on the electronic screens around the station and makes her way to Platform One. She spots her group huddled around a table in the corner surrounded by luggage and beach umbrellas. As always, the girls are immaculately dressed with sleek hair and flawless nails. Anoush, Claire and Rashida nibble on bacon and egg muffins, while Mathieu is folded over with his head resting on the table. Zain isn't with them.

'Hey hey!' Samira says, suddenly self-conscious about her denim shorts. 'Early start to get here, huh? Everyone excited?'

The girls look up with bleary eyes framed by thick lash extensions.

'Hey, Samira,' Anoush mumbles with a yawn.

Claire grimaces. 'Who thought the train was a good idea?' She brushes crumbs off her flowing dress. 'This should be classified as torture.'

'Is it too late to book flights?' Rashida asks.

Mathieu utters a pained groan.

Samira blushes, fingertips reaching for her lanyard. She'd wanted to save everyone money to spend on their beach-house accommodation and activities-packed schedule so had chosen the cheapest train. No-one had cared when she'd checked with them before booking. Now, it feels like a problem.

'It'll be worth it, promise ... and I have everyone's party passes,' Samira volunteers in an attempt to shift the mood. 'They're, like, your most prized possession this week. You'll need them for the smash room this afternoon.'

'Nice,' Anoush says, taking hers and looping it around her neck. 'I'm going to slam a teapot so hard.' She turns to the girls. 'I hope we meet some hot guys this week. There's something about a beach holiday that's so romantic.'

Rashida winces, pointing at Mathieu scratching himself. 'We need fresh meat, one thousand per cent.'

Samira hands the passes out to the others, still standing because there isn't a chair for her. The group fall into silence, yawning and checking their phones.

Samira looks around. 'Where's Zain?'

Anoush points in the direction of Platform Two. Samira walks around the corner and finds Zain standing in front of a vending machine. As she gets closer, she sees his packet of chips is caught. His hands grasp each side of the machine and he shakes it, but the packet doesn't budge. He swears and runs his fingers through his tousled dark hair.

Samira bounds over and places her hands over his eyes. 'Guess who?'

Zain peels her hands off his face. 'Hey babe,' he says.

She leans in for a kiss but she gets caught in his backpack straps and his lips miss hers and catch her earlobe instead. They laugh awkwardly as they pull apart.

'Pumped for the trip?' Samira asks.

He covers a yawn. 'Yeah.'

'Me too. So much! But everyone seems flat.'

'The early start to get here was brutal.'

She cringes. 'Oh.'

'So how are you, babe?'

'It's the week. *The* week,' Samira says, arms flailing with excitement. 'I can't believe it, I can't.'

Mathieu saunters up behind them, holding out a half-empty bottle of orange juice. 'Yo, can't believe what? Oh shit, you told her already, man?' His eyes widen. 'Samira, I can't believe it either, none of us can, but some things aren't meant to be.'

There's a lingering pause. Samira looks to Zain for answers, but he avoids eye contact. She fiddles with her party pass. 'What's going on?'

'Mat, it's chill,' Zain says to Mathieu. A frozen fake smile is locked on his face.

'Tell me,' she says, wrapping the lanyard so tightly around her finger that it burns red.

Mathieu winces. 'I'll go catch up with the others. Unless you want some juice, Samira?' Zain glares at him. 'You know what, I'm out. Sorry, man. I'll be over there.'

Zain rolls his eyes as Mathieu lopes off. 'Great. Thanks.' His gaze fixes on a muddy footprint on the tiles.

Samira steps in closer. 'What am I missing?'

'My mind's everywhere,' Zain shakes his head. 'I don't know how to do this.'

Samira feels a burning sensation spread across her cheeks. 'You're dumping me?'

Silence. He kicks at the ground.

'Zain?'

'I hate the word "dumping". Maybe we could chill out for a bit?'

'That's the thing you say when you're too scared to break up with someone.' Her bottom lip quivers. 'You told me you wanted to be my *first*. I booked us a hotel for my birthday night. And you said you loved me, like, yesterday. Look!' Samira scrolls through her phone desperately. 'Well, I can't find the message now, but you said it. I know you did.'

The loudspeaker system interrupts her. The train is due in five minutes.

Zain groans. 'I didn't want it to go down like this, babe. Mathieu should've kept his mouth shut.'

'Is this so you can hook up with other girls?'

'I don't know! Maybe it's so we can *both* be with other people. It's your week too.'

'Don't pretend you're doing me a favour.' Samira's lip trembles again. 'I can't believe Mathieu knew before me.'

Zain hangs his head. 'Forget that. Let's try to stay friends, babe.'

'Stop calling me that.' Samira can't hold her emotions in any longer. 'Just leave me alone.'

Tears streaming down her cheeks, she makes her way back to the group. Claire's and Rashida's gazes stay low; Mathieu has filled them in.

Anoush walks over. 'What happened?'

'He broke up with me,' Samira says. She swipes away tears and stares at the black mascara staining her fingertips. 'We're over. He wants to be with other people.'

Anoush shakes her head. 'Oh, girl, I'm sorry. This is unbelievable.'

'I feel like a loser. Omigod, here I am planning this trip for us and ... bam! Dumped.' A knot hardens in her stomach. 'This is a nightmare, Anoush. How am I going to survive this week?'

Dahlia

Day 1: 12.38pm

Dahlia's head is as fuzzy as if it were dancing in the clouds. She's frozen in the plane aisle, unable to tear her gaze from the vacant seat next to Florence. Stevie's seat.

Dahlia's back teeth grind as she imagines a stranger squeezing past her to curl their body into the space where Stevie was supposed to be. She grasps at the fine gold chain with the 'S' pendant laced around her neck. It was given to her a year ago, just after the funeral, and she's only taken it off once.

There's a sharp dig in the small of her back. It's Kiko, nudging her forward to their row.

'You're with me, lady,' Kiko tells her. She checks her ticket then slides into the window seat behind Florence's row. 'Coming?' she asks.

Dahlia looks again at the empty seat next to Florence. 'But then Florence is by herself.'

Florence shrugs. 'It's the tickets' wishes. Well, for now. The air-con is freezing so I'll need a warm body to spoon for some of this trip.'

'This is what a two-seater world serves up for groups

of three,' Kiko says, stretching out her hand to Dahlia and drawing her into her seat. 'It's a logistical mess. We'll rotate.'

Kiko drapes a jacket around her shoulders as she and Florence crack jokes over the seats. Their laughter about an older couple they saw making out in the departure lounge bounces around the plane. The noise draws some looks, but they don't seem to care. No-one claims the empty seat next to Florence, so she piles it high with carry-on luggage.

Dahlia sinks back into her seat, twisting her fingers through the pastel pink hues of her pixie cut. She runs her tongue over her braces, overwhelmed by all the sights and sounds. Her journal — her usual outlet for daydreaming and untangling her feelings — is stuck in her check-in luggage but that doesn't stop her mind from wandering. And, as they often do, her thoughts drift to Stevie. It's been a year since they said goodbye. A year since the girls got drunk and wrote *Fuck cancer* on the wall of the bathroom at Stevie's wake. A year since their hearts broke.

Not that Stevie let the brain tumour get the last word. After her death, Dahlia, Kiko and Florence discovered that she'd left each of them a small sum of money to put towards a week away after school finished to mark their graduation and ring in a new life chapter. After endless teary and grief-fuelled arguments, the girls agreed to spend the majority of the money on flights and added the rest to a shared kitty for the week.

Money had always been tight in their world so Kiko and Florence were on board with Stevie's idea from the beginning. Dahlia was less than thrilled. She'd give up the money, the trip, the necklace, all of it, to get her best friend back. She can't imagine surviving the week without her.

Her thoughts need somewhere to escape to so, with her journal trapped in her checked-in luggage, she settles on writing on her phone instead.

5 Things I'd Rather Do Instead Of This Holiday
Be chased by a bear in the woods
Walk on fire/nails/broken glass
Spend time with Dad's new girlfriend
Swim with great white sharks
Eat pig brains

There's something about the ordering and categorising of a list that soothes Dahlia, even if she's not sure why. All she knows is that her top-five lists soften the sharper edges of life.

Florence's and Kiko's laughter hits a crescendo and snaps Dahlia back to reality. With the sound of their happiness in her ears, she begins her usual flying rituals to manage her growing anxiety. Checking and rechecking her seatbelt. Avoiding eye contact with the flight attendant as he details what to do if they land in the sea. Drawing in deep breaths as the plane whirs and hums on the runway. Another check of her seatbelt. She silently curses Stevie for putting her through this, then immediately feels guilty.

As the plane soars into a sky of pale blue, Dahlia tries to shrug off her concern about how she'll endure the long-haul flight overseas when she packs her life into a backpack to work as an au pair for a year. She'd considered cancelling the gap year because the original plan had been for her and Stevie to go together.

When Stevie told her about the opportunity, it had seemed like a dream come true. The hiring families covered airfares and accommodation, and they'd have every second weekend off to explore neighbouring cities. But then tragedy struck and Dahlia barely made it through the final year of school without Stevie. It seemed impossible to accept what a future beyond that might look like. Staying close to home was being close to Stevie.

Even now, the thought of moving overseas without her seems so hard. Dahlia's free weekends won't be full of adventures with Stevie. Her days won't be buoyed by Stevie's brightness. She won't be known as Stevie's best friend. Instead, she'll be the girl whose best friend died. Every memory seeped into the soil of their hometown will be left behind.

The thought of that happening is unbearable. Dahlia bites the inside of her cheek as the plane passes through a scattering of clouds. It's hard enough to hurt, but not hard enough to draw blood. Her right hand reaches for the top of her head, fingering the fairy-floss-shaded strands closest to the roots. She gently pulls like she's in a trance, then yanks harder, feeling a strand of hair rip from her scalp. She tugs at another. This time, the hair breaks off halfway.

She tousles her hair to disguise it and quickly glances at the others. They're in their own worlds. Kiko is humming and staring out the window. The blunt ends of her black bob kiss her collarbone as she plays with the dainty stud in her nose. Florence's headphones are on and she's slumped back and snoring. Dahlia notices Stevie's prized lightning-bolt brooch is pinned to the front of Florence's satchel. Her heart pounds as she hopes the brooch is clipped on properly.

'You okay?' Kiko asks.

Dahlia nods, but her watery eyes can't lie.

Kiko reaches for her hand, but the movement startles Dahlia and she jolts forward, hipbones straining against the seatbelt.

'Sorry, sorry,' Kiko says. She peels off her jacket and drapes it over Dahlia's lap. 'Try to close your eyes and think of the beach. We're nearly there.'

It's a lie, but Dahlia appreciates it. 'How high are we?'

'The beach, the beach,' Kiko repeats with a smile. 'Swimming, relaxing, partying … That's all you need to think of until we land.'

'Stevie would be proud of your bossiness.'

'I learnt from the best,' Kiko says.

'We all did.' Dahlia relaxes into her seat and takes a deep breath. 'Fine, you win. Stevie wanted this for us. Beach, swimming, blah, blah, blah. I'm in.'

'Tray tables down, please,' a voice booms above them.

The girls look up and the flight attendant passes them lunch.

'This mystery meat might kill me,' Kiko says, poking at the hunks of brown meat swimming in red sauce. 'I would have preferred Mum's world-famous tamagoyaki as my last meal on earth, but at least I'll have died eating.'

'Do you have to talk like that?' Dahlia asks.

Kiko's eyebrows shoot up in surprise. 'Like what?'

'Like death is funny. Like it's all a joke.'

'For once can you not make everything about—' Kiko catches herself. She exhales. 'Sure.'

'Thanks,' Dahlia murmurs. 'Sorry, I didn't mean to sound so …'

She doesn't know how to finish the sentence. Despite keeping a journal since she was eleven, Dahlia often can't conjure the words she needs to explain how she feels.

'I get it. Besides, now who's bossy?' Kiko adds with a grin to soften the mood.

Dahlia returns her smile, then grimaces at a sudden digging in her abdomen. She lifts up her T-shirt to adjust her mum's old money belt from when she'd backpacked in her twenties.

'That thing is hilarious,' Kiko teases her. 'Very retiree-on-holidays chic.'

Dahlia laughs. 'Shut up. Lady, you're jealous because I — oh *shiiiiiiiiiiiiiiiiiiiiiiiit!*'

Without warning, the plane plummets a hundred feet. Loose items go flying. Screams shatter the air and red sauce drips from the cabin ceiling. A girl across the aisle is bleeding from her cheek. She whimpers as a friend presses a serviette against the gash.

Dahlia clings to the armrests. Her stomach flip-flops and the taste of bile hits the back of her throat.

The attendants are calm but firm, directing everyone to stay in their seats as they stagger down the aisle to their assigned spots and wrestle with their seatbelts.

Hands trembling, Dahlia dares to reach out for a sick bag. But before she can open it up, the plane drops again.

Dahlia's hands snap back onto the armrests as they're tossed around the sky. The screaming this time is higher, shriller, although maybe it never stopped from the first time. A boy a few rows ahead has thrown up on himself, while the couple behind them sob as they say how much they love each other.

This time, Dahlia reaches for Kiko's hand. They lace their fingers together and Dahlia's eyes clamp shut, blocking everything out. For a split-second she sees nothing but the darkness of the back of her eyelids.

The plane lurches.

She yelps, imagining it hurtling through the clouds.

'This is it,' she murmurs, gripping Kiko's hand tighter.

'I'm here,' Kiko says. 'Don't let go.'

The plane shudders before levelling out. But then it drops again. This time it's hundreds of feet in seconds.

The plane is vibrating so hard that Dahlia is convinced it's moments away from cracking apart into a million pieces and raining down into the ocean. Her brain feels scrambled as she struggles to recall a single word of the flight attendant's instructions about what to do in case of an emergency.

Dahlia looks at Kiko. They're still holding hands tighter than she's ever held a hand before. Their hair is laced with red sauce. She tries to stop seeing it as blood oozing from a wound on Kiko's head but can't. She closes her eyes and inhales through her nose, deeply, slowly, like a counsellor at a grief support group taught her last year, but keeps catching herself holding her breath.

'Dahlia,' she hears Kiko murmur.

She can't seem to move her lips to reply.

'Dahlia?' Kiko repeats. 'Dahlia Raine Valour, can you hear me?'

'Mmm?' Dahlia manages. She doesn't open her eyes.

'We're okay,' Kiko says. Dahlia feels their knees gently bump together. 'Join us out here in this mess.'

Dahlia's eyelids crack open slightly. Kiko's face is blurred and up close to hers.

'You good?' she asks.

'Mmm-hmm.' Dahlia looks down. Their fingers are still laced together.

'Keep it if you want to,' Kiko tells Dahlia with a wink.

Dahlia blushes and looks away. They unfold hands. Neither mentions the sweatiness of her palm. 'That was ...' Once again, the words are missing.

'Intense, right?' Florence blurts from the row in front of them. She has no problem summoning the words she needs — and often some she doesn't. 'I thought we were going to have to land on some tiny island, then we'd be stranded there for weeks. And it would start off being kind of brilliant, but then we'd all have to eat each other to survive and ... well, that wouldn't be brilliant.'

Kiko shakes her head. 'Can you not?'

'Right?' Dahlia adds. 'My stomach is churning enough.'

'I wouldn't have eaten either of you,' Florence says, twisting around to grin at them through the gap in the seat. Red sauce is spattered over her fine butterscotch hair. 'But can you hear those guys behind us talking about how they'll use this experience to pick up girls? If we end up trapped on a deserted island then I'm turning them into juicy steaks, no worries.'

Samira

Day 1: 4.09pm

Graffiti covers the walls of the darkened smash room. An old dented washing machine lies on its side on the concrete. Beside it there's a crate of plates, bowls, mugs, teapots, vases, ceramic statues and wine bottles.

Samira's goggles dig into the side of her face but she's too fired up to care. 'Pass me the baseball bat,' she calls out over the thrashing rock music. 'Anoush, you better move out of the way.'

Anoush grimaces instead of handing her the bat. 'Maybe this isn't a good idea.'

'It's a *great* idea,' Samira says, adjusting her gloves and coveralls. 'I'm going to smash the mugs first. Zain's mum has a set just like them.'

'Are you sure this is what you want? It's been a big day.'

The train trip had dragged so much that Samira had wondered if they were travelling back in time. She'd spent hours slouched in her seat, wondering how she'd ever thought she was ready to lose her virginity this week to a boy who almost put his neck out looking in the opposite direction whenever he walked past. The others were oblivious as she blinked back tears and wished she could disappear beneath her seat. She might have done if it weren't for the unknown sticky substance coating the floor.

Anoush purses her plump lips. She looks over her shoulder through the small glass window cut into the heavy bolted door. Rashida and Claire watch on, trading disapproving glances.

'Maybe you should call your mum first?' Anoush suggests. 'Talk things out?'

'Later. This first.' Samira stretches her arms above her head and clicks her neck to each side. She fishes her phone out of her pocket and holds it out to Anoush. 'He's already changed his status to "Single".'

'That blows. It does. But it's accurate. And, on the plus side, you're single too. We can meet hot boys together.'

'I can't even think straight,' Samira says, tightening the straps on her hard construction hat. It pushes against her throat, making it hard to breathe. 'Bat, please.'

Anoush passes it to her then steps out of the way. Samira lines up six mugs on top of the washing machine and takes a few practice swings.

The sound of shattering glass erupts from the room next door. Despite her clunky helmet, goggles and safety gear, Samira can't tune out Zain's and Mathieu's euphoric cheers. Her grip tightens on the bat and, despite the heat in the smash room, goosebumps erupt on her body. She reminds herself that it's over, that she can't walk into the next room and lace her fingers through his like she has hundreds of times before. The bat swings loosely from her hand as her goggles fog up. She takes them off and wipes them out.

'What's up?' Anoush asks, coming closer. 'Are you crying?'

Samira gestures to the laughter next door. 'Listen.'

'I know it's rough, but, like, try to ignore it.'

'How? We'll be underneath the same roof for a week.'

'I ... I have no idea. I guess it's just something people say.'

'Did you know?'

'Know what?'

'That he wanted to break up.'

Anoush stiffens. 'No, of course not.'

'Mathieu said something about none of you believing it and I ... Sorry, I'm being paranoid now.'

'It's okay.'

They don't speak for a few moments as the boys' cheering echoes through the walls.

'You know what, smash the life out of those ugly mugs,' says Anoush. 'You need this.'

'Thanks,' Samira says, sniffling. 'No-one else has said much to me since it happened.'

'Forget about them, they're in their own party bubble.' She leans over to help Samira grip the bat a little higher. 'Now, bend those knees and give it everything. I'll line up the dinner plates next.'

Zoë

Day 1: 4.39pm

Zoë's phone finally gets reception. Instantly, it floods with notifications. Eleven text messages from Dad. Three text messages from Mum. Seven missed calls from Dad. Another two text messages from Mum. Three voicemails from Dad. One voicemail from Mum. Zero emails about early acceptance.

Her face crumples.

'Thoughts and prayers for your inbox, Tiny Sloth,' Luca says as he drives them along the highway to the coast. It's been Luca's nickname for Zoë since she was fourteen and fell asleep at eight thirty at a sleepover while everyone else partied and talked until the sun rose. He's never let her forget it and has teased her affectionately ever since.

'About time we got reception,' Violet mutters, scrolling through her messages and feed. She smooths down her heavy fringe, then takes a selfie and plays around with the filters.

Zoë cringes as more notifications come through. 'Is this the worst thing I've ever done? Don't answer that.'

'I feel like we're your kidnappers,' Luca says with a nervous laugh.

'Maybe we should take you home,' Violet says. 'We can use Mum as a human shield.'

'Aunty Caro would make it a thousand times worse,' Luca says. 'Can you imagine the drama? Besides we're nearly there.'

'Well, Aunty Rosette and Uncle Gian are probably about one minute away from turning this into a full missing persons investigation,' adds Violet, not looking up from her phone. 'Just saying.'

Zoë groans. 'Or sending a bounty hunter out after me.'

'That's more likely,' Luca says with a smirk. 'A quick request from your handsome driver: can someone put chocolate in my mouth?'

'I can't go home,' Zoë says, glaring at her phone. 'I can't.'

'Well, you could,' Violet says, 'but Aunty Rosette will kill you on arrival.'

'Chocolate!' Luca repeats, opening and closing his mouth like a fish.

Zoë snaps off two cubes and pops them into his mouth. 'They promised me this. They said I could go. It's not my fault they're scared I'm going to go wild. As if I even would or could!'

'You said it.' Luca gives her a grin.

'Fact.' Violet nods. 'You'll be tucked up in bed at sunset every night.'

'The shade,' Luca laughs. 'But that *is* how you roll, Zo.'

Zoë shrugs. 'I'm not arguing! I do the right thing. I always have.'

Her phone buzzes. Dad again.

Chickpea, where are you? Contact me NOW or you're grounded for a month.

'Grounded? Has he forgotten I won't even be living at home soon?' Zoë asks.

'It's not only you. Our whole family's obsessed with all of us leaving,' Violet says. 'Mum said she sometimes sneaks into my room to watch me sleep. Stalker alert!'

'I busted Mum looking at old baby photos of me the other day,' Luca adds, pushing a curl back from his forehead. 'Get a hobby, Elena! Start knitting.'

They crack up so loudly Zoë almost doesn't hear her phone buzz again.

I'm not joking. Call me. NOW!!!

Zoë gulps. She pictures her dad pacing the house, his heavy work boots pounding on the floorboards. Her fingers hover over the phone but nothing helpful comes to mind. Nothing seems like enough.

Call me right NOW.

Then another message immediately after.

NOW, ZOË!!

Zoë looks out the window. The evening drags darkness across the sky.

'What's up, Zo?' Violet asks. 'Is it Uncle Gian again?'

'Yeah.'

'Need me to call my mum?' Luca chimes in. 'She can run interference.'

'I'm handling it,' Zoë says. She types out a text.

I love you both. I'm safe. I'll see you next week, Zxx

Luca shoots her a look. 'You are staying with us, right?'

'Keep your eyes on the road.'

'Are we nearly there?' Violet asks with a yawn. 'I'm convinced you've been driving the wrong way for hours.'

'Happy for you to take over,' Luca snaps. 'Oh wait, that's right, you don't have your licence yet and Zoë is terrible with directions.'

Zoë sniggers. 'Remember when you took the wrong turn driving us to Aunty Caro's and we got stuck in traffic on the bridge for over an hour?'

'I'm about to toss you both from the car,' Luca says. 'But first, check this out.'

He winds down his window as he turns into the wide sweeping driveway of the resort. Thousands of fairylights twinkle in the trees lining either side of the road.

They all scream with excitement as they get deeper into the property and see the lush green gardens. A hint of an aquamarine infinity pool that seems to go on forever. The swim-up bar with thumping music. The packs of young people filling the walkways, getting ferried with overstuffed luggage in golf carts, hanging by ping-pong tables and playing with the giant outdoor chess and checkers sets.

Zoë's phone vibrates. Her dad is calling.

She stares at the screen, fingers frozen above the 'accept' button. Before she answers, it's rung out. She glances out her window, jaw dropping at the grand white pillars at the entrance to the main building.

She opens up her messages and sends one more.

PS: I'm sorry x

Then she turns off her phone. 'I'm so dead.'

'Then you've got nothing left to lose,' Luca says with a devilish grin.

'I hope it's worth it.' Zoë slides down in her seat. 'It'll be worth it, right? This is *the* week.'

The car pulls into a space in front of the large marble lobby.

'We'll be living like royalty,' Violet murmurs, nose pressed up against the window. 'Prakash and Akito have dropped us a ton of messages about how it's incredible inside, like something from a movie set.'

An attendant rushes to their car and opens a door. 'Welcome to the Grand Southwell on Saldana Strip,' he says with a sharp nod. 'Please allow me to help you with your bags.'

'Sweet,' Luca says. 'I mean, thank you, good sir.'

The girls fight back laughter.

'Your suites are ready,' the attendant continues. 'As a special welcome, I trust you will enjoy the complimentary chocolates.'

'I'm sure we will,' Violet says.

Zoë's skin tingles as she stares at the colossal lobby. 'This is …'

'One thousand per cent going to be worth it,' Luca declares, wrapping his arm around her shoulder.

Dahlia

There are only three items left on the baggage carousel. A large grey bag with a plastic lily hanging off the handle. A faded backpack. A small black suitcase. Kiko collects the bag with the flower and checks the padlocks, while Florence pulls on her backpack.

'Yours, Dahlia?' Florence points at the suitcase.

'Mine's a red backpack. Mum's old one.'

'It's probably getting unloaded,' Kiko says with a hopeful tone. 'I bet they're behind after all the delays. I lost track of how long we were stuck on the runway.'

Dahlia looks around, gnawing on her thumbnail. Her stomach still churns after the shaky flight. The crowd has thinned out and the carousel has stopped moving.

There's a stinging at the corner of her thumb. She glances down to see broken skin. A tinge of blood stains the creases of her knuckles.

5 Failed Attempts To Quit Nailbiting
An expensive manicure
Practising mindfulness

Wearing Mum's foul-tasting nail polish
Snapping an elastic band on my wrist to replace the
    habit
Grossing myself out at the thought of germs
    (worked temporarily)

'Hey, I checked and no more bags are coming from that flight,' Kiko pipes up. 'I'm so sorry.'

'Shit.' Dahlia's luggage holds some of her most meaningful possessions — things that can't be replaced; things she couldn't bear to leave behind.

She feels cracked open without all the things that usually help when her mind is on fire. Her bedroom, oils and affirmation cards. Her mum, who is pulling double shifts as a nurse at the hospital all week. Her dad, even though his girlfriend's laugh sounds like fingernails on a chalkboard. Her psychologist, who she's booked in to see after the trip but right now feels so far away she might as well be in an alternate timeline. And an old notebook that she and Stevie filled with letters to each other, which she's been using to journal her thoughts for the past year.

'The airline has your number and the hostel's,' Kiko says. 'We'll keep calling to check on your luggage too.'

Dahlia feels trapped within a swirling chaos. It makes it almost impossible to think clearly. She hates that Stevie would've known what to do but Dahlia can't ask for her advice.

'Maybe go to the hostel without me and I'll sort something out,' she says. 'I need my bag.'

'We're not leaving without you,' Florence says, readjusting her backpack.

Kiko nods. 'I've got our emergency credit card if you want to buy supplies, and you can borrow our clothes and make-up.'

'What's mine is yours,' Florence adds.

'Thanks,' Dahlia murmurs.

Kiko squeezes her hand, only for a second but enough for Dahlia to feel the warmth of her fingers. 'I know this is a tough week. We've got you, lady.'

'And your luggage will be here before you know it,' chimes in Florence. 'This happened to my neighbour a few years ago and it worked out fine.' She pauses. 'Actually no, that's wrong, it never showed up. Ignore me.'

'Moving on,' Kiko says with a groan. 'I vote we go to the hostel.' She waves a printout of their confirmation in Florence's face. 'Room 22, let's do it.'

Florence yawns. 'Great plan. I need a nap.'

'You slept half the flight!' Dahlia says.

'It's the last day of my period and I had big sleep plans for that flight but the turbulence crashed my style. Nap. *Now.*'

The girls find a shuttle to their hostel — a white van that reeks of cigarettes and stale fried food — and spend the drive trying not to vomit on the cracked vinyl seats.

When they spill onto the sidewalk in front of their hostel, Florence gags. 'That was foul.'

Dahlia, also close to throwing up, looks away. Her gaze locks on Florence's satchel. The brooch is missing.

'The lightning bolt! Where is it?'

'What's wrong?' Kiko asks.

Florence tugs at her T-shirt. 'It's here.' The brooch is pinned high on the left side. 'I moved it.'

'Oh.' Dahlia blushes. 'Sorry.'

'It's alright,' Florence says, shooting Kiko a look that Dahlia isn't supposed to see.

Kiko screws up her nose. 'Okay, you two ... on a scale of one to ten, how much red sauce from the plane do I still have on me? You're both pushing a twenty,' she says, trying to soften the mood.

It works. They talk and laugh as they drag their gear through a gate and down a thin concrete path to the hostel reception. Old-school hip-hop blasts from a speaker but there's no-one behind the front counter.

Kiko and Florence head for the bathroom, while Dahlia takes in the overlapping flyers, postcards and photos on a corkboard in the common room. A group of backpackers lounge in discoloured beanbags in the corner.

One of them, a guy about their age with thin-framed glasses, calls over the music. 'You wanna check in? The clowns here are *way* behind. We've been waiting for hours. Dorms are still being cleaned.'

'What about the private rooms?' Dahlia asks. 'Room 22?'

He shrugs. 'Same deal, I guess.'

Dahlia's right hand grazes the crown of her head. She wonders again when she'll be reunited with her luggage, then catches herself holding a torn-out strand of pastel pink hair.

Swallowing hard, she storms into the bathroom and talks to Kiko and Florence through the cubicle doors. 'Our room isn't ready, and I can't even find someone who works here to ask for help. First the flight is a disaster, then my luggage goes missing, and now we don't even have a room. I'm starting to feel like it's all a bad omen! Maybe we shouldn't have come. This is the anniversary — and I feel like I'm spiralling, I really do. Maybe I'll get a bus back or something, because I can't afford a flight. Or maybe I should try to—'

The sound of the toilets flushing drowns out her outburst. The girls step out of their respective cubicles and lather up their hands with soap.

'Lady, we love you,' Kiko says. 'And you can do whatever you want. Sure, Stevie wanted you to have a good time — and we want you here too. But if it's too hard and too much, then we get it. We have your back.'

'We do,' Florence adds. 'It's a lot.'

There's a heavy silence for a few beats.

'*Did* Stevie want me to have a good time?' Dahlia asks.

Kiko tilts her head in confusion. 'Of course.'

'By guilting me into a beach holiday with you two?' Dahlia jokes, flashing a weak smile. 'She knows my skin burns under a desk lamp.'

The girls smile, relief on their faces.

'I'm not going to pretend the past year hasn't been a horror show,' Kiko says. 'But you know you can talk to us about anything, right?'

Dahlia nods. She does, but she rarely knows how to voice what's burning inside her, even to her friends. The mental gymnastics are exhausting, and her emotions feel so swollen with pain that she worries she'll drown the girls in a wave of darkness if she dares to speak the truth.

Florence applies tomato-red lipstick, then pecks Dahlia on the cheek.

'Come on,' Kiko says. 'We'll work something out if we stay together. It's what we do.'

Back at reception, there's still no-one behind the desk.

Dahlia peers out through the large flyscreen sliding door. 'Did you see the pool out there? The sun's still out, and there are lounges and umbrellas too.'

Kiko smiles. 'That's more like it.'

Florence slides open the door and charges ahead, bumping into a group of boys in board shorts. The footpath in front of them is littered with surfboards and backpacks. With a quick wink at Dahlia and Kiko, Florence confirms it's fine for them to go on without her.

Dahlia and Kiko dawdle towards the pool, which is surrounded by faded blue and white striped umbrellas.

'I might call the airline again,' Dahlia says, leaning against the pool fence. 'Maybe they've heard something.'

'It's only been an hour,' Kiko says. 'And everything you need is right here.'

'A new toothbrush?'

'There's a supermarket down the road.'

'And clothes.'

'My suitcase is your suitcase, remember? Same with Florence's.' Kiko sighs. 'I wish you didn't only look for the bad signs.'

Dahlia clenches her fists, nails digging into the skin. 'That's unfair.'

'Maybe. But your blinkers are on. You're shutting everything good out.' She pauses. 'Shit. I'm making this worse and that's the last thing I'd ever want to do. I might give you some space.'

Heart racing, Dahlia grabs at Kiko's arm. 'No. Wait.'

Kiko's face softens. 'Yeah?'

'I know I'm cloudy right now. But when I saw that empty seat on the plane ...' Her fingers find the delicate gold chain at her neck.

'I know,' Kiko says, pulling her in for a hug. 'Me too. It was another reminder Stevie isn't here, and we get enough of those every day. But we're doing this for her.'

'You're right.' Dahlia smiles. 'I hate that.'

'It's tough always being right, but it's a burden I have to live with,' Kiko teases. 'Hey, you know what else I saw on that plane?'

'No, what?'

'I saw you,' Kiko admits. 'Facing your fears, stepping outside your comfort zone. It's amazing.' She pauses, then stammers in a rush, 'And ... and I saw Florence of course.'

Dahlia is too stunned to speak. Their gazes lock for a moment and she notices that Kiko's chocolate-brown eyes are dusted with flecks of green.

'Thanks,' she manages, looking away. 'That means a lot.'

'Stevie wants us to look for the good stuff too, that's all I'm saying,' Kiko tells her. 'Anyway, there's a spare hat in my bag if you want it.'

Before Dahlia can stitch together a reply, Kiko is marching over to Florence, who's now sprawled on a lounge in her bikini bottoms and a faded T-shirt, the fine golden hairs on her thighs twinkling in the sunshine. The boys she was talking with have dumped their belongings on nearby lounges.

'Dahlia, water looks good!' Florence calls out. 'You joining us?'

The sun kisses Dahlia's shoulders as she watches Kiko strip down to her vintage polkadot swimsuit. Kiko catches her looking and a small smile slips out of the corner of her mouth.

Samira

Day 1: 7.01pm

Mathieu and Zain barrel into the beach house behind Samira, hurling their backpacks down in the spacious living room that opens up onto a huge balcony overlooking the water. Everything in the house is white or cream, from the pristine carpet to the shaggy rug beneath the coffee table and the accent chairs scattered with cushions.

Samira cringes as the boys stomp through the carpeted hallway and up the staircase to shotgun bedrooms on the second level.

'I've got a bad feeling,' she mutters, scoping out the white walls and glass ornaments on the hallway table. 'Everything looks so …'

'Beautiful?' Rashida offers, handbag swinging dangerously close to a crystal vase.

Samira winces, remembering the damage at the smash room. 'Breakable.'

'Hope they have insurance,' Anoush says as she charges past with her suitcase to race up the stairs. 'Oi, Mathieu!' Her voice echoes through the house. 'Samira booked this trip so the master bedroom is ours.'

Samira smiles, grateful to have Anoush on her side. She potters at the island bench in the kitchen while the others argue and sort out sleeping arrangements.

Her phone buzzes with a message from her mum.

Darling, just checking you're alive and got in safely? Hope you're having the best time. Love you xxx

It buzzes again.

PS. Teta says hi and don't forget to take photos.

Samira stares at her phone, unsure how to reply. She wants to tell her mum everything and craves hearing her voice, but she's so far from home and doesn't want her mum to worry, not when she's already been through so much.

Her dad and mum began dating in high school and broke up when Samira was two years old. They managed to stay close, despite extended family and mutual friends in their close-knit community believing it to be impossible. They'd simply fallen out of love at the same time, as people sometimes do. When Samira's dad packed up his clothes and moved out of the house, Teta settled into their spare bedroom and that's the way it stayed. It was the new normal.

Samira loves her dad, and now that they've moved for her mother's work, he comes to visit her on weekends. Sometimes he even stays the night on their couch to maximise their hours together. She feels her parents' mutual respect for each other every time they speak about her; she's the link that holds them together. But

47

day to day, Samira is in a jigsaw puzzle of three: Teta, Mum, Samira. They fit together perfectly.

Before she's worked out what to type, raucous laughter fills the house and the others jostle down the staircase.

'This place is stunning,' announces Claire, squealing as the boys thunder past her. She pauses on a step to check out her reflection in an enormous ornate mirror and smooth her hair. 'I'm never leaving.'

The guys cheer in agreement and line up tequila glasses on the countertop.

Samira shrugs away the praise for the beach house like she hasn't spent every spare second in recent months getting the trip organised. She rifles through her handbag looking for the itinerary and her fingertips graze the unopened packet of condoms she'd thrown in at the last minute. She shoves the packet deeper down into the bag before anyone notices.

Blushing, she pulls out the itinerary and places it front and centre on the fridge.

'What's the plan tonight?' asks Anoush, pouring herself and the girls glasses of pink sparkling wine.

Samira takes a small sip of hers, trying to hide her disgust at the dry taste. 'We can head to the beach party near Saldana Strip,' she says, setting the drink aside.

Rashida screws up her nose. 'The all-ages one? But aren't they, like, every night?'

'The boys want to check out the clubs,' says Claire, slurping her drink.

Anoush tops up their glasses. 'You've still got your cousin's ID, right, Samira?'

She nods, struggling to remember the details: her cousin Mary's middle name, date of birth, star sign. It's all a blank. Cheeks reddening, she fishes the ID out of her wallet.

Rashida snatches it from her and looks it over. 'That'll work,' she says.

'Maybe,' Claire says. 'Samira's eyebrows aren't as defined as hers, but ... they're passable.'

Samira takes another sip of her drink, feeling the burn down the back of her throat.

'You have to come, Samira,' Anoush says, gulping down the rest of her wine and topping it up again. 'Think of all the new boys we'll meet. We'll *all* be there.'

* * *

By nine o'clock, Anoush is slumped asleep on the couch. Legs splayed, eyelashes meshed together, one heel on, one heel off. Drool clings to her lower lip.

'Oi,' Claire says, tickling the skin behind Anoush's knee. 'Get up, Anoush.'

Anoush lets out a short, sharp snort that rolls into a rumbling snore.

Mathieu recoils. 'She sounds like a bear in hibernation.'

'She sounds like you, man, with that snoring,' Zain adds.

'Messy,' Rashida says, stroking Anoush's cheek. 'What a little lightweight. What do we do?'

'She's out of it,' Samira says. 'We can't leave her alone.'

Claire purses her lips. 'But it's night one! I'm not missing tonight.'

'I'll stay with her,' Samira volunteers. 'You all go and I'll make up for it tomorrow at the foam party.'

No-one resists the idea and a mistimed rallying cheer ripples through the group as Claire and Rashida tussle for mirror space, and Mathieu rushes around trying to find his wallet. In the disorganised chaos, Samira and Zain end up in the kitchen together.

Her palms sweat as Zain forces an awkward smile, mumbles, 'Okay, then,' and adds something about needing to get his phone. Neither of them mention he's holding it before he disappears down the hallway.

Eventually, the group barrel out of the house in a cloud of perfume and cologne, leaving Samira and Anoush alone in the lounge room. Samira drags a blanket over Anoush's body and gently tucks it in around her. She sits a mixing bowl from the kitchen beside the couch and dims the lights in the lounge room. Anoush lets out another snuffle, before nestling deeper into the couch.

Yawning, Samira heads out onto the balcony and curls up on a sunlounge, admiring the twinkling fairylights and buzz of cicadas in the air. Lively laughter from the house next door punctures the night, followed by the opening bars of a blaring pop song.

I nearly ran away
To start things over
Instead I'm gonna
Take what's mine

Live your way
Live your way
Live your way, sweet baby

Live your way
Live your way
Oh, oh, live your way, baby

Samira recognises it as Alotta Peach: a flamboyant singer with two tracks in the charts, enough wigs to fill a semi-trailer and a large birthmark under her right eye. Alotta Peach even has the headliner spot at the end-of-week stadium spectacular, a much-hyped event that Samira organised tickets for months earlier.

She strains to see into next door's backyard, but can only make out three figures in costumes dancing and singing around a fire pit. They move fast around the flames but from what she can tell, there's a pirate, a queen and a robot. Mouth ajar, Samira watches as the Pirate climbs onto the Robot's shoulders while the Queen twirls and cheers them on.

There's a fire
Inside my soul

Getting up, getting out
Like I want

Live your way
Live your way
Live your way, sweet baby

Live your way
Live your way
Oh, oh, live your way, baby

Samira edges closer to the railing for a better look. The Queen sports a high red ponytail and a flowery tattoo that runs from thigh to knee. The Pirate's face is caked in thick make-up. The Robot wears heavy purple boots. Their playlist ticks over to another Alotta Peach track, which sends them into a fresh round of rapturous dancing.

Swallowing hard, Samira glances behind her to the quiet, darkened house. Alone on the balcony, her fingers trace the corners of the VIP party pass around her neck as the sound of her neighbours' unrestrained joy washes over her.

Day 2

Dahlia

Day 2: 8.13am

The sun beats against the blinds of the musty hostel room. Dahlia, in the top bunk, traces the cracked ceiling with her finger then rolls to face the wall, shielding herself from the light piercing the sheer fabric. Her head pounds from lack of sleep and the slippery anxious thoughts that come and go. She shakes off macabre improbable possibilities, draws in a deep breath and exhales, bringing herself back to the moment like her psychologist has helped her to do many times.

A bright white sneaker sails through the air, strikes the wall and lands on the floorboards, snapping her to attention. She curls onto her side to see Florence grinning from her top bunk on the other side of the cramped room.

'Wakey wakey, everyone. Ready to go to this theme park or what?' Florence asks.

Kiko groans from the bunk below Dahlia. 'Slow down! WonderWorld is open until ten tonight.'

Dahlia's stomach churns at the sound of Kiko's voice. Her memories from yesterday are blurred and messy, like they've been swirled around on a paint palette. Kiko's delicate fingers laced through hers on the plane. The unwavering, caring look that felt strong enough to split Dahlia in two. A knowing smile by the pool as Kiko stripped down to her swimsuit. Some fragments have faded to soft watercolours, but others remain bold and vivid. Biting her bottom lip, Dahlia pulls the sheet tight around her body and wonders if Kiko felt it too.

'Think of the fairy floss,' Florence says, waving another shoe in their direction. 'Those sausages on sticks. Chucking up on the rollercoasters. Let's get moving.'

'What's the rush?' Kiko replies, before breaking into a grin. 'Oh, don't tell me …'

Florence pulls on her denim shorts and a crop top. 'What?' she asks with a playful wink.

'Those boys from the pool yesterday,' Kiko says. 'Any chance they're in attendance today?'

Dahlia gasps. 'What did I miss? What happened?'

Florence laughs. 'Nothing … yet. But Seiji said he and Mitch will meet us there.'

'Oh great, randoms tagging along,' Kiko teases her. 'Your pick-up skills are next level.'

'It's nothing, we're just hanging.'

'With you, nothing is always something.'

Florence throws the other sneaker and Kiko lets out a squeal.

'They leave tomorrow anyway,' Florence adds. 'Seiji's chin dimple is hot though, huh?'

'If you say so,' Kiko says.

Florence walks over to Dahlia's bunk and tweaks her nose. 'Hey sleepyhead, you coming with us?' She opens the blinds and sunlight streams into the room. 'I'm heading down for bacon and eggs now.'

'Just waking up,' Dahlia says.

'Excellent.' Florence claps her hands. 'Okay, WonderWorld! WonderWorld! WonderWorld!' She drags back Dahlia's sheet, then takes Kiko by the hands and pulls her out of the bunk. 'Let's get maximum rides in before the boys show up.'

'I need a shower first,' Kiko says, pulling out a towel from her bag. 'Dahlia, help yourself to my clothes and I'll meet you both at breakfast.'

The girls leave the room and Dahlia climbs down the ladder, wincing as her feet push against the hard wood. She takes a deep breath as she crouches down at Kiko's open bag, feeling as though she's prying. She unzips the bag a little wider, hands accidentally fumbling over a lacy black bra. Blushing, she shoves it deep beneath a pile of sundresses and bikinis.

She selects a pair of ripped cut-off shorts and holds them up to her waist. As she gets to her feet to slip them on, a folded piece of paper falls out onto the floorboards. It's torn in half but held together with sticky tape that's brown at the edges. She plucks it up off the ground then freezes when she recognises the messy handwriting. Dahlia has letters written in the same script, marked *D & S only! Private! Read at your own risk!* She's seen it on school assignments. On forged notes to get out of athletics carnivals. On the pages she tore from their notebook and stuffed in her bottom desk drawer before turning the book into her journal.

Dahlia sinks onto the floorboards, back pressed against the hard brick wall. She hasn't dared look at Stevie's handwriting for so long she thought she'd forgotten it, just like she worries about forgetting the sound of Stevie's voice, but every scribble feels like home again. She tries to smooth out the creases in the paper, taking in the familiar loopy swirls and jagged angles of the lettering.

The Too Late List.

Dahlia didn't know this list still existed. She'd assumed it had been thrown away or shelved like the rest of Stevie's personal belongings her family couldn't bear to keep in the house any more. She definitely didn't know Kiko had it.

In another lifetime, Stevie would be the pressure valve on this holiday. The rock, the cheerleader, the one cracking everyone up with hilarious stories about when she caught her parents having sex in the home gym, or the time she wet herself at school camp from drinking too much hot chocolate. But, like every other day this year, she's not here. The tumour dragged at her and drained her, transforming the girl Dahlia grew up with into a skeletal form of herself. But her spirit never diminished. Stevie was always the loudest in the room in life, and she was determined to be the same in death. Even at the awful end, she found ways to tease and boss the girls around, to enchant them with her every word.

'I'm over having relatives I barely know talking to me in whispers,' she'd once groaned to Dahlia. 'Are they afraid of blurting out the wrong thing? What could they possibly say that's worse than the fact I'm dying? I'm over it! It's not up to me to help them accept the fact it's the last Christmas lunch where I'll be stealing the pork crackling, you know?' Stevie laughed because she always laughed, but Dahlia knew she wasn't joking. 'If this is all I get in life, then I want my time here to be real. I don't want to waste any of my final seconds.'

Stevie became obsessed with perfect last times and wrote them up in the Last Time List. No matter the weather or mood, there was always something for her to do each day. Visit the beach. Eat a block of chocolate in one sitting. Kiss a cute boy. Smoke a full cigarette behind the bushes on the oval.

'It tastes like a bin but I'm dying anyway, right?' she spluttered as the girls doused her in perfume to hide the smell.

It was a happy list and it buoyed Stevie every day.

But the crumpled torn page in Dahlia's shaking hands isn't that list. The spidery handwriting dancing across the lines isn't her final catalogue of perfect endings, goodbyes and last times. Stevie was equally fixated on the things she'd never get to do. Despite her mum's pleading not to, she also wrote another document. The Too Late List.

Some people found it morbid, but in typical Stevie style, she didn't worry about what others thought. She wasn't depressed by the list, which seemed to grow longer every day. She was simply fascinated by the possibilities humans have on offer in a lifetime.

'No-one can experience everything,' she announced to Dahlia one rainy afternoon as she tinkered with the list in bed. 'It's not like I'm the only person who misses out on stuff. It's how life is designed.'

'Totally ... So, ah, you want to watch a movie or something?'

Stevie groaned. 'Dahlia Raine Valour, did you change the topic? Everyone acts like my problems will go away if I shrink myself down and stay quiet. Don't you dare be like everyone else, don't you dare.'

Dahlia's lip trembled. 'I'm sorry, I'm sorry, I won't. I'm listening.'

'Good. Because I'm sick, and I need someone to talk about it with. I need you.'

Dahlia nodded for Stevie to continue.

'Thank you. So this is my theory: life is filled with crossroads and if you choose one path, then the other path, as it was, closes up.'

'So you're saying life is the most hectic game of choose your own adventure?'

'Yes! Only in life you can't flip back to chapter one and start over. You can't read it again to experience every possible ending.'

'I've never thought of it like that.'

'No-one gets *everything*. You make your choices and have to live with them. I think it's why so many adults are moody — they're too busy moping about those closed-off paths. Well, and bills.'

The girls cracked up.

'Oh, and you know what I'm not sad to miss out on when I'm old?' Stevie added. 'False teeth.'

They laughed so hard that afternoon that Stevie's mum knocked on the bedroom door to check everything was okay.

Dahlia watched Stevie add experiences to her Too Late List for weeks.

Meet a celebrity
Skinny-dip
Meditate
Fall in love
Get married
Visit a haunted house
Travel to Fiji
Get a tattoo
Save a life
Try radical honesty
Learn the guitar
Skydive

The list went on and on. Daydreaming and talking about it kept Stevie occupied for months through all the scans, surgery, chemotherapy, radiation, the poking and prodding.

Things were slow at first, but then they got fast when Stevie was moved into palliative care. She never made it to Christmas lunch.

'Thank you, my people,' she croaked to Dahlia, Florence and Kiko through split, whitened lips on their final day together. 'We're still us and always will be.'

They clung to each other's hands, hers, theirs. Stevie's were alarmingly cold but the girls didn't let go until the nurse asked them to leave so Stevie could rest. Stevie's eyes glistened as the girls stroked her forehead and told her they'd see her tomorrow.

The next day, Stevie's mum called Dahlia to say Stevie had passed away in her sleep that morning.

The girls all wore blue, her favourite colour, to the funeral and snuck a bottle of wine out of the wake to drink in her honour on Florence's verandah while her father and step-mum pretended not to notice. The next day, Stevie's mum dropped off some of her personal mementos. For Dahlia, her necklace. For Florence, her brooch. And for Kiko, her Polaroid camera.

Stevie's mum also told them about the money Stevie had left for them to take a trip together. Life went on, just as Stevie had said it would. But it hadn't felt the same since.

Dahlia takes a deep breath and presses her back against the wall. She scans the list for the first time in over a year, fighting back tears at seeing all the things Stevie never got the chance to do. Knees to her chest, she nibbles on the skin next to her thumbnail, biting until it bleeds.

Samira

Day 2: 12.03pm

Samira's nose crinkles at the stench of sweat in the marquee. She and the other girls wade through waist-high foamy bubbles towards an empty table near the bar, slipping and laughing as their bling-covered sandals stick to the floor.

Anoush releases a pained groan as she wrings out her skirt. 'My head hurts,' she says, sinking onto a stool. 'I don't think I can face this.'

Rashida sips her drink. 'No bailing, girl.'

'You already missed last night,' Claire adds, pursing her lips in disapproval. 'Find your second wind.'

'I'll get you some water, Anoush,' Samira offers.

As she fills a glass at the bar, her gaze locks on Zain on the opposite side of the room. He and Mathieu flash toothy grins as they flirt with two girls with long damp hair and side-swept bangs. One of the girls, a redhead in a soaking wet miniskirt, looks at Zain like he's a roast dinner with all the trimmings. Stepping in closer, the girl scoops up a handful of bubbles and blows them in his direction.

Samira returns to the table. 'This song sucks,' she shouts over the thumping track, glancing at Zain and the redhead twisted together in the corner. His arms are around her waist. Her hands are everywhere.

Samira's throat burns with the lump she's been trying to push down since yesterday. She dares to steal another look. Zain's and the redhead's limbs are entwined now in a mess of foam and wet hair as they gyrate to the music. Their lips meet, and the girl's hand snakes up the back of Zain's head to pull him in even closer. When they break apart, his mouth cracks into a smile. Then his lips brush against hers again.

'I'm about to be sick,' Samira murmurs.

Anoush whimpers. 'Me too.'

Samira smiles at her. 'You're a good friend.'

'No, I need to throw up,' she gags, hand covering her mouth. 'Right now.'

Anoush sprints towards the marquee exit, disappearing into the ocean of foam and people. Samira follows, weaving and bumping against sticky hands and elbows, before spilling out the exit and onto a stretch of parkland running alongside Saldana Strip. She spots Anoush hunched over under a weathered tree near the rows of portaloos.

'You alright?' Samira calls, rushing over to hold back Anoush's shiny long hair.

'Don't look at me, it's hideous,' Anoush groans, pulling her hair into a topknot. When she sees the portaloos, she gags again. 'I think it was better inside.'

Samira holds out her water. 'Here. Take it.'

'Thanks,' Anoush says, taking a small sip. 'Hey, we've got a girls' day tomorrow, right? You and me.'

'Sure do, it's on the itinerary.'

'Nice.' Anoush collects herself and applies some lipgloss. 'Let's go back in and find the others.'

Samira pauses, remembering Zain and the redhead's passionate kiss. Her stomach churns at the thought of having to see them again. 'I might hang out here a little longer. Enjoy the quiet and fresh air.'

Anoush gestures to the portaloos. 'Really?'

Samira laughs. 'You know what I mean. I'll see you soon.'

She joins the queue to the toilets. Two girls standing in line in front of her take selfies, pouting and smiling and stopping to check their angles. Samira pulls out her phone and scrolls through her camera roll. A photo of last night's sunset. A photo of Anoush jumping on their bed in her furry lion onesie. A photo of Claire's shoulder sunburn.

Before the trip, Samira imagined taking hundreds of photos with Zain, with Anoush, with the group. But like everything this week, nothing's going to plan. She doesn't know if she even wants to remember the trip, let alone collect photos that will transport her back to this feeling. A single tear escapes.

'Toilet's free,' a bubbly voice announces.

A girl wearing a plastic gold crown, singlet and puffy tutu stands in front of Samira. Her dyed cherry-red hair is pulled into a high ponytail that cascades down her back, and her wrists are loaded with colourful bangles that rattle with every theatrical hand movement.

'I can't even tell you how hard it is to wee in this,' the girl adds, tugging at the tutu. 'My fault for guzzling two jugs of water! Ten out of ten do *not* recommend.'

Samira can't help but smile. 'I'll keep that in mind.'

The girl cocks her head to one side. 'Hey, you poor thing, have you been crying?'

'No, all good,' Samira fibs, letting the girl behind her go ahead in the queue. 'Just got some of the foamy bubbles in my eyes.'

'Ouch!' The girl fishes a pair of cheap yellow sunglasses in the shape of sunflowers from her bag, and passes them to Samira. 'Here, take these. Sounds like you need them more than me. Anyway, have fun!'

She pirouettes away, trips over her feet mid-spin and lands on the grass. It's only then that Samira recognises the flowery tattoo stretched across her thigh.

'Wait, *you're* the Queen!' she gasps. 'From next door!'

The girl struggles to her feet. 'I mean, this is my everyday crown, not my evening crown, but that's me. Wait, you're at that massive house next door? You're fancy.'

'Not even a little bit. But I did see the fire pit and the dancing.'

'You should have come over!' The girl beams so brightly it's like someone has turned on all the lights. 'It was our Alotta Peach Appreciation Fire Pit. You know her?'

'She's headlining this week, right?'

'It's why we're here.'

'You're, like, her groupies?'

The girl cackles. 'Peaches. We follow her around. I saved up all year for a meet-and-greet at this week's concert and I already know it will be the best five minutes of my life.' She slips off a colourful bangle and passes it to Samira. 'It's yours. I have heaps at the house.'

'More stuff? Thanks,' Samira says, slipping it onto her wrist. The bangle features a row of cartoon peach illustrations, a pastel AP logo and the line: *Live your way, baby.* 'You're a walking gift shop.'

'I also answer to the name Tilly.'

'Oh, um, I'm Samira,' she says, letting another girl go ahead of her to the toilets.

'Sounds like a pop star!' Tilly's indigo eyes glitter in the sun. 'I can picture the letters up in sparkling lights with thousands of fans in the audience.'

'You really like pop stars, huh?'

'I really like most things.' She grins. 'Hey, can I call you Sammy? You seem like a Sammy.'

'That's what Mum calls me. Go for it.'

There's a sharp tap on Samira's shoulder. She turns to see a long queue of girls with wet clothes and matted hair.

At the front, a short girl taps her boot on the grass. 'You going?' she barks. 'We're nearly wetting our knickers here. Shut up and get on with it.'

Tilly smiles. 'Hey, there's no need for that. Why don't we all—'

'Pipe down, freak,' the girl in the boots snarls.

Samira swears. 'Don't talk to her like that. She's done nothing wrong.'

'Her outfit is all kinds of wrong,' the girl sneers, gesturing to Tilly's tutu. Behind her, other girls titter. 'Tell her to go back to the circus.'

Samira's jaw drops and she feels a fury building inside her. Tilly mutters for Samira to ignore her, but she's fixated on the girl. 'What's your problem?'

'Your friend's a freak,' the girl says, spitting on the grass near Samira's foot. 'And newsflash, you're a loser. How do you like that, loser?'

Samira steps in closer, rage bubbling beneath the surface. For once, the words come to her at the right moment. 'Say that one more time.'

'*Loser.*' The girl pushes Samira's chest, sending her flying backwards onto the grass. She hits the ground hard.

Tilly rushes to her side. 'Sammy! Sammy! You okay?'

She nods, a little winded, as Tilly pulls her to her feet and helps her brush off dirt and grass from her clothes and elbows. When they look back to the queue, the girl has disappeared into the crowd.

'Sammy, there are more toilets around the corner,' Tilly says, glaring at everyone in the queue who stayed silent. 'Come with me.'

Afterwards, in the park, the girls sit in the sun eating triple-stacked rainbow ice-cream cones from the food truck parked outside the marquee.

'How's your bum?' asks Tilly, licking droplets off her wrist.

'As bruised as my pride. I've never been in a fight before and it shows.'

'You were a real-life superhero, but you didn't have to do that,' Tilly says. 'I'm used to people treating me that way.'

'That's terrible.'

'Dressing how I feel on the inside is the world's worst crime apparently.' Tilly pauses. 'Other than my two best friends, you're the first person to stand up for me.'

'Ever?'

'Correct. So thank you,' she says, clinking her ice-cream with Samira's. 'And sorry about the sore bum.'

'It'll survive.' Samira grins. 'I better get back to the party. My friend Anoush was in a world of hurt when I saw her last.'

'Well, the boys probably think I've snuck into Alotta's dressing room to steal her wigs.'

Samira snorts. 'Thanks again for the gifts.'

'No problem, neighbour,' Tilly says, jumping to her feet. 'Come over sometime.'

Samira's fingers trace the Alotta Peach bangle on her wrist as she watches Tilly skip away.

Live your way, baby.

Zoë

Day 2: 1.06pm

Akito plunges his finger into the baba ganoush, laughing as Zoë rolls her eyes. He licks off the dip, unfazed, and reaches towards the bowl again.

'What's wrong with you?' Zoë smacks his hand away as she reaches for a cracker.

'I didn't realise a queen was here at the Grand Southwell,' he teases in a high-pitched voice, lounging back on the couch next to Prakash. 'We must be on our best behaviour for Queen Russo.'

Prakash rolls his eyes. 'Come on, man.'

'Why aren't you lot dressed for the party?' Akito asks, sizing up the girls' outfits.

His new friend Darius, who's staying in the penthouse suite above theirs, called out over the balcony twenty minutes earlier and invited them all to his traffic light party. The rules are simple according to Akito. The colours relate to relationship status: green is single, red is in a relationship or not interested, yellow is maybe interested but unsure.

Violet raises an eyebrow. 'Excuse me? *You're*

70

critiquing us,' she says to Akito, gesturing to her pink bodycon dress and Zoë's purple off-the-shoulder top and miniskirt.

The girls have been picking out clothes, trying them on, and swapping them all morning. Their rooms look like they've been ransacked.

'Luca, tell him what's what,' Violet adds.

Luca grins as he tops up everyone's drinks. 'You look fierce, Violet. No further comment.'

Akito runs his hands through his jet-black hair. 'You girls look nice but I'm not seeing any green, red or yellow.' He pops the collar of his green polo shirt, then points at Prakash's shirt with a yellow abstract design down the front. 'See, yellow! Even P's into it.'

Violet shrugs. 'Green does nothing for my skin tone.'

'And yellow washes me out,' Luca says with a wink. 'I'm not changing.'

Zoë rifles through Violet's costume jewellery and slips a ring with a ruby red gemstone onto her middle finger. 'There,' she says, sticking her finger up in Akito's face. 'Red. Happy now?'

He rubs his palms together. 'Party time.'

They cram into the penthouse suite one floor up with a sea of strangers draped in red, yellow and green. The lights are low and the air stinks of sweat and salt and cigarette smoke. There's no sign of the mysterious Darius who has apparently invited half of paradise.

Zoë and Prakash splutter at the stench, covering their mouths.

The group quickly splits apart. Luca and Violet make a beeline for the food table, while Akito slinks across the room to a leather couch in the corner. Wads of cash are piled on the coffee table for a strip poker game. Akito slips on a shiny green poker visor and nestles among a group of girls in skimpy dresses and guys undressed down to their shorts. He waves at Prakash and Zoë to join him.

'Want to?' Prakash asks.

Zoë's throat is scratchy from the smoke. 'Can we get some air?'

They head towards a full-length sliding glass door that leads onto an enormous balcony. A cool breeze licks Zoë's skin as she steps onto the tiles. Music from inside thumps behind her, and a handful of boys are flopped on a daybed playing cards in the corner. Prakash gives them a polite nod, but Zoë walks on, squeezing past a dining setting and rows of sunlounges.

The bright sunlight stings her eyes but she forces them to stay open to take in the view. Saldana Strip, the ocean brushing the skyline, the mountains in the distance. She slips her phone out of her tote and takes a few photos of the soft pastel swirls of the clouds and the glowing sun cracked open above the sea. She exhales. This is the escape she's been holding her breath for all year long, but thanks to the guilty churning in her stomach she wonders if she should have followed her parents' orders and stayed home.

Out of habit, she checks her emails to see if there's any news about her university acceptances. Nothing.

'Zo. You're doing life admin at a party?'

'Fine.' She raises her phone to take a photo of Prakash grinning at her. But before she can, it buzzes in her hand.

Hey, how's your week? I'm home for a few days and wanted to check you're okay too? Greta x

'Look who's keeping tabs,' Zoë says, rolling her eyes. 'She's rushed home to be by their side! This text translates to: *You're a terrible daughter, now tell me every naughty thing you're doing so I can rat you out. PS: I'm their favourite.*'

Prakash smirks. 'Projecting much?'

'No! Perfect daughter Greta is on a mission to torture me. Wasn't it enough for her that she blitzed school and got into the Gifted and Talented Program *and* made Mum and Dad happier than they've ever been?'

'More is more. She's trying to out-Greta herself.'

Zoë sighs and scrolls through her latest messages from her dad. They range from furious, to guilt-inducing, to playing it cool. She wants to tell him that she's tired and burnt-out and this week is hopefully going to help rebuild her before studying begins again. But instead she sends this:

I only ever wanted to stick to the plan we agreed on. I'm ok. Promise. But I need this. Love you x

She pauses, then adds:

Tell Mum I'm sorry again.

She turns off her phone before any replies arrive to spin things upside down.

'Prakash?' she says.

'Yeah, Zo?'

'Do you think your parents are proud of you?'

He exhales. 'Big question. Maybe … sometimes.' He breaks into a grin. 'At least until they find out I actually want to be an actor. Then I'll be disowned.'

'No way. You're their precious baby boy!'

'Yeah, yeah,' he says, gently shoving her shoulder. 'But I'm no academic whiz, unlike someone on this balcony.'

'You got top marks all year in English.'

'Almost top. You beat me half the time. And there's no medical degree in my future. Now *that* would have made them proud. I bet your parents are so proud of you. Well, until you ran away and ruined everything,' he adds with a smirk.

'Shut up!' She elbows him in the side and he pretends to wince. 'I don't know, P. My parents are hard to read, especially Mum. Nothing feels good enough. It's exhausting.'

Behind her, the glass door slides open. It's a guy wearing a camouflage-green shirt that strains against his tattooed arms.

'That's him,' Prakash whispers.

The enigmatic Darius. He steps out onto the balcony, shutting out the party raging behind him. Zoë waits for him to join the boys playing cards but he saunters in their direction. He stops a few metres away and leans against the balcony.

'Cigarette?' he asks, holding out a packet.

'All good, thanks, man,' Prakash says.

Zoë wrinkles her nose.

'Bad habit,' he mutters but lights up anyway.

'Darius, right?' Prakash says. 'We're Akito's mates. This is Zoë, I'm Prakash.'

'He said you might be out here.' Darius swivels his head towards Zoë. 'So what does purple mean?'

Zoë winces as smoke trails in her direction. 'Ah, historically it's regal, I think, but it can also be seen as romantic. Plus, scientists now know it's the most powerful visible wavelength of electromagnetic energy.'

'Huh?' Darius cocks his head to one side. 'You're at a traffic light party so I meant *that* purple.' He gestures to her off-the-shoulder top.

'Oh, right. I guess it means I got a last-minute invite and red isn't my colour.' She flashes the ruby ring on her middle finger. 'But I did my best.'

'Red, got it,' he says, inhaling another breath of the cigarette. 'You two been together long?'

Zoë's eyes widen. 'We're friends.'

'And barely that,' Prakash adds with a cheeky grin. 'She checks emails at parties.'

Darius nods. 'You're that bored, huh?'

Zoë waves away the smoke. 'No, it's fine,' she splutters. 'I … I better find the others. I'll see you later.'

She hurries inside and spots Luca and Violet dancing in a corner of the lounge room.

'Where have you been?' asks Luca, leaning in closer. 'You reek of cigarettes.'

'Can we leave soon?' Zoë asks.

Violet gestures around. 'It's the penthouse. What's wrong with you?'

Zoë shrugs. 'I got a text from Greta. Guilt's kicking in.'

Luca sighs. 'Aren't you tired of trying to please everyone?'

'I'm drained watching you do it,' Violet adds.

'You don't know what it's like to have her as a sister.'

'True, but I don't see Greta, or anyone, here judging you. You're doing it to yourself.'

Darius suddenly appears with a tray of colourful drinks topped with cream and paper umbrellas. Violet adjusts her dress and leans forward, plucking a pina colada off the tray.

'Why thank you,' she says, batting her thick eyelashes. 'This is your party, right?'

'You know it,' he says with a grin. 'Just dropping off a special delivery for my new pal Zoë.'

'What the ...' Luca mutters. 'Zo, what is happening?'

'Nothing,' she says.

Luca takes a sip of his cocktail and gasps. 'How much alcohol is in this? Not that I'm complaining.'

Darius shrugs. 'Lost track.'

'So, are you going to the foam party too?' Violet asks him, eyeing off the tattoos lining his arms.

'Maybe.'

'You should,' Luca adds. 'Zoë will be there.'

'We'll *all* be there,' Zoë corrects him, swirling her drink with the cocktail umbrella.

'Shut up and think of the free drinks,' Luca mutters under his breath.

Violet takes a big slurp of her cocktail and holds up the empty glass. 'Zoë never knows how to have fun. This is wasted on her. Here, give me that.' She takes Darius's phone and presses a few buttons. 'That's my number. Message us if you come.'

While the others fall into conversation, Zoë looks around, spinning the red ring on her finger. She spots Prakash playing strip poker in the corner with Akito and a group of strangers. Prakash's shirt is wrapped around his waist and he looks as uncomfortable as she feels. His gaze meets hers and they poke their tongues out at each other.

Dahlia

Day 2: 1.59pm

There's only half a metre separating Dahlia and Kiko but there may as well be oceans. They drag their sneakers along the cobbled footpath at WonderWorld in silence, passing friends licking dreamy clouds of fairy floss, parents wrangling their toddlers into a double pram, and a young couple walking hand in hand.

Kiko pulls out a map of the theme park. 'Ferris wheel?' She unfolds it and squints at the crumpled paper. 'I don't think it's too far away.'

'Trapped in a tiny cage perfumed with puke?' Dahlia crinkles her nose. 'Nah.'

'Dodgem cars?'

'Whiplash in the making. Plus the puke thing again.'

'We could meet up with Florence and the boys at the water slides?'

'I'm okay. You go though.'

Kiko shrugs. 'I don't want to cramp her style. So what then?'

'Not sure.'

They dawdle along, falling quiet again. Dahlia hasn't

brought up the Too Late List yet, but she can't get it out of her head. Everything seems like a possible new entry for something Stevie didn't get to do. Did she ever come to WonderWorld with her family? Dahlia hates that she can't remember.

They walk by the screaming thrills of the tilt-a-whirl, before turning the corner to see long queues for the river rapids and log rides. A red tourist choo-choo train steams past, filled with waving kids and exhausted-looking parents.

Dahlia sighs. A deep, slow sigh.

Kiko stops abruptly in front of a flickering kiosk sign. 'That's it!'

'What?' asks Dahlia, wincing at the blinking lights. 'Do you want a WonderWorld showbag?'

Kiko dismisses the kiosk with a dramatic flick of her hand. 'You know, Dahlia, if you don't want to be here, you don't have to be.'

Dahlia's jaw drops. 'Excuse me?'

'The blunt comments, the sighing, *the mood* ... You're acting like you're spending time with your worst enemy.'

'I'm ... I'm good,' Dahlia says. 'We're having fun.'

Kiko raises an eyebrow. 'Are we?'

'Fine.' She pulls out the list from her denim cut-offs and thrusts it in Kiko's face. 'I found this.'

'And?'

'It was crumpled in these shorts in your luggage. Like it's nothing.'

'That's unfair. I'm keeping it safe.'

Dahlia's bottom lip quivers. 'How could you not tell me you had it?'

'Her mum left you three messages,' Kiko says. 'You never gave her an answer and she couldn't look at it any more. I thought you knew.' She pauses. 'Stevie's mum needed it gone, Dahlia, and it means something to me too.'

'I wasn't in a good place then,' Dahlia says.

'Me either. We all lost Stevie.'

'I know that.'

'Sometimes, and I don't think it's deliberate, but I think you forget.' Kiko juts her chin out a little. 'And while we're being honest, I'm working my way through that list. Checking things off.'

'Why? It's hers.'

'It's *for* her now. She'd want that, like she wanted us to take this trip.'

'How do you know?'

Kiko shrugs. 'Gut feeling. Guess I don't know for sure. But I'm positive about one thing: she wouldn't want to see you like this. Scared. Angry. Hiding.'

'I'm not!'

'This isn't you. I don't get why Stevie dying means you have to stop living? You're suffering twice.'

Dahlia's cheeks burn red as she folds the list up into a tiny square and stuffs it into her pocket. 'I don't need any more therapists in my life.'

Kiko locks eyes with her. 'Fine. I'm sorry. But you brought it up.' She exhales. 'So where to now? You've vetoed half the park.'

Dahlia looks away, hands trembling so much she loops her fingers together. Over Kiko's shoulder looms the WonderWorld Spooky House of Horrors, an old-looking building covered with spider webs, rusty chains and fake blood dripping down the walls. Dahlia's heart races. Stevie had a haunted house on her Too Late List.

'You want to tick something off?' she suggests, pointing.

Kiko's jaw drops when she turns around to see the haunted house. 'I didn't think that was your speed. Angry vampires and decapitated mummies and corpses and all that.'

'You want me to face scary stuff,' Dahlia says, then nudges Kiko to soften the mood. 'Besides, all those sombre ghouls — I'll fit right in, huh? Oh, and wait.' She pulls out the folded list and passes it to Kiko. 'It's yours. Thanks for taking good care of it for her.'

'My pleasure,' Kiko says, slipping the list into her pocket. 'Now let's find us a werewolf.'

As they walk closer to the entrance, they can hear shrieking and rattling coming from inside.

'Maybe we *should* go to the ferris wheel,' Dahlia murmurs.

Loud screaming echoes from deep within the house. An *Enter if you dare* sign hangs on the wall next to the ticket counter.

'Dare you,' whispers Kiko.

'Dare you back.'

They step inside. Cobwebs hang from the ceiling and a deep creaking noise reverberates in the distance. Faded portraits of wizened old men and women line the entrance, their dusty frames lined with a thick red substance.

'Is that blood?' hisses Kiko, linking her arm through Dahlia's.

'It's fake, all for effect,' Dahlia whispers. 'Keep moving.'

They turn a corner and enter a long shadowy hallway lined with spindly glow-in-the-dark skeletons. They edge past peeling wallpaper and long jagged scratch marks on the wall. The air smells dank with a hint of wet wood.

A large vampire mannequin stands in one corner. As they pass, it hisses and bares its fangs.

Kiko clings tighter to Dahlia. 'That hunk of plastic scared the hell out of me!'

A shiver goes down Dahlia's spine. She feels a cold breath on the back of her neck.

'Stop breathing on me, Kiko.'

'I'm not! My hand is over my mouth — I've nearly chewed my nails off!'

Dahlia stops. 'Seriously? You're not doing it?' Her hand flies to the back of her neck. 'Then what was … Shit, let's keep going.'

The sound of wailing fills the room behind them as they approach a door. As they argue about who should open it, the wailing gets louder.

'It's getting closer,' Kiko whimpers.

Dahlia swings open the door and links her fingers through Kiko's. 'Come on.'

Rubber snakes drop from the ceiling at their feet. They scream and surge forward into a thick fog, spluttering as they swipe at cobwebs all around them.

'I can't do this!' Kiko says. 'Where's the exit? I think I'm having a heart attack. I can't, I can't—'

'You can,' Dahlia says, holding up their interlinked fingers. 'I'm here. It's just a fog machine — we're nearly done.'

The temperature drops as they round another corner. Fake blood is splattered on the floor and ceiling and four mummies wrapped in thick bandages line the wall.

'I see you!' Kiko yells at the first mummy. 'I know you're up to something!'

'Keep walking,' Dahlia says. 'Remember the vampire? Fake, fake, fake.'

They pass the mummies and walk towards a glowing light.

'The exit,' Kiko cheers.

'See! That wasn't so bad,' Dahlia says. 'A few more steps then we're—'

An icy hand grazes her shoulder. She gasps, causing Kiko to shriek, and they jolt around to see the four mummies lurching at them, arms out, heads locked at disturbing angles.

The girls stumble backwards, their cries lost beneath the mummies' howling. Kiko almost snaps Dahlia's wrist as they cling to each other's hands. A cloud of wispy cobwebs wraps around them as, flailing and shrieking, they dash towards the exit.

Still holding hands, they sprint into the sunlight. Panting, Kiko leans over, trying to slow her breathing. Dahlia is laughing, still in shock.

'Did you see them?' Kiko asks, breathless. 'We could have died!'

Suddenly one of the mummies charges out of the exit behind them, arms out, lurching in their direction. It expels a deep roar, and Dahlia and Kiko leap together and scream.

'Nope!' yells Kiko, half-giggling, half-terrified, as she pulls at Dahlia's hand. 'Nope, nope, nope!'

They laugh as they run down twisting alleyways and pathways, past a merry-go-round and fairy-floss stalls.

'That was ...' Kiko's face is as pink as Dahlia's hair. 'Amazing.'

'It was, hey?' Dahlia wonders if her cheeks are as rosy as Kiko's. 'Should we go again?'

'Absolutely, positively, definitely a thousand times no way! Once for Stevie is enough for me.'

'How do the actors playing the mummies not get punched in the face fifty times a day?' Dahlia asks. 'I was about to clock them!'

'You were my hero in there,' Kiko says. 'I couldn't have done it without you.'

Dahlia blushes. 'You did the same for me on the plane.'

They swap little smiles before breaking eye contact.

Kiko skips ahead, passing food trucks and stalls, and pauses in front of a van to order a blueberry slushie.

She slurps the drink and passes it to Dahlia. 'Your turn,' she says, her lips stained as blue as the sea. 'I know you'll like it.'

'Confident.'

'Well, I know you.' Kiko pauses. 'I think I do.'

Dahlia takes a sip. 'You do,' she admits. 'And I really am sorry. I've been unbearable.'

'You don't have to apologise. Grief. It goes on and on, and swells and fades, and even disappears sometimes, only to come roaring back when you least expect it.' Kiko tilts her head. 'Stevie wrote a big list — she dreamt big. I'd get through the things on it quicker if I had someone to do them with.'

'Interesting.' Dahlia's lips slide into a smirk. 'Are you taking applications for the position?'

'Know anyone?'

'I have someone in mind.'

They walk in silence for a few steps before Kiko jolts in excitement. 'Photo booth! We have to do it!'

They squeeze inside the tiny booth, thighs pressing together, and fumble at the buttons. As the timer counts down, they laugh hysterically and debate how to pose. Then the light flashes, locking in the moment.

The photos spit out of the machine and the girls huddle in close for a look. Dahlia's breath catches.

In the first shot, Kiko is winking with a crooked grin, while Dahlia flashes a smile so luminous it's like she's remembered how good things can feel if you let go.

Samira

Day 2: 3.22pm

The foam party has escalated. An inflatable slide bounce house is rigged up in the centre of the area, with a ball pit below it surging with rainbow plastic balls. Two organisers in fluoro T-shirts stand on a high platform to manage the growing crowd hurling themselves down the soapy slide. It's already sagging in the middle, weakened by the river of foamy bubbles rushing along it.

'Oh yeah, Saldana Strip! Who else wants to have the slide of their life?' a cheesy voice booms over the loudspeaker. Another surge of people race to line up.

Samira's mouth cracks into a smile. 'Hey, should we go on the—'

Claire elbows her in the side. 'Oh my Beyoncé, check out Zain and that girl again.'

The knot in Samira's stomach constricts. She glances over at the pair locked in a passionate kiss, then looks away, tightening her arms around her middle.

'They're going for it,' Anoush says, a little in awe.

Rashida whistles. 'Now with added levels of sloppy.'

'Can we forget about them?' Samira asks, trying to stay upbeat. 'Let's do something fun. Just us girls.'

'Love it,' Anoush says. 'Like what?'

'Like that.' Samira gestures to the inflatable slide where a guy is zigzagging down headfirst on his stomach. He collects a faceful of foamy bubbles before somersaulting into the ball pit.

Anoush's eyes widen. 'Maybe ... not.'

Claire crinkles her nose. 'It's a no from me. I want to look good and I will not look good doing that.'

'It'd ruin my hair,' adds Rashida.

'Sorry, Samira,' Claire says with a flippant shrug that shows she's not sorry at all.

Anoush throws Samira an apologetic look.

'I really can't bribe one of you to ...' Samira's voice trails off when she feels someone's gaze on her. She turns to see a boy with long lashes smiling at her. It suddenly feels like there's something trapped in her throat. A choked 'Hi' escapes.

'Hey,' the guy says. There's a small gap between his front teeth. 'Can I ask you something?'

Samira's palms are sweating so she links her fingers together. 'Anything.'

'I don't want the whole room to hear.'

Samira moves towards him, feeling the girls watching her.

'Can you ask your friend if she wants to kiss me?' he whispers.

'Of course,' she says, leaning in before clicking to what he actually said. 'Wait, *what*?'

'All good, I'll ask her myself,' he says before turning to the others. 'I clearly have no moves.'

Samira plasters on a toothy smile, half in shock she misinterpreted the situation, half-relieved the others can't read her mind.

Rashida and Claire bat their eyelashes at him but he steps towards Anoush. 'Would you wanna kiss me?'

'Is this a dare?' Anoush asks.

He looks over his shoulder to where a group of guys are egging him on. 'Kinda. They thought I'd be too chicken to come over. But I do want to kiss you. If *you* want to.'

'Well ... alright!' Anoush giggles.

They hold hands, fumbling for a second, then their lips touch briefly before Anoush steps back.

'Hey,' he says to her softly.

'You taste like spearmint,' she says, blushing as she leans in to kiss him again. This time, they don't pull apart so quickly.

Samira looks away, clearing her throat to hide her embarrassment, while Rashida and Claire squeal with laughter.

A huge roar erupts from the growing crowd centred around the base of the inflatable slide. They're shouting one word on repeat: 'Zoë!'

A girl with cat-eye glasses — Zoë, Samira assumes — stands at the top of the slide, waving at the crowd. She claps in time with the chanting, then freezes. 'I can't, Prakash!' she cries out to the guy behind her. 'It's too high!'

The crowd roars even louder, and Prakash scoops a handful of bubbles from the top of the slide and plops it on Zoë's head. She squeals and bats him away — and her feet slip out from under her. She skids backwards down the inflatable slide, arms and legs flailing.

Prakash's jaw drops. Then he jumps, clutching his knees to his chest, and careens down the slide to join her in the ball pit.

Cheering echoes around the marquee as the girls trade horrified looks.

'Still want to go on that germ-infested slide, Samira?' Rashida asks. 'That could have been you tripping.'

Anoush giggles, her shoulders bumping against the mystery boy's broad frame.

Samira shrugs as she looks over at the girl called Zoë. Her friends have surrounded her in the ball pit, laughing and dancing, and the grin on her face stretches from ear to ear.

'Did you see her fall?' Claire sniggers. 'She looked so trashy.'

The others purse their lips in agreement and an ache in Samira's chest deepens. 'That's such a nasty thing to say,' she tells Claire, her voice quiet but strong. It's the second time today she's found the right words when she's needed them, rather than days later when the moment is gone.

Anoush lowers her head a little.

'Excuse me?' replies Claire, hands on hips.

'She's having fun.' Samira gestures to Zoë, who's climbed onto her friend Prakash's shoulders so he can run with her around the pit. 'We don't even know her. Why do you care?'

'Whatever,' Claire sniffs. 'I could say the same to you.'

'I care because it's mean—'

'Well, I didn't ask your opinion.'

'Let's all take a breath,' pipes up Anoush.

'Drama in aisle five,' Rashida says. 'I repeat: drama in aisle five.'

Just then, Zain and Mathieu rock up. Their arrival cuts through the tension and the girls leap up to greet them. Samira forces a fake smile and avoids eye contact with Zain.

'Yo, we're moving on to that all-hours club on the corner,' Mathieu says, gulping down the last of his drink. 'The one with the podiums and no windows. You girls in?'

'The Capitol?' Samira asks. 'We've got a limo booked later in the week to take us there.'

'But we can still check it out now,' Mathieu says with a shrug. 'It's around the corner and this party blows.'

'We're in,' Anoush says. The mystery boy is still super-glued to her side. 'Everyone, this is Dan. Dan, this is everyone. His friends might come too.'

As the group saunters towards the exit, Anoush whispers to Samira, 'Got what you need for the Capitol?'

'I do,' Samira says, her fingers finding the fake ID in her handbag.

'Excellent.' Anoush skips ahead to link arms with Dan and meet his friends.

Samira is stuck walking behind Rashida and Claire, who hasn't said a word to her since their disagreement. By the time they join the queue at the Capitol, Anoush, Dan and the boys are already inside. The entrance is roped off and operated by a bouncer with tattoos on his knuckles. Yawning, Rashida scrolls through her phone, and Claire snaps pouting selfies to check her make-up.

Samira turns over the fake ID in her palm. 'My cousin doesn't even look like me,' she whispers to Rashida. 'I don't think I can do this.'

'You're overthinking it,' Rashida hisses. 'Pull it together, *Mary*, before you get us all refused.'

'Your IDs aren't fake,' whispers Samira. 'What if he can tell?'

'Play it sweet. We'll see you inside.'

The girls reach the front of the line. Claire pushes out her chest and shows her ID. The bouncer doesn't even notice, just lifts the rope for her.

Rashida hands over her ID, continuing to play with her phone as she's let in.

'Your ID, miss?' the bouncer asks Samira.

She tries to convince herself this moment means nothing to him and she's yet another faceless brunette in line. That he has no idea her real name is Samira not

Mary, or that her mum and Teta will ground her for life if they discover she's broken the law.

'ID, miss?' he repeats, this time a little louder.

'Sure,' Samira mumbles to disguise her shaking voice and passes him the card. 'Here.'

She sees the *Live your way, baby* bangle hanging from her wrist and, before the bouncer can read the birthdate on the fake ID, she snatches it back.

'Sorry, I've realised I … I've left my hair straightener on,' she stammers. 'I have to go.'

And she flees, her sandals smacking loudly against the concrete footpath.

Zoë

Day 2: 4.03pm

Zoë sinks deep into the ball pit again and scoops through the foamy balls, flinging them in every direction as she searches for her phone. 'It has to be here,' she mutters, pushing back wet strands of hair.

Prakash wades towards her. 'No luck in this direction. Violet's triple-checking the portaloos outside.'

'We've been looking forever,' Zoë says, scouring the sea of rainbow balls. 'Maybe it's on our table and I missed it?'

'It's not!' Luca calls out. 'Checked there. Although I did see Darius making out with someone.'

Prakash grins. 'I saw that too! The girl with the spiky green hair and big hoop earrings?'

'No hoops and this girl had curls down to her bum.'

'He's doing the rounds then,' Prakash says, before noticing Zoë glaring at him to focus. 'Sorry, Zo, I'll call your phone again.'

Zoë melts into a grateful smile. 'Thanks, P.'

'Move it, slowpoke,' Luca tells Prakash. 'There's a drink at the bar calling my name.'

'Hey, don't rush me, I can't get it out of my pants,' Prakash says, his palm stuck in his jeans pocket, before realising how that sounded.

The trio collapse into laughter and grab at each other to stop slipping over.

'Help me!' Zoë sinks backwards into the balls, wheezing between bursts of giggles.

Luca's and Prakash's hands find hers and they pull her to standing position.

'You're a liability,' Luca says.

They turn to see Darius and Violet snapping a photo of themselves kissing. She's on her tippy-toes with her arms laced around his body.

Luca rolls his eyes. 'Doesn't Violet realise he's hooked up with half the foam party?'

Prakash holds up his phone. 'It's going straight to voicemail, Zo. I've called your number seven times.'

As they dig through the pit again, shouting erupts behind them. They turn to see Darius waving a phone high above the crowd. Violet stands beside him, grinning from ear to ear.

'Missing something?' Darius shouts.

Zoë jumps in the air. 'Yes!' she says, turning back to Luca and Prakash, who scoop her into a group hug. They lose their grip and all crash backwards into the ball pit. This time, Zoë doesn't care. 'Yes, yes, yes!'

Darius appears above them, his head blocking out the strobe lights painting streaks through the air. 'It's for you,' he says, holding out the phone. 'Your dad.'

Zoë's hands race to her mouth in shock. '*What?*'

'Uncle Gian called?' Luca looks at Zoë's phone like it might detonate and blow up the marquee. 'Leave me out of it, Zo! I accept no responsibility for driving you here.'

'The phone was over there,' Darius says, gesturing to the opposite side of the pit. 'Buzzing right under some random chick's feet! We answered it and the guy said he was looking for Zoë. Case closed.' He holds the phone out for Zoë again. 'Seems like a good guy, your dad.'

'He's my uncle, Violet's uncle too,' Luca says with a smirk. 'Meeting the family already, huh?'

'This is bad,' Zoë mutters, taking the phone. Her hand shakes as she imagines what her dad might rant down the line: *Chickpea, you're not leaving the house until you're fifty! You won't study medicine, you're banned from seeing the cousins and you'll live in our spare room forever!*

She fantasises about throwing her phone back in the ball pit, changing her name and never returning home to avoid the conflict with her family. But then she imagines her father waiting on the other end of the phone line, most likely sick with worry, and she decides it's time to face the inevitable outrage.

'Dad?' she begins.

Behind her, people roar as giant beach balls rain down on them. She's deafened by the crowd surging in the ball pit and thumping on the dance floor.

She can't hear a word he's saying. Then again, louder. 'Dad?'

It cuts out.

Zoë swears at her phone.

Luca's shout pierces through the chaos and she looks up. He's pointing to the corner of the ball pit. 'Gross! A guy's peeing! A guy is *peeing*.'

Everyone squeals and clambers over each other to escape the area.

'I should call Dad back,' Zoë shouts in Prakash's direction as she kicks foamy balls out of her way and veers towards the exit.

'I'm coming with you!' Luca calls, lunging for Zoë's arm. 'Don't leave me with these animals!'

Outside the marquee, they find a quiet spot away from the crowd.

'Calling Uncle Gian is a terrible idea,' Luca says. 'I vote you pass me the phone, get a drink and pretend everything is fine.'

Zoë laughs. 'I have to deal with this. The guilt is getting to me! May as well be now.'

'How about never? Never sounds good to me.' He sighs. 'Well, it's been nice being your cousin, Zo.'

'You too, sometimes,' she teases. 'By the way, you're in charge of organising my funeral.'

Her throat feels dry as she makes the call.

'Zoë!' It's Greta's voice that answers. 'Are you there? What's happening?'

Zoë freezes. She was expecting a fiery conversation with their dad, not a sparkling welcome from her older sister.

'I ... Yeah, I'm here. Where's Dad?' Zoë's heart races as she hears the rise and fall of her parents arguing in the background.

'He's with Mum in the kitchen. They're talking things out.'

'Sounds like more than talking.'

'Mum's pretty fired up. We'd finally calmed her down, then that random guy answering your phone set her off again.'

'Oh shit,' Zoë says.

'Listen, Dad got your messages and he's been thinking about it and talking about it with me. And, well ... he's starting to think you're right.'

There's a long pause, then Zoë says, 'This must be a bad connection. I swore you said he thinks I'm right.'

Luca pinches her arm. 'What's happening?' he mouths. 'What's Uncle Gian saying? Has he hired a hitman?'

Zoë mouths back, 'It's Greta! I think Dad's high!' She mimes smoking a joint.

'*What*?' Luca tries to press his ear close to the phone to listen, but Zoë shoos him away. He gestures that he's going back to the party for another drink and stomps off.

'Zoë?' Greta's voice cuts through. 'You still with me?'

'Just taking it all in.' She swallows. 'Can you put Dad on? I ... I need to talk to him.'

'Sure. Give me a second.'

There's rustling and hushed whispers before her father's deep voice says, 'Chickpea.' He sounds so warm that it instantly throws her.

'Dad, I don't know what to say.'

'Are you safe?'

'I am. And I'm so, so sorry.'

'Those hours before you texted back were the worst moments of my life.'

'*Dad.*'

'And if it were up to your mother, you'd be grounded forever.'

'Or dead,' she mutters.

He chuckles. 'Oh, Zoë. You should never have run away. But your mother and I have spoken, endlessly so, and I don't think we played fair either. We never should have changed the plan so abruptly.' His voice cracks. 'Sometimes I think we forget that you're not our little girl any more.'

'I am though.'

'In some ways. But you're moving on, Chickpea. You're going to be a doctor, for God's sake!'

'Maybe, Dad. I'm still waiting to find out.'

'If freedom is what you want,' he says, 'then it's yours.'

'Dad, I never wanted freedom. Just a break.'

'Well, you've got it either way — and everything else that comes with growing up. Responsibility, liability, accountability. It's all yours.'

'Is this a trap?' Zoë asks.

'No, not at all. We'll see you in less than a week.'

'And Mum's on board?'

'She'll get there. Greta's helping her prepare dinner now.'

'Of course she is,' Zoë says, stomach churning at the thought of her mother and Greta in the kitchen talking about her.

'Now, now. You're in debt to your big sister — she's come to the rescue this week, more than you could ever imagine. Really helped me to see how short-sighted we'd been.'

Zoë's mouth feels dry. 'I'm going to make you proud one day too, like Greta does. I promise.'

There's a pause before her father says, 'You already do, Chickpea, all while giving us a heart attack. Now, look after each other at the coast. Your mother can't handle any more surprises.'

When Zoë hangs up the phone, she opens the message from Greta. Guilt panging in her chest, she fires off a short reply.

Thanks x

Samira

Day 2: 4.46pm

Samira weaves through side streets, heart pounding, before eventually stopping on a corner to catch her breath. She looks around. Everyone is in pairs and groups. She's the only one alone.

She messages Anoush but there's no reply. Fifteen minutes pass, but it feels like fifteen hours. She calls her and it immediately clicks over to voicemail.

'Hey, it's Anoush. I'm busy doing something awesome. I only check this thing about twice a year so Mum, if that's you, text me instead! Okay, byeeeeeeeeeee.'

Samira stares at her phone, willing it to ring or vibrate, anything to prove her friends are missing her or worried about where she's gone.

Her phone buzzes, but it's a message from her mum.

Hope you have the best time tonight! Have lots of adventures (but not TOO many). Keep enjoying your special week xx

Another buzz.

PS: Call me in the next day or two! I miss your voice

Samira's fingers trace over the phone's buttons as she tries to drown out the cacophony of sounds on Saldana Strip. She wants to call her mum and tell her everything. But she doesn't dare admit the truth: this week's perfect plan has already fizzled into a mess. She thought she'd felt alone before, but there on the Strip, surrounded by hundreds of happy people, Samira has never felt lonelier. In that moment, she wants nothing more than to curl up in bed as her mum gently strokes her cheek to help her fall asleep like when she was a little girl.

And then she hears a voice that lights up the afternoon. 'Sammy, this is meant to be! Hello!'

Samira turns to see Tilly and her friends wearing slight variations of the bold, bright costumes from the previous night: the Queen, the Robot and the Pirate.

'What are you up to?' Tilly asks, glancing at the shop behind Samira. It's closed.

'Um, my group and I got separated,' Samira fibs. 'They're late, but I'm sure they'll be here soon. We're … we're on our way to a party.'

'Sounds fun,' Tilly says. 'Isn't this the best week? We didn't make a lot of plans, we just dress up and see where the day takes us. And hey, it's taken us to you.' She turns to her friends. 'Hey Peachies, this is that fabulous girl I was telling you about. Sammy is my superhero. She gives good loo chat too. Great loo chat.'

The Peachies laugh, clearly used to Tilly's enthusiasm.

'Hey, I'm Kris,' says the Robot.

'And I'm Harry,' adds the Pirate. 'And you obviously know the Queen herself.'

Tilly curtsies. 'She does.' She points at Samira's bangle. 'Sammy's a Peachie in the making. I'm thinking "the Warrior".'

Samira blushes. 'I don't know if that suits me.'

'You fought for me!' Tilly says. 'I can't believe we've run into you! I was telling these guys you give off good vibes left, right and centre.'

'I ... I do?'

'Ten out of ten aura.'

Samira grins. Tilly seems to have that effect on her. 'Um ... thanks.'

'So we're heading to a dumplings place two streets back if you're interested,' Tilly adds.

'The all-you-can-eat one?'

'You know it. Want to bring your friends?'

Kris smirks. 'Stop trying to recruit more Peachies into your cult, Tilly.'

'At least so obviously,' adds Harry. 'Shameless.'

'That sounds awesome,' Samira says before she can stop herself. 'But my friends and I have those, um, those plans.'

'Sure, all good! Pop your number in here,' Tilly says, passing Samira her phone. 'In case you get a craving later.'

As Tilly and the Peachies walk off, arguing over which song Alotta Peach will open her set with at the concert later in the week, a new number pranks Samira's phone. She saves it under *Tilly the Peachie*, then stares at the screen, wishing Anoush would reply.

* * *

Twenty minutes later, after still nothing from Anoush, Samira stands in the doorway of the hole-in-the-wall dumpling bar, watching the Peachies laughing and arguing and feeding each other with chopsticks.

They spot her and wave her in, round up another chair, and heap steamed dumplings onto a plate for her.

Within an hour, Samira's startled to realise she's told them everything: about Zain, Anoush, the fake ID, all of it. The words tumble out and they listen, really listen, and the night rolls on.

It's Tilly's idea to hold an exorcism at midnight. 'A "Good Riddance to Zain" exorcism,' she says.

Kris and Harry roll their eyes at the suggestion. But Samira, despite having no idea what Tilly's talking about, agrees.

Zoë

Day 2: 10.17pm

Zoë and the others are down to their underwear and packed into Darius's rooftop hot tub like sardines. Foamy bubbles spill over the edges and onto the deck, and music blasts from a speaker in the corner, competing with the songs blaring from other suites in the resort.

Luca takes another sip of his cocktail and leans in closer. 'Say it again, Zo.'

Zoë beams. 'Not grounded!'

'No yelling from Aunty Rosette?' Violet chimes in, sloshing her drink everywhere. 'Or crying from Uncle Gian?'

'None,' Zoë says, and widens her eyes for emphasis. 'Dad even said he loves me.'

Prakash wipes water from his thick brows. 'I can't get over it. You're in the clear?'

Luca pretends to bow down. 'So clear it's translucent! Zo, this is your permission from *everyone* to forget about exams and have fun.'

'He's right for once.' Violet props herself up in the tub

to better show off her lacy pink bra. 'This is a once-in-a-lifetime shot.'

'I know, I know,' Zoë groans, rolling her eyes. 'We only get this holiday once.'

Luca stands up, sending water spraying everywhere. 'Zoë!' he declares, ignoring the girls giggling at his sopping wet boxer briefs. 'You don't seem to understand the gravity of what you've pulled off. I thought you were dead-cousin-walking, but you've escaped without a lick of punishment. It's a miracle!'

Akito cheers. 'The universe wants you to party!'

'Nay!' says Darius, sliding into the tub and passing around more drinks. '*Needs* you to party.'

Prakash and Zoë swap smirks.

'Yes, needs,' Luca repeats, high-fiving the boys. 'Listen to us, Zo.'

'Let's do something outrageous then,' Violet says. 'Come get a tattoo with me tomorrow.' She holds out her phone. 'Look at this butterfly design.'

'Not a chance!' Zoë says.

'But it looks so adorable.'

'And clichéd,' Luca adds.

While the cousins argue, Zoë slips out of the hot tub and pulls her towel around herself.

'Zo, you better not be going to bed after our inspiring pep talks,' Violet yells, splashing water at her. 'Uncle Gian might've gone easy on you but I won't.'

Zoë walks towards the balcony door before pausing in front of the speaker. She slowly looks over her shoulder with a crooked grin, then leans over and turns up the volume, before whipping off her towel and twirling it in the air.

Violet's hollering fills the night sky as Zoë throws the towel onto the deck and dances under the yellow glow of the fairylights.

Day 3

Samira

Day 3: 12.10am

Samira stares at the fire pit, hypnotised by the flicker and spark of the burnt orange flames. They cast eerie shadows across the beach house's courtyard.

Tilly's voice cracks through the dark. 'It's after midnight, Samira. You ready to do this?'

Samira's gaze falls to the *Live your way, baby* bangle again. 'I think so.' A nervous laugh slips out. 'But also no. Just one second.'

She can't believe she's at the Peachies' house in the middle of the night. This isn't part of the plan. She checks her phone. Still nothing from Anoush, despite Samira texting and calling her after fleeing the Capitol earlier that day.

'Hey!' Tilly's voice snaps Samira back to reality. 'Phone away, Sammy. I need your full attention at this exorcism of your ex.'

The moon glows high among speckled stars, and the boys crowd around Samira, waving sparklers in the air.

'Are they necessary?' Samira cringes as the sparklers pop and fizz uncomfortably close to her hair.

'Don't they look fabulous?' Tilly claps her hands twice. 'Let's begin. Silence!'

Samira, Kris and Harry swap wide-eyed looks and stifle laughter.

Tilly clears her throat. 'We're gathered here today—'

Harry snorts. 'It's not a wedding.'

'Right, right,' Tilly says, hushing them. 'We're here tonight, at, twelve past twelve precisely — wow, that's got to mean something, right? — to banish the bad vibes that this so-called Zain—'

'That *is* his name,' Samira says with a grin. 'But you're correct on the bad vibes.'

Tilly nods. 'Right. Basically we're all here because Zain sucks. He broke the heart of the amazing Sammy, the Warrior among us, and she deserves one million times better. My Peachies, Kris and Harry, will serve as witnesses to this momentous event,' she continues, 'and it will go down in history as a night to remember. A night when good overcame evil. When the hero beat the villain. When true love — self-love — won all.'

It's Kris's turn to crack up. 'Move it on. I'd love to get to bed before the sun rises.'

Tilly turns to Samira. 'Where are the items I requested?'

Earlier in the night, Samira had collected a few things: Zain's passport photo, which she'd kept tucked in her wallet; an item of his clothing (she'd snuck next door into his room to borrow a sock); and a love letter. Zain had never written one, so Samira scribbled out one of his nicer texts on the back of a takeaway menu.

'Here they are,' she says, emptying the items out of her handbag onto the bench in the courtyard. 'Hope they're okay.'

Tilly strokes each piece — cringing when she realises she's fondling a stranger's sock — before placing it back on the bench.

Kris and Harry snigger.

'Perfect,' Tilly says, glaring at the boys. 'Sammy, first select the item of Zain's clothing.'

Samira picks up the sock.

'What does this represent to you?' Tilly asks. 'Think deeply.'

'It's his sock … so … feet?' Samira shrugs.

'No, no.' Tilly shakes her head. 'Like, socks, feet, shoes, shoes are made for walking, walking, walking, walking away, walking all over someone, walking the talk, walking the walk …'

'Is she having a stroke?' whispers Harry.

'Think, Sammy,' she insists. 'Why did you pick this sock? What does this sock say about Zain?'

'If that sock could talk, we'd all be millionaires,' Kris cracks.

'Fine.' Tilly rolls her eyes. 'Just throw it in the fire.'

'I thought I was only borrowing it,' Samira says.

'Nope. Fire. Now.'

Pinching the sock between two fingers, Samira tosses it into the fire.

'Anyone else feel sorry for the sock?' Harry asks. 'What did it ever do to us?'

Tilly claps her hands again. 'Silence! Next, the love letter. Read it out, please, then add it to the pit.'

'It's just a text, and not that lovey,' Samira says, picking up the menu. '*Babe, you looked so hot tonight. See you in my dreams.*'

Kris cringes. 'That's it? Pass the spew bucket.'

'Writing romantic texts obviously wasn't Zain's strength, but I'm sure he had lots of qualities that made Samira fall for him,' Tilly says. 'Not that we're focusing on his good qualities! This is a bad-qualities-only exorcism.'

Samira holds the menu over the fire. The edges catch alight and then it's sucked into the flames.

Tilly hums as she throws a feather, a leaf and a black and white shell into the pit.

'What do they mean?' Samira whispers.

Harry leans in. 'She has no idea.'

'Everyone, stop trying to micro-manage the purging!' Tilly says. 'Sammy, pick up the photo of Zain. And look at it. Really eyeball this tyrant.'

Kris stifles laughter behind his hand. Tilly shoots him a warning glare.

Samira picks up the photo and stares at it, taking in Zain's soulful expression. He looks so serious, because he wasn't allowed to smile for the passport photo.

She remembers the day the photo was taken. They'd sipped on chocolate milkshakes before going to the local post office. Samira didn't even need a photo. She only got one because Zain didn't want to go alone. It would be boring without her, he'd said.

They'd fought afterwards because he'd flaked on their plans to have a picnic in the park, going instead to Mathieu's to play video games. Later that evening, he'd surprised her with a bouquet and a mumbled apology. Cringing, Samira remembers how she'd been so annoyed with how he'd treated her, but she'd let him shower her with kisses and didn't mention the flowers looked suspiciously like Teta's roses from the front garden. She wishes she could go back to that moment in a time machine to call him out.

'What are you thinking, Sammy?' whispers Tilly. 'Wait, that's personal — you don't have to answer that.'

Samira looks at the photo again, then looks at Tilly. Every sense is sharpened, from the smell of the fire, to the sound of partying in the distance.

'I don't think I can do this,' she admits. 'He was my first proper boyfriend.'

'Didn't he hurt you though?' Harry asks.

'Hear, hear!' Kris adds. 'He sounds like a douchelord.'

'Quiet, you two,' hisses Tilly.

'I don't know, I guess,' Samira says. 'But I had this perfect week planned out for us. It was even colour-coded with themes. And matching stickers.' She sniffs, half-laughing, half-crying. 'No wonder he dumped me.'

'I, for one, love a good sticker,' Tilly says. 'But it's time for a new plan. With new colours! If you're ready to move on, rip up that photo of Zain and throw it in.'

'For real?' Samira asks.

'You don't need it any more.' Tilly switches to a softer, more ethereal tone. 'Rip up the photo, throw it in the fire and let these words wash over you: "Burn, Zain, burn. Burn, Zain, burn".'

'But I don't want him to *actually* burn.'

'No, this is, like, metaphorically,' Tilly says with a grin. 'You're burning him from your heart so something majestic can rise from the ashes. A life you truly want!'

Samira nods and tears through the photo until it's just a scattering of tiny pieces in her palm. With a lump in her throat, she sprinkles the shreds into the fire. They shrivel into blackness, until they're nothing but a pile of ash.

Dahlia

Day 3: 2.31am

The smell of salt is heavy and there's only a hint of light from the moon shimmering behind a mass of charcoal clouds. Dahlia and Kiko trail along the sand behind Florence, Seiji and Mitch as soft waves lap against the shore. The boys laugh and joke with Florence, the trio taking turns piggybacking each other.

Dahlia and Kiko have settled into a slower pace, their fingertips gently brushing as they swing their arms. Even the slightest touch makes Dahlia feel like she's plugged into a power socket. Electricity crackles through her body. But there are no clues in the dark. No way to decode Kiko's expression, to know if she feels it too.

'What's the plan, Florence?' Kiko calls out, shattering Dahlia's dreaming. 'Have you got us lost?'

Florence bounds over and stops between them, splitting them apart. Even in the darkness, Dahlia sees the glint in Florence's eyes.

'Something's brewing,' Dahlia says. 'I know that look.'

She first saw it when Florence dared the girls to join her in mooning her cranky old neighbour after the street's

Halloween party — and Stevie was the only one who got busted with her underwear around her knees. Or the time Florence was headed to a senior's house party on a Friday night but told her step-mum she was going to a school book club. She even wore her uniform. Despite Florence's eyelids heaving with glitter, her step-mum believed her and spent the next fifteen minutes blabbing about the novel on her bedside table. Stevie, Kiko and Dahlia muffled giggles behind their hands, but Florence never cracked; she smiled and nodded at her step-mum in all the right places, never losing the glint in her eye. The second she was in the back of Kiko's car, she stripped off her school uniform and slithered into a miniskirt. Florence's glint always leads to something intoxicating. Something rule-bending. Something unforgettable.

Now, Florence gestures around the deserted beach. 'Isn't my plan obvious?'

'*Obviously* not,' Kiko says with a shrug.

'Skinny-dipping in the ocean.'

'No way!' Dahlia's hands race to the sundress skimming her thighs.

The girls giggle at her reaction.

'Mitch and Seiji are in,' Florence shares with glee. 'Are you two?'

'Are you kidding?' Dahlia replies, breaking into laughter. 'No way.'

'Your loss.' Florence sweeps off her top to reveal a red bra covered in strawberries.

'What if someone sees you?' Dahlia asks.

'It's pitch-black, so if someone is squinting to get a look then they're the Pervy McPerve *not* me,' Florence says, sliding off her shorts so she's left in her underwear.

Kiko looks around. 'It *is* dark, Dahlia.'

'And the dark hides many secrets,' Florence says. 'It's just a body. I have nothing to be ashamed of, and neither do you. We're all skeletons getting around in fleshy skin suits.' She grins. 'If I was in charge of this country, I'd let people walk around naked.'

Kiko flicks Florence's bra strap. 'You'd really want to see your step-mum and dad walking around with their bits out?'

'Whatever. I'm proud of my body, imperfections and all — and you should be proud of yours.'

Dahlia laughs. 'I get that, and I am, but can we be proud of our bodies in our hostel room or something?'

'You ask a lot of questions,' Florence says. With a high-pitched shriek, she flings off her bra and drags down her underwear, covering her lower half with one hand before sprinting towards the water.

Mitch and Seiji bellow with laughter as they strip down to nothing too, their bums glowing luminous under the moonlight, and follow her. Florence dives beneath a rolling wave, while the boys edge in slowly and splash each other.

'Our girl,' Kiko says. 'She can't be tamed.'

'I wish I was more like her,' Dahlia says as Florence's laughter rings out from the ocean.

Kiko raises an eyebrow. 'You wish you were in your birthday suit with two nerdburgers right now?'

'Maybe not that, but Florence is fearless. She doesn't worry about consequences or what people think. She doesn't worry at all. I'm praying the police don't lock her up for public nudity — meanwhile, Florence doesn't even care where she flung her bra.'

Kiko lets out a little snort. 'She'll care if she can't find it later.'

'I don't think so. I want to be more like that. Stevie was like that. Brave.'

'You are brave,' Kiko says. 'What about the haunted house?'

Dahlia shrugs. 'A one-off.'

'Well, you saved me. And next time, remember that. Do the thing you think you can't. Take the smallest step.'

'That's the problem — there are so many things,' Dahlia says. Her hand reaches to tug at a strand of pink hair but she catches herself. 'I wouldn't know where to begin.'

'Start with the one thing you can't stop thinking about.'

Stillness hangs between them. It's so weighty Dahlia feels like she could reach out and pop it with a pin.

'I loved today,' she admits.

'I thought you might have.' Kiko reaches into her wallet and pulls out the pictures from the booth. She turns on her phone light. In all the photos, they're huddled in close, knees and shoulders touching, with beaming smiles. 'Evidence, see.'

'Shut up,' Dahlia says with a giggle.

'Your smile is radiant,' Kiko says. 'You look so happy.'

Dahlia stares at the photos of them wedged in close, arms and legs twisted together in a flurry of poses. 'I guess I do.'

'So, are we doing it?' Kiko asks.

Dahlia's heart nearly stops. '*It?*'

'Joining Florence and the boys in the water.'

'Oh, right.'

'It's on Stevie's list, and you said you wanted to be brave.'

'I don't think I can,' Dahlia says. 'I could barely change out of my gym clothes at school.'

'It's all good, lady. We'll stay here.'

'I don't want to hold you back.'

'I'm where I want to be,' Kiko says with a soft smile. She sits and buries her bare feet beneath the sand. 'This is nice.'

'Looks it.' Dahlia shifts from foot to foot, drawing an infinity loop in the sand with her toes. Her heart flutters.

Before she can change her mind, she peels off her sundress. Now all she's wearing is a mismatched bra and undies. It's thrilling.

Kiko breaks into a grin. 'Are we going in?'

'I'm not,' Dahlia admits, still pacing from side to side. 'But this is a small step, right?'

Kiko looks up at Dahlia for what feels like a long time. The air is warm but Dahlia is shivering.

'Hey, you're shaking,' Kiko says.

'I feel strange. Like I'm out of my body. Or on another planet.'

Kiko jumps to her feet and pulls off her T-shirt, revealing a sports bra and bare belly. 'There. Now there are two of us on your planet.'

She's so close Dahlia can see the tiny mole on her collarbone and hear her breath catching. Kiko reaches out, lacing their fingers together.

Dahlia edges in cautiously, like she doesn't want to make a sudden move that might risk splintering this moment into reality. Their toes kiss in the sand.

Kiko gently traces her fingers over Dahlia's cheek. 'Is this okay?'

Dahlia nods.

Kiko leans in and brushes her lips against Dahlia's. They're soft and warm, sending fizzing sparks through her body.

But just as quickly, Kiko pulls away. 'Sorry,' she says. 'I don't want to rush you.'

Dahlia softly cups her face. 'I said it's okay.' Her voice is barely a whisper.

She pulls Kiko towards her and this time they sink into the kiss. The ocean swells behind them as they lace together, mouths moving as one, breath tangled.

Even when they break apart, they stay close, fingers entwined. Dahlia leads Kiko down to the sand, and they sit together, Kiko resting her head on Dahlia's shoulder.

'Is this even real?' Dahlia murmurs. 'Where have you been all this time …?'

Kiko gives a little shrug. 'Here. But you see me now.'

'Why didn't you tell me? I had no idea. Florence is going to freak out.'

They're so close the tips of their noses are touching.

'I doubt it, let's just say you're the last person in the universe to know,' Kiko murmurs. 'And Florence is right: you do ask a lot of questions. Now kiss me again before you think of anything else.'

Zoë

Day 3: 3.11am

Someone is shouting Zoë's name. Blood rushes to her head as she peels off her eye mask. They call out again. It's one of the boys, but she can't tell who.

Yawning, she stumbles in the dark down the hallway and through the kitchen, fumbling to find the light on her phone. She follows the sound of her name until she reaches the balcony. Her jaw drops at the sight of Akito whimpering and swearing as he writhes on the ground, his arm bent at a disturbing angle. Prakash kneels beside him and Darius is there too, calling out Zoë's name.

'Oh, you're up!' Darius exhales in relief. 'Akito fell. You'll know what to do.'

'What are you doing here?' Zoë's surprised to see him in their suite. 'What's going on?'

Akito lets out an anguished moan. 'Zo!'

Zoë crouches down to inspect his contorted arm.

'Is it broken?' Prakash asks, gagging.

'I think so. Or dislocated,' Zoë says. 'He needs a doctor urgently.'

'Can't we wrap it up?' Darius asks. 'Don't you know this stuff?'

Zoë rolls her eyes. 'I've done a week of work experience.' She gently touches Akito's shoulder. 'Everything is going to be alright but it's time to get you to a doctor. Right now.'

She turns to the boys. 'Make yourselves useful and help him up.'

Darius's eyes are wide. 'Then what do we do?'

'Isn't it obvious? Take him to a hospital. We'll get a ride out front.'

Prakash stands a little taller. 'Zo, we've got this, you go back to sleep. Sorry you were woken up — it's been a massive day.'

'It's fine,' Zoë says.

Akito moans as Darius helps him walk through the apartment.

Zoë grabs Prakash by the elbow. 'You alright? Especially with trainwreck Darius in tow.'

He winks. 'If he gets his way, we'll sort it and be back in time to party.'

'What even happened?' she asks. 'Akito fell over?'

'Five words: breakdancing on the balcony table.'

Zoë shakes her head. 'Natural selection at its finest. I still can't believe that boy's going to be an engineer.'

Samira

Samira wakes up sweltering on the couch in the Peachies' living room. She kicks off the blanket that Tilly had given her earlier and reaches for her phone, but the battery is drained. The moon glistens through the window as she tiptoes around the darkened room for a charger. No luck.

She wanders through the kitchen and finds a charger wedged beside the kettle. Her phone reboots and the loading screen lights up. It's 4.12am. She squints out the window to the courtyard and sees the mound of grey ash from the exorcism. It wasn't a dream.

Her stomach churns. It had been a joke at first, but now it feels like something real went down in those hours. She wonders if maybe Tilly's outrageous ritual did help in some way. That maybe everything will work out in the end.

'You okay?' Tilly's whisper breaks through the dark. 'I haven't placed a hex on you, have I?'

Samira offers a wry smile. 'I'm under the Peachies' spell.'

'Do you think Zain's gone? Banished?'

Samira pauses. 'I can't explain it. But something feels different.'

Different is an understatement. Last night she became a Warrior, and stood in the courtyard with a Queen, a Pirate and a Robot burning the belongings of her ex-boyfriend.

'This is amazing. It worked!' Tilly enters the kitchen, her Alotta Peach bangles jangling on her wrist. 'We have to celebrate. What are you doing right now?'

Samira laughs. 'Don't you ever sleep?'

Her phone flashes and she glances down. The screen is full of notifications from Anoush. Three missed calls and a flood of drunken messages riddled with spelling mistakes and exclamation marks.

sammira, were r u???? i'm back fform club
ym phone died!!!!
thoght you hmoe to bed
(at th beach house not actually homee!!!!!!!!)
dan here on couch (im in love)
call me k

Samira's stomach lurches. 'I better go,' she tells Tilly. 'It's my friend.'

'All good,' Tilly reassures her.

Samira hesitates. 'Can I say something weird?'

'I love weird.'

'It feels like we've known each other for ages.'

'I know! I had so much fun.' Tilly grins. 'But I shouldn't say that, should I? Not when it was a whole dramatic ex-boyfriend situation.'

'I had fun too,' Samira says. 'I'll see you around.'

'Hope so.'

Samira slips out the sliding door and tiptoes across the courtyard, cringing at the cold tiles beneath her feet.

The lights are out when she enters the beach house, but she can make out pizza boxes cluttering the kitchen bench and the sleeping bodies of people scattered through the lounge room. A rattling snort comes from a guy dozing in an armchair in the corner and she stifles a giggle as she creeps up the stairs.

Samira opens the door to the bedroom and freezes. Anoush and Dan are fully dressed and lying on top of the covers. Their limbs are entwined and they are snoring softly. One of Dan's sneakers rests on a folded pile of Samira's clothes on her side of the bed.

Sighing, she closes the door and creeps back down to the lounge room. She uses her phone light to scan the darkened space and squeezes into an empty spot on the couch beside a boy who is splayed out and drooling on a cushion. With her knees pinned to her chest, Samira closes her eyes and falls into a restless sleep until the sun rises.

Zoë

Day 3: 9.38am

Facts dart through Zoë's pounding head. Humans are bioluminescent. Some tumours grow their own hair and teeth. Chloroplasts enable photosynthesis. There are about two hundred and seventy bones in the body at birth. Potassium chloride is an ionic compound soluble in water.

She groans and flips the pillow over to the cool side. Everything feels unbearable.

'Morning!' Luca swans in and flops onto the bed beside her. 'Violet thought she heard stirring in here.'

'What time is it?' Zoë murmurs, fumbling for her eye mask.

'Twenty to ten,' he says with a yawn. 'The boys got back from emergency a few hours ago.'

'How's Akito?'

'Dislocated it, broken it, can't remember.'

She swings her legs over the side of the bed, wincing as the back of her throat burns with bile. 'We should check on him. He was in a bad way.'

'It's alright, Dr Russo, he's sleeping it off,' Luca says. 'Prakash had it all under control. Check the chat. It was like minute-by-minute commentary.'

Zoë gives a wry smile. 'Prakash was turning green when I saw him.'

'They'll be sleeping for ages,' Luca says. 'Should we hit the pool? I can't be bothered walking so I'll arrange some golf buggies to drive us after breakfast if you want?'

Zoë flops back on the bed and pulls the pillow over her head. 'Make the call. I'm so tired that I can't even remember where the pool is.'

After visiting the decadent breakfast buffet, where Zoë could hardly look at the food, let alone eat it, the cousins arrive at the Grand Southwell's tropical pool and swim-up bar. It's surrounded by lush green plants, palm trees and sunlounges.

Violet sits on the side of the pool and dangles her toes in the water. Zoë and Luca slide in, flinching as the cold stings their skin. Moments later, Darius bombs into the water, spraying it over the girls.

Violet squeals. 'Stop it!' She points at the No Diving Or Bombing sign by the pool. 'You'll get us kicked out.'

'Or mess up your hair?'

'Whatever. I thought you'd be asleep after last night's excitement.'

Darius grins. 'I'll sleep when I'm dead. Plus, you texted me. So what are we up to? Truth or Dare?'

Zoë groans. 'It's too early.'

'I'm in,' Luca announces.

'Me too,' Prakash calls out, walking down the path with a towel over his shoulders.

'Aren't you exhausted?' Zoë asks. 'How's the patient?'

'Sleeping it off. His arm's broken in two places.'

Zoë's eyes widen in shock. 'Poor guy.'

'I, however, am excellent, thank you for asking.'

Zoë splashes water at him but sends a wave in Violet's direction instead. Violet screeches as droplets drip from her hair.

'You're all dead in Truth or Dare,' she threatens before diving beneath the surface.

'I'm out,' Zoë says. She yawns, slips out of the pool and curls up on a sunlounge, half-listening to the others playing the game as she drifts in and out of sleep.

Luca admits he kissed someone at the foam party yesterday. He can't remember his name, only that he ended up with his chewing gum in his mouth.

Prakash downs a mug full of tomato sauce, orange cordial, water, salt and pepper from the breakfast buffet before spluttering it everywhere.

Violet crab-walks to the towel stand and back, getting plenty of confused stares from people milling about the pool.

Darius removes his board shorts, gives himself a wedgie and walks over to an unsuspecting older gentleman settling onto a sunlounge and says in a fake posh accent, 'Sorry to interrupt, dear chap, but do you have the time?'

Luca reveals he has a favourite sibling but insists he'll never say who.

Darius admits he once cheated on a school essay by paying his sister's friend to write it. He got the second-highest mark in the class, which set off alarm bells for the teacher but they couldn't prove it.

That jolts Zoë awake. 'You did what?' she calls out from her sunlounge.

'Look who's finally joining us,' Darius teases. 'Wasn't my finest moment.'

'Didn't you feel guilty?'

Violet waves it off. 'Let's not make a thing of it.'

'Fine, but it seems like a thing to me,' Zoë says with a shrug.

'Don't worry, you're still the smartest person we know, Tiny Sloth,' teases Luca.

'It's pretty bad,' Prakash agrees. 'What's the worst thing you've done, Zo?'

'Not sure.' Zoë pauses. 'When I was seven I told the girl across the street that she couldn't play with my favourite doll. She cried. Like, full-on sobbing.'

'You were seven, it's fine,' Luca scoffs.

'We need to get a few more naughty items on that list,' Darius says.

Zoë wrinkles her nose. 'I did this.'

'What do you mean?' Darius asks. 'Fall asleep after drinking one and a half lolly waters?'

'No!' Zoë bristles. '*This.*' She gestures around at the resort. 'Coming here.'

Luca whistles. 'Tiny Sloth is a fugitive. She risked it all.'

'And here she is, lazing away this opportunity,' Darius says, pulling out a tiny flask from his pocket and holding it towards Zoë. 'Swig?'

'I'm fine,' she says, dismissing the offer with a flick of her wrist. 'After last night, I can't even look at alcohol without wanting to vomit.'

'If you won't, I will,' says Violet, reaching over for the flask and taking a quick mouthful.

'Join us for Truth or Dare at least?' Darius presses Zoë.

'Fine,' she says with an eye roll. 'Truth. Please.'

Prakash grins. 'Lovely manners, Zo.'

'Have you ever picked your nose and eaten it?' Violet fires at her. 'Do you fold or scrunch toilet paper? How many times did you and Prakash kiss when you were kids?'

'Gross! I fold. And mind your own business.'

Darius slaps Prakash on the back. 'Player.'

'We were eleven,' Prakash says with a snort. 'It was barely two kisses.'

'Someone give me a dare then,' volunteers Zoë.

'That's more like it!' Darius says. 'I dare you to cartwheel over to those girls putting on sunscreen and squeal, "I believe in fairies".'

'That's so ridiculous,' says Luca.

'Ridiculously perfect,' adds Violet.

It's been years since Zoë has done a cartwheel. But at least it isn't a nudie run around the pool. She adjusts her swimsuit. 'I'll do it.'

'Didn't you nearly break your neck during gymnastics?' Luca asks. 'And that was only a forward roll.'

Zoë pulls a silly face. 'Don't make me bring up your attempt at cricket, Luca.' She stretches her arms and shrugs her shoulders. Her head still throbs. She takes a quick sip of water. 'And no photos, Violet.'

'I don't make promises I can't keep.'

The sky turns upside down as Zoë cartwheels towards the girls. Once, twice, three, four, five times she spins. Behind her, the others wolf-whistle and cheer her name. She lands in front of the girls, almost tipping backwards onto the hot concrete. Red-faced, she regains her balance, then leaps into a lopsided star position.

'I believe in fairies!' she squeaks.

The girls' jaws drop. One of them clutches her tote a little tighter.

'You're high, right?' the other girl whispers, leaning in closer. 'Can you hook us up?'

Zoë's eyebrows shoot up. 'I'm sober.'

The first girl chokes back surprise and places her tote on the ground. 'I don't know if that's better or worse.'

Zoë's friends scream with laughter.

She whips around to face them. 'Whatever! I did it! Everyone can get off my back now!'

Suddenly she feels a lurching in her stomach. Her throat burns red-hot. She scans the tropical pool area for a bin, a patch of dirt, anything, but there's nothing but lush greenery, manicured bushes, spotless tiles and metres of crystal blue water.

Panicked, she lunges forward and sprays the girls' legs with chunks of bright orange vomit.

Samira

Anoush flashes a smile at Samira and gestures to the sign at the mini-golf counter that says they can play nine, eighteen or twenty-seven holes.

'How many should we do?' she asks, her voice light and breathy. She's on her best behaviour; usually she says what she wants. 'You two pick. I'm happy with whatever.'

Samira nearly cracks up over that lie. Her brain ticks over the list of things she and Anoush had originally planned for their girls' day today. Getting their nails done. Massages. Milkshakes. Checking out the markets. Hiring bicycles to cycle up to the lighthouse overlooking the ocean. Zero mention of mini-golf with a random guy from the foam party. So much for the girls' day.

Samira and Dan trade uncomfortable glances. It seems neither knew the other would be here. They answer at the same time.

'Just nine holes,' Samira says, slightly louder than his, 'Twenty-seven holes.'

'You're keen,' she adds.

His cheeks redden a little. 'Is it that obvious?'

Samira immediately softens at his palpable affection for her friend. 'Meet in the middle and do eighteen?'

'Great.' Dan's shoulders relax. 'Sweet.'

Anoush cheers their compromise with so much enthusiasm it's like she's won the lottery. Samira can tell she likes Dan. A lot.

They walk to the start of the course. There's a little wooden rainbow over the first hole and a sign that states they should be able to complete it in two strokes. The girls gesture for Dan to go first, so he places his golf ball down on the marker.

Anoush pulls Samira aside so sharply that her nails graze her skin. 'He's nice, right?' she whispers.

'Yeah,' Samira says, grip tightening on her golf club. 'He's into you. So much for a pash and dash though.'

'Samira, we made out for, like, hours. My lips still hurt, but, like, in the best way. I think I'm in love.'

'It hasn't even been twenty-four hours,' Samira points out.

'Summer romances wait for no-one! And he's got friends ...'

'Not interested,' Samira says. 'But do I need to, like, state the obvious here? I'm a total third wheel. You two are on a date and I'm, like, your chaperone.'

'No, this is fab,' Anoush says. 'I feel terrible about the mix-up at the Capitol last night, so this way we can all be together.'

Samira rolls her eyes. 'Throw in a pair of glasses and a snarky comment about what you're wearing and I'm your mother right now.'

Anoush laughs. 'Stop it.'

Dan strides back to them. 'What's so funny?'

'Just Samira being Samira,' Anoush says.

'The one and only,' Samira says, taking her spot on the green. She hits the ball and it careens towards the rainbow. It slows to a stop next to the hole.

'Nice one, Mum,' Anoush whispers.

They swap positions on the green. Anoush swings her club but misses the ball, which leaves her and Samira in another fit of giggles.

'You've got this, Anoush,' Dan tells her in earnest. 'We won't count that one.'

She swings again, sending the ball bouncing down the green. It hits the side of the rainbow, then rolls into the hole.

Dan and Samira cheer, both leaning in to high-five her at the same time. Anoush's palm claps with Dan's, leaving Samira's mid-air by itself. She shakes her head at the ridiculousness of it all.

The game passes in the way mini-golf usually does: laughter, swearing, balls dropping into holes, balls lost in bushes.

Dan lets Anoush cheat and flirt her way to a win, while Samira crawls on her knees in the hedge beside the ferris-wheel-themed eighteenth hole looking for her ball.

'Got it!' she declares as she gets to her feet. 'I'll hit it in the last hole then we can go and … Oh.' Anoush and Dan are locked in a kiss.

Samira averts her gaze, not wanting to stare. 'I might just …' Her voice trails off and she dawdles back to the clubhouse by herself.

She buys a bottle of sparkling water to kill time.

'Student?' asks the woman behind the desk as Samira sips her drink. 'Bet you'll never forget this week, am I right?'

'You could say that.'

When Anoush and Dan join her inside, they're flushed and holding hands. Anoush is giddy with joy. Dan seems to be the same.

'Drink, anyone?' Anoush asks, gesturing to the vending machine.

Dan nods and says, 'Thanks,' and she slips around the corner out of sight, leaving him and Samira alone.

Samira wonders if there's enough small talk in the world to fill the quiet.

'That was fun,' Dan offers.

'Yeah, for sure. Was great.'

'If I'd known you were by yourself I would have brought along a mate,' he adds.

She can tell he means it in a nice way, but the words 'by yourself' sting. She searches for a topic they have in common, but all she knows about him is that they attended the same foam party and he likes her friend.

'So …' she says.

'So …' He drums his fingers on the table.

'Omigod, want to hear a funny story about the foam party?' Samira offers up.

Dan seems relieved. 'Oh yeah?'

'Well, and this is the funny part,' she leans in closer, 'I thought you were walking over because you liked *me*. How hysterical is that?'

His eyes widen, just a little. 'Oh really?'

Samira realises, seconds too late, that her filter has failed her. This isn't hilarious. It's humiliating.

'It's nothing though, right?' she stammers, wishing the floor would swallow her up. 'Forget it. Not funny. It was confusing though.'

'Right.' He nods. 'But was it?'

'I mean, maybe a little, or even a lot. You approached me and for a second, like, literally a second, I thought you were coming to chat. To me, I mean,' she rambles, her nerves getting the better of her. '*Obviously* you were coming over to chat, just not to me specifically. And now we know you were coming over to do more than chat, right? Although you did come up to me, I guess, which is probably why it was so confusing in the first place.' She swallows. 'But then you kissed Anoush so it, um, all became clear.'

By now Dan's cheeks are a deep shade of red.

'Isn't that funny?' Samira adds, forcing an upward inflection into her voice.

He fakes a laugh as Anoush barrels over to them.

'Not telling Dan all my secrets, are you, Samira?' she asks, passing him a bottle of water.

'If only I'd thought of that,' Samira says, gritting her teeth. Anything would be less awkward than the conversation they'd just endured.

'What should we do next, itinerary queen?' Anoush asks.

'We could hire bikes?' Samira notices Dan's nose screw up at the suggestion. 'Or hang at the little beach near our place?'

Dan's hand finds Anoush's. 'The beach — that reminds me! My mates signed me up to a volleyball competition later this arvo down at the beach by Saldana Strip. The free shuttle goes right there. Want to come?'

'Absolutely,' says Anoush, before glancing at Samira. 'I mean, what do you think, girl?'

'Balls flying towards my face has never been my favourite way to pass the time,' Samira says, still aching with embarrassment from her conversation with Dan. 'You two go and I'll catch up with you later.'

'We can sunbake while they play?' Anoush offers.

Dan scoffs. 'Please! With that competitive streak I saw on the mini-golf course?'

'Competitive? Me?' Anoush tosses her hair over her shoulder. 'Never.'

'You have to come,' Dan says with a grin.

Anoush flashes a smile. 'Fine, I'm in.' She turns to Samira. 'You're coming too. Girls' day, remember?'

Samira remembers. But she's not sure if Anoush does.

* * *

Samira's palms are clammy as she takes in the picture-postcard scene. Brilliant orange sun beaming down. Glistening waves rolling onto the sand. Dan's friends in bikinis and board shorts, playing volleyball like they were born to do it.

'It'll be fun,' Anoush whispers to Samira while Dan coats his bare chest in sunscreen. 'We'll just play a game or two.'

'Are your resuscitation skills up to scratch?' Samira asks. 'I don't want my tombstone to read *Samira Makhlouf died doing what she hated: organised team sports in the burning sun.*'

Anoush strips down to her bikini. 'Look at all the hotties,' she hisses. 'There'll be someone to give you mouth to mouth, guaranteed. Why should Zain get to have all the fun?'

Samira bristles at his name. 'I'm so done with him,' she says, thinking about the exorcism.

She pulls off her T-shirt, throws it onto the sand and follows Anoush onto the court. As she adjusts the straps of her bikini, a volleyball sails towards her head.

'Yours, Samira!' Dan shouts.

'Kill me now,' she mutters under her breath.

Gritting her teeth, she dives forward and, with clenched fists pressed together, blasts the volleyball up and over the net before face-planting into the sand.

Zoë
Day 3: 5.57pm

It's when Darius stuffs a lipgloss, some batteries and two packets of lollies into his pockets at a convenience store that Zoë realises the game-playing has escalated.

'Are you *shoplifting*?' she hisses, elbowing Violet in the side to draw her attention to what's going on. The three of them are supposed to be on a snack mission for the group. 'That wasn't the dare. Put it all back.'

Darius turns and gives Zoë a ghoulish clown grin. Earlier in the day, Violet was dared to decorate his face with cheap facepaints from a two-dollar shop, and he's completed the look with a red plastic nose and curly green wig.

'Just clowning around,' he says, but doesn't empty his pockets. 'Hey, where's your red ring?'

'My what?' Zoë asks, looking at her bare fingers. 'Oh, from the traffic light party? I gave it back to Violet.'

'Nice. I like your green top too,' he says. 'Does that symbolise what I think it does?'

She raises an eyebrow. 'Excuse me?'

'Just checking,' he adds with a smirk. 'I guess not.'

'The party was yesterday,' she says, moving away from him to eye off the colourful packets of chips lining the shelves. 'My green top means nothing.' Her stomach grumbles. They haven't eaten since brunch.

Darius slides up beside her again, sending a chill down the back of her spine. 'Dare you to take a packet and run,' he whispers in her ear. 'Something to add to your naughty list.'

Zoë's eyebrows shoot up. 'No,' she hisses back. 'What is wrong with you?'

He laughs. 'I'm kidding.'

Violet appears behind them holding two bottles of soft drink. 'Chill, Zo, he's messing around.'

'Check his pockets then.'

'Who's this hurting?' Darius asks.

Zoë dares to look at the young man standing behind the counter. 'That guy, probably — you could get him fired. I'm out. Violet, you're coming with me. Now.'

The girls leave without buying any snacks or drinks.

Outside, Violet rolls her eyes. 'You've seriously overreacted. Can't you play it cool for one second?'

'There's something off about him,' Zoë says. 'You get that, right?' Her stomach growls again and she swears. 'I need food. My stomach is eating itself with hunger but we're not going back in there.'

'Fine,' Violet grumbles as they walk along the footpath. 'But I don't think he's that bad.'

'I figured that when your tongue was halfway down

his throat yesterday,' Zoë says, peeking through the windows of a stretch of restaurants.

'Hunger makes you sassy, Zo.'

'I need a burger and then I'll be happy again.' Zoë bites her lip. 'You know he's kissing other people, right?'

'Duh. Of course I know. It's not like I want to marry the guy.'

'I'd object.'

'You'd hurl a bowl of Aunty Rosette's puttanesca in his face, for sure,' Violet says with a snigger.

'With extra olives and anchovies. I don't know how to say this, but I swear he was hitting on me in there.'

'You wish,' Violet says, laughing again as they walk along. Then she comes to a sudden halt. 'Look.'

They're in front of a tattoo parlour. Zoë takes in the neon red piping on the signage, the window displays and the walls overloaded with designs. A sign saying *We accept walk-ins* hangs next to the door. A loud high-pitched buzzing echoes from inside.

'Burgers will have to wait,' Violet announces. 'I need you to dare me to do something first.'

'Get a tattoo? No way.'

'Just say it.'

'The game's over.'

'Fine.' Violet fires off a message into the group chat: *Someone dare me to get a tattoo*

Her screen floods with messages.

I DARE YOU TO GET A TATTOO RIGHT NOW!!!!!!

Do it!

Double dare you

TRIPLE DARE YOU WITH A CHERRY ON TOP

Do it, Violet!

Violet grins at Zoë. 'They accept walk-ins.'

'But Aunty Caro will—'

'Never know it exists based on where I'm planning on getting it.'

'I'm not doing your eulogy,' Zoë says, opening the door and ushering her cousin in.

Zoë watches the tattoo artists wielding the needles with ease and precision, while Violet sits down on a metal bench and flips through a folder of designs.

'Just looking?' calls a woman with a blunt silver fringe and full-sleeve arm tattoos, pausing her work on a back tattoo of a lion. 'Or do you want ink? I'm nearly done here.'

'Just looking,' Zoë stammers at the same time Violet says, 'Want ink.'

'There's a two-for-one deal if you're interested,' the woman says. 'Applies to piercings too.'

Violet looks at Zoë, whose hand is shoved in a jar of free lollies on the countertop. 'We could do it together, Zo. Wouldn't that be unbelievable?'

'If "unbelievable" means "unlikely" and "improbable", then yes,' Zoë says through a mouthful of lollies.

She joins Violet on the bench and they flip through the pages of designs.

'Which one do you like?' Zoë asks.

'A butterfly maybe, but now I'm not so sure,' Violet says. Her jaw tightens as she watches the woman with silver hair finish the tattoo. 'It looks like it hurts,' she whispers. 'Do you think it hurts?'

'Affirmative. Ooh, I like this one.' Zoë holds up a page displaying a small and dainty heartbeat design.

'A heartbeat? I know you're not in love so tell me that's not related to doctor stuff, Zo.'

Zoë shrugs. 'So what if it is?' She walks over to stuff her hand back in the lolly jar. 'Are you getting a tattoo or not?'

'I don't know now!' Violet says. 'I'm confused.'

'Want to think about it over a burger? That way you're taking longer than a minute to decide on something that will last a lifetime.'

Violet groans. 'Making decisions is so overwhelming. You're going to be a doctor, Luca's signed up to a business diploma, and I still don't even know which courses to register in at fashion college!' She sighs. 'How am I meant to commit to something forever?'

'My thoughts exactly,' Zoë says, taking her hand. 'Food time.'

'But everyone's hyped for me to do it.'

'You're allowed to change your mind. They'll get over it, and I don't see them volunteering to get tattoos on their bums.'

They hurry towards the exit. Violet keeps her head low.

'No ink tonight?' the silver-haired woman calls out.

'No ink,' Zoë says. 'But beautiful work … ah, keep it up.'

'Move it,' hisses Violet, her cheeks flushed red.

She drags Zoë out the door back onto Saldana Strip. In one direction, people lounge around on the grass in front of an ambulance and first-aid tent. In the other, rows of bars pulsate with lights and music even though the evening is young.

'Burgers, burgers … Ooh! I see something up ahead,' Violet says, lurching towards a line of food trucks parked further along the Strip.

Zoë steps forward to follow and feels blood rush to her head. She holds out her hands, trying to steady herself against the dizziness, but her vision goes blurry and she collapses on the concrete.

Dahlia

The girls stand on Saldana Strip and watch the glowing orb of the sun edge its way towards the ocean. A brilliant sunset paints the sky with smoky oranges and pinks.

'It's so beautiful,' whispers Dahlia.

'Selfie?' asks Florence.

'Let's try to enjoy it,' Kiko says. 'Be in the moment.' She pauses, taking in the technicolour night again. 'Yeah, quick selfie!'

They huddle together, squashing in close for the photo.

'Turn more,' directs Florence, waving her phone. 'Keep turning, keep turning.' She whistles. 'Dahlia, may I say, my jumpsuit looks fierce on you.'

Dahlia grins. 'The one benefit of my luggage disappearing into an unknown vortex.'

'Now get ready,' Florence says as they all pose. 'Keep smiling — I'm taking a hundred. We can show these photos to your kids one day, lovers!'

Kiko scrambles for the phone but Florence waves it around, still snapping photos.

Dahlia laughs, straining on her tippy-toes. 'Let us see, lady. We need approval!'

Over Kiko's shoulder, she spots a girl who's frantically crouching, then standing, then crouching again and screaming for help. She's a blur of colour and movement and it takes Dahlia's eyes a while to focus and realise there's another girl lying on the concrete at the first girl's feet. She looks limp, lifeless.

'Hey!' Dahlia reaches out to Kiko and Florence, who are still scuffling over the phone. 'I think someone's hurt.'

Kiko's eyebrows furrow. 'Who?'

Florence scans around in the opposite direction.

Holding her breath, Dahlia watches as people closer to the two girls walk on, either oblivious or too afraid to get involved. An indescribable feeling washes over her. There's no time to worry or overthink.

'Quick,' she says, waving to Kiko and Florence to follow her. 'We better help.'

Dahlia legs it across the grass towards the girls. The first girl looks like she's about to throw up. 'Is your friend alright?' Dahlia asks her.

'I ... I don't know,' she stammers. 'She fainted out of nowhere! She's my cousin ... I don't know what to do.'

The girl on the ground groans. Her right hand shakily reaches to touch her temple.

Her cousin kneels by her side. 'I'm still here, Zoë,' she says, stroking the girl's forehead. 'It's Violet.'

Zoë's lips crack into a small smile. 'I know it's you.' She tries to move, but can't seem to lift her head from the footpath. 'I told you I needed a burger.'

'What do I do?' Violet whimpers. 'I don't want to leave you.'

'We'll help,' Dahlia says, sucking in a breath. Her tone is strong, but her stomach is doing somersaults.

'Do we move her? I knew I should have paid more attention in first-aid but that instructor was hot!' Florence babbles. 'He had that offbeat, broody vibe.'

'Florence,' murmurs Kiko, bringing a finger to her lips.

'No moving,' Zoë says, wincing.

Violet's eyes widen. 'She'd know. Zoë's going to be a doctor and save the world.'

Dahlia points further down Saldana Strip. 'I think that's an emergency tent.' She squats down next to Zoë. 'I'll run over and get help while Violet and my friends stay here. No-one's leaving you.'

'I'll wait here too,' Zoë says, attempting a weak joke.

Adrenaline courses through Dahlia's body as she runs along the walkway towards the first-aid tent. Her sandal straps strain against her skin. She arrives at the tent in a blaze, cheeks flushed red and heart thrashing in her chest.

Inside the tent, her breath catches. A boy lies in the recovery position attached to an intravenous drip. His friend holds the IV bag. Two girls sit side by side on plastic chairs, their faces buried in sick bags. Another boy lies on his side on a bed, whimpering and clutching his stomach. He's by himself. A girl swears as a nurse takes a blood sample.

Dahlia collects herself and hurries over to a first-aid person sorting medicines in the corner. Her words spill out in a rush. 'Help, it's my friend! Well, she's not my friend, but this girl, this nice girl, she's fallen and hit her head.' She points back to where Zoë's lying on the concrete. 'She's over here ... well, over there ... it's hard to explain. I don't know if there's blood but she needs help. She needs help now!'

The rest happens in a blur. The workers in the tent discuss options, and within seconds a doctor is jogging with Dahlia back to the others.

A small group of people huddle around Zoë. Violet is still whimpering, while a boy is holding Zoë's hand and drawing circles on her palm. Three other boys stand nearby, all hardened jawlines and furrowed brows. Kiko and Florence hang on the edge of the group, careful not to intrude.

The doctor urges everyone to take a few steps back as she presses a wet washer to Zoë's forehead.

As Violet wipes away tears, she notices Dahlia and gives her a small smile. A thank you. Dahlia smiles back, then her gaze catches Kiko's and Florence's. They gesture for her to come with them, having done what they can.

'That was intense,' Dahlia says, exhaling as they stroll along the walkway. 'Do you think Zoë will be okay?'

Kiko links her arms through Dahlia's and Florence's. 'I do, because she's in good hands now.'

'She looked helpless, didn't she?' Dahlia adds.

Florence nudges her. 'Listen, when Zoë retells this story, you'll be the heroic stranger who sprinted to get help. I bet by the hundredth retelling she'll have you performing surgery on her on Saldana Strip.'

Kiko's mouth breaks into a grin. 'This might be too soon, but does this experience count for Stevie's list?' She pulls the list out of her bag. '*Save a life.* I know it's a stretch, but what do we think?'

Florence nods. 'It counts. Tick!'

'And thanks to the haunted house and Florence's skinny-dipping, we can cross two more things off,' Kiko says.

Florence beams. 'You're welcome. Tattoos next?' she suggests, waving towards a nearby tattoo parlour.

As they look over, a girl and guy walk out. 'I knew I shouldn't have listened to you,' the girl rages. 'They didn't even spell your name right!' She sticks both her middle fingers up at him and storms off. The boy hurries after her.

Kiko sniggers. 'Maybe not?'

Dahlia reaches for the list. 'What else is left?'

They huddle around for a better look.

'Meditate?' Kiko suggests.

'I can already do that,' Dahlia says. She took a three-day meditation course to try to help with managing anxious thoughts.

'Then tick,' Florence says, reading over the list. 'I can't believe Stevie wrote *Fall in love*. No pressure! She may as well have put *Learn to levitate* because we'd need some serious magic to pull that off.' She winks. 'Right, girls?'

Dahlia doesn't dare turn her head but she feels Kiko's eyes on hers for a split-second. A tiny smile slips out and the air suddenly feels hot and sticky.

'Moving on,' Kiko says, taking back the list and holding it to her chest. Dahlia sees her cheeks have reddened. 'I think Stevie would be happy with our progress.'

Florence leans over Kiko's shoulder to scan the list again. 'And there's *Get married* too? Marriage is an out-of-date, unnecessary tradition and I am *not* marrying some drunk stranger just for the list.' She pauses. 'Although maybe I would ...'

'Never say never, right?' Dahlia replies. 'It could be a hilarious story for the memoirs.'

Florence's jaw drops. 'Indeed. And just like that, the student becomes the master.'

Day 4

Samira

Day 4: 2.03pm

Samira grimaces at her tired eyes in the downstairs hallway mirror and touches up her mascara.

A pre-paid snorkelling trip had been planned for earlier in the day, but everyone had been too tired and hungover to care that they'd lose their non-refundable holding deposits. Even Anoush, who'd insisted Samira include snorkelling on the itinerary, groaned and rolled over in bed, dragging the sheet up over her face. Samira had held back tears on the phone to the tour operator as she profusely apologised for cancelling. Afterwards, she had nibbled on a piece of bacon and gazed at the tickets, wondering whether she should still go. Then she pictured being alone on the boat surrounded by strangers laughing and joking together. Her chest tightened in shame and she stuffed the tickets away.

Now, in the afternoon, the others are ready to party again. Anoush has overridden Samira's plan to go to the beach cinema and clubbing at the all-ages nightclub and instead invited them to a party at Dan's resort.

Rashida swans past, swirling a drink in her hand. 'Coming to the soiree?' she asks in a haughty voice.

'Yeah, Anoush mentioned it,' Samira says. 'If by soiree you mean the keg party with a bunch of bros.' She giggles but Rashida doesn't. 'Um, yeah, so I'll be there. You?'

'Wouldn't miss it. Dan's friends are h-o-t,' Rashida says, eyeing Samira up and down. 'Big afternoon ahead, better get changed.'

'I'm ready,' Samira says.

Rashida takes an extra-long sip of her drink. 'Oh. Well ... you look fine.'

There's an awkward pause.

'So ... I'll, ah, catch you soon,' Rashida says and snakes away up the staircase.

Samira is simmering at the catty remarks when her phone buzzes. Her shoulders relax when she sees it's a message from Tilly.

Hope you're having a fab day!

Samira writes back.

You too. About to head out with everyone x

She tugs at her dress, which is inching up her thighs, then looks in the mirror again to fluff her long thick hair to accentuate the waves. 'It looks alright,' she mutters, before realising she's talking to herself again. In a house full of people, she's spending a lot of time alone.

She steals another glance at her reflection, self-conscious after Rashida's sharp comments. 'Maybe I'll do a brighter lip,' she mumbles, turning and climbing the staircase.

As she walks towards the master bedroom, she hears Claire's and Rashida's muffled voices rising and falling through their closed door. She holds her breath and listens.

'... I know,' Claire groans. 'It's embarrassing, she's so out of her depth.'

'Right?' Rashida adds. 'Like, we had *the* most awkward encounter of my life downstairs.'

Claire giggles. 'What happened?'

'Oh, don't make me relive it.'

'Poor clueless Samira.'

The words hit Samira deep in her chest.

'Someone needs to teach her how to be less weird, but, like, that's not our job,' Rashida continues.

'Some things can't even be teached, girl.'

Rashida snorts. 'The word is "taught", Claire. That's true though. She's a lost cause.'

'That colour-coded itinerary too. Like, who is she, our teacher?'

'She doesn't fit in.'

'Right? She's not one of us, no matter how much she wants to be.'

'Hey, that's harsh.' Anoush's voice cuts through the bitchiness.

Anoush is in there? Samira nibbles on her thumbnail.

'You were the one whinging after she almost blew your date with Dan with all her awkwardness,' Claire says. 'What did she say to him again?'

'Something about the foam party ... it doesn't matter.'

'It does!' Claire says. 'Like, chill out, Samira. Be the wing-woman. It's not that hard.'

'I think she was bummed we didn't do the girls' day,' Anoush says. 'I feel bad that I bailed on it, especially after the mix-up at the Capitol.'

'Don't. She's obsessed with you, Anoush,' Rashida says. 'It's not your fault the teachers paired you up.'

'Serious stalker,' Claire adds, giggling again. 'It's tragic.'

'No, she's nice!' Anoush says. 'And a good person.'

'Bor-ing,' says Rashida in a singsong voice.

'She's just …' Anoush pauses.

'A loser?' More giggling.

Samira chews on her bottom lip.

'No, not a loser,' Anoush says.

The others snort with laughter.

'I'm not joking!' she insists. 'But I think I'm her only real friend. It's a lot of pressure.' Anoush sighs. 'All this stuff with Zain breaking up with her has made this week extra hard.'

'I thought he was dumping her months ago?' exclaims Claire.

'Me too,' Anoush moans. 'It's such a mess.'

Samira shakes her head in disbelief. Anoush *did* know about Zain. She'd lied to Samira's face.

'Here, Anoush, have another drink. Something tells me you're going to need it at the party,' Rashida says. 'You'll be babysitting Samira before you know it.'

'Stop it,' Anoush says, but Samira can tell she's laughing.

'I'm just saying what we're all thinking,' Rashida adds.

'All this party talk reminds me I need a cute dress, like, now,' Anoush says.

'Go on then, girl,' Claire chimes in. 'You have to look smoking.'

It clicks that Anoush is about to burst into the hallway. Samira rushes into their shared room and burrows beneath the bedcovers.

Moments later, Anoush walks in. 'Oh hey. You having a nap?'

Samira fakes a whimper. 'I don't feel so good.'

'What's up? Are you okay to come to Dan's?'

'I ... I don't think so. It's my stomach, my head, my back ... It's like I've been stabbed in the back.' Samira can't resist the secret dig.

'Is it period pain? Do you need painkillers?'

'No, it's mainly the stomach and head thing,' she says, silently berating herself for buying into dramatics. 'I'll be alright. I think it's better if I lay low. Rest up and try to get over it.'

Anoush pauses. 'If that's what you think. Can I do anything?'

'No, you've done enough. Thanks.' Samira's lip quivers.

'Want me to come back early from the party?'

'I can handle it.'

'If you're sure, because we might end up crashing there to save on transport,' Anoush says, pulling on a sparkly dress. 'Feel better, okay? We'll miss you.'

Samira gives her a tiny smile.

'Bye, girl. Rest up.'

She manages to hold back her tears until Anoush has left the bedroom.

* * *

The house is still when Samira finally ventures downstairs. She makes a cup of tea and curls up on the couch, feet tucked beneath her, to drink it. She contemplates calling her mum, only she can't imagine how to begin that conversation. They've never had secrets from one another, but now they seem to be piling up.

When she places her empty mug in the kitchen sink, she notices her crumpled itinerary stuck to the fridge. Only the top is visible behind the takeaway menus, a certificate stating Mathieu and Zain are in the Stinky Bill's VIP Club for completing the Big Beef Challenge by eating a two-kilo steak, bread roll, chips and salad in under an hour, and photo booth prints of Claire, Anoush and Rashida. The sight of the photos cracks her open. The group had pleaded for her to organise their dream trip and she'd exhausted herself factoring in everything they wanted. Initially, she didn't mind how much work it was because she thought they were grateful. But now she knows the cruel things they say behind her back.

She glares at the fridge then heads down the hall to

the bathroom. She pauses outside the door to Zain's room, wondering what would be the worst that could happen if she knocked. The mess began with him; maybe it can end with him too.

But she shakes off the feeling, silently congratulating herself for the self-control, and walks on towards the bathroom. She yanks open the door and a pained gasp slips out.

Zain is locked in a steamy kiss with a girl against the bathroom sink. The girl's sharp fire-red nails rake against Zain's back and she's wearing nothing but the oversized T-shirt that Samira bought him for his birthday.

Zain pulls back, eyes widening in shock. 'Samira?'

'Get out!' the mystery girl snaps.

'I ... I didn't know you were in here,' Samira stammers, stepping back so quickly she bumps into the hallway table. A small vase filled with flowers crashes to the floor, shattering glass over the tiles.

'Omigod,' she gasps. 'There goes my deposit.'

'Samira, wait.' Zain steps towards her. 'It's okay.'

The girl's eyebrows narrow. 'Is this your girlfriend, Zeke?'

'No,' he mumbles, without correcting her. 'She's not.'

'I'll go,' Samira says. 'I'm going.'

Emotions pinball through her as she storms into the kitchen to grab the dustpan and brush. The sound of Zain and the girl arguing stings her brain as she kneels down in the hallway and sweeps up the shards of glass.

Cheeks burning, Samira pours the glass into the bin, then pounds up the staircase and into her bedroom. She calls her mum, but there's no answer, so, fighting tears, she collects her make-up bag from the ensuite and drags her suitcase onto the bed.

Dahlia

Day 4: 4.07pm

Hundreds of people dance on the sand while inflatable palm trees bounce in the air above them. Music pulsates and the crowd swells.

Nearby, at the beachside pool, the girls are stretched out on a daybed. Dahlia adjusts the denim shorts Kiko lent her, savouring the feeling of the sun on the back of her calves. There's still no news from the airline about her luggage, even though she's been checking in every day.

'This bed is bigger than our room,' Florence says, rubbing sunscreen onto her nose and cheeks, which are softly dusted with freckles. 'Worth every cent.'

'I'm never leaving, we have everything we need to survive,' Kiko says, gesturing to the oversized striped umbrella above and the bowl of sweet potato fries between them.

'Totally worth emptying the kitty and living off canned tuna for the rest of the week,' Dahlia jokes, not looking up from her phone.

The screen is hidden from the others, so she opens up the album filled with videos of Stevie, puts on her headphones and presses play. The shot zooms out to reveal Dahlia sitting on the edge of a pool, her feet dangling in the water. She looks at the camera and asks how many days to go before they're overseas. From behind the lens, Stevie tells her six hundred and thirty-one days. Dahlia whines that's too many, and Stevie tells her to be patient.

The video crackles and blurs as Stevie sits down next to Dahlia. Suddenly Stevie flips the phone camera and their faces fill the screen. She kicks the water, spraying droplets over them both, and they burst into laughter.

They lean in close so their heads are in the frame and argue over who's going to be the best au pair the world has ever seen. Dahlia thinks it'll be Stevie because she's hilarious and entertaining. Stevie thinks it'll be Dahlia because she's kind and funny and everyone loves her, even if she doesn't realise it. A little smile sneaks out the corner of Dahlia's mouth as she reminds Stevie everyone loves her too, even though her feet stink and she never flosses.

Stevie brings the camera up close to her face and sticks her tongue out. Dahlia does the same then says the world isn't ready for them, but Stevie says it'll have to be. She pauses and everything goes quiet, before she tells Dahlia it'll be the best thing she's ever done, made even better because she's doing it with her best friend. Dahlia rests her head on her shoulder, then Stevie cracks a joke about her breath and they break into laughter again. The footage cuts out.

Dahlia wipes a bead of sweat from her forehead. She knows the date of the clip by heart. Stevie was diagnosed with a brain tumour five weeks later.

Stomach churning, Dahlia turns off her phone to stop herself from watching another video. When she glances up, Florence and Kiko are sword-fighting with their sweet potato fries.

'So what's next on Stevie's list?' Kiko asks. 'I've lost track, but we can cross off *Attend epic beach party*. This is next level.'

'Stevie would be jealous of the daybed,' Dahlia adds. 'I wish she could see it.'

The girls lapse into silence.

'So ...' Kiko says, 'the list?'

Florence stuffs a sweet potato fry into her mouth. 'You had it, right, lady?' she asks Dahlia.

'Oh yeah,' Dahlia says, reaching into her shorts' pocket. She pauses. Digs deeper. 'Wait ...' Her heart races as she checks the other side. 'That's strange.'

The girls sit up, watching her.

'Is it in your bag?' Kiko asks, leaning in closer.

Dahlia pulls everything out of her tote and lines it all up on the daybed. 'No. It's not here.' She takes a deep breath before checking her pockets again. Still nothing. She swallows. Checks her wallet. Nothing. The bottom of her tote. Her wallet again. Her pockets again. Her tote again. 'Shit. Are you sure you don't have it, Kiko?'

Kiko feels inside her pockets and bag. 'I swear I gave it to you after we had those vegie burgers at the park. I'd spilt the sauce on it and you wanted it for safekeeping, remember?'

Dahlia does. She'd been so worried about the list being ruined and now she's lost it.

She nibbles the inside of her cheek as she silently catalogues her thoughts.

5 Lost Things In Order of Least to Most Important
Bobbypins (all of them, ever)
Hair ties (all of them, ever)
Matching earrings (all of them, ever)
The ring Mum gave me for my sixteenth birthday
Stevie's Too Late List

'It's alright, it'll show up,' Kiko says, nudging the bowl of fries closer to Dahlia. 'You've probably put it somewhere extra safe.'

'Maybe it's back at the hostel,' Florence chimes in.

'It was with me,' Dahlia says. 'It was here.' Her chest tightens as she scans the throbbing party. 'I can't believe this. It's all we have left of her.'

'That's not true,' says Kiko. 'The necklace, the brooch, the camera. Plus, photos, letters, our memories ... we have so much.'

'But we're meant to be ticking things off the list, like you said.' Dahlia's fingers tug at her hair. She stops herself. 'Her mum trusted us. I can't be the reason we have to stop now. I can't, I can't, I—'

'Breathe, Dahlia,' Kiko says. 'We'll work it out.'

Florence picks up her phone. 'What was left on the list?' she asks, tapping away at the screen. 'I'll write them down.'

Dahlia's head feels hollowed out. She can't think or remember. 'I don't know ... there was the haunted house ... and Florence did skinny-dipping ...' Her voice trails off. She can picture Stevie's scrawled handwriting in her mind but can't make out any of the words. 'I think *Swim under a waterfall* was on there too.'

'Or did she do that with her parents?' Kiko asks. 'I swear I've seen a photo.'

Dahlia closes her eyes and tries to visualise Stevie's family's living room. Her mother had photos cluttering the mantelpiece, lining the walls, hanging off the fridge. In most of the shots, no matter her age, Stevie's eyes were often closed, her hair always messy, and her mouth wide with laughter. Dahlia tries to pinpoint a photo of Stevie beneath a waterfall but she can't.

'I don't remember seeing it,' she says, a desperate note to her voice.

She doesn't dare mention that she's not sure if that's because it doesn't exist or because she's starting to lose Stevie. Memories already seem fuzzier, their details so blurred that sometimes it's hard for her to know what's real and what she's rewritten in her mind during the past year. It's why she watches the video clips on repeat. Saying goodbye to Stevie was hard enough the first time. She can't bear to do it again.

'Hey!' Kiko says, reaching for her hand. 'It'll be alright.'

Dahlia nods, biting the inside of her cheek again. She's aching to admit that she's struggling and that she's sorry. But for some reason Kiko's caring gesture makes it even harder to summon the right words.

The music from the beach party throbs around them, which only compounds Dahlia's tangled thoughts. Beside her, the girls struggle to piece together their scrambled memories of Stevie to form a new list.

'What else?' Kiko murmurs.

Florence grimaces. 'No idea. Dahlia, can you think of anything else Stevie wanted to do?'

Dahlia locks eyes with Kiko, her heart aching when she sees them glistening with worry. But she can't take another second of the noise.

'I'm sorry, I can't hear myself think,' she stammers, standing up and shoving her belongings into her tote.

'Dahlia, wait,' Kiko says. 'Talk to us.'

'I'll meet up with you later, okay?' Dahlia loops her bag over her shoulder. 'Don't hate me.'

She hears Kiko and Florence calling for her to stop, but Dahlia is already running across the golden sand and into the crowd.

Zoë

Day 4: 4.48pm

Bags of chips. Wheels of cheese. Blocks of chocolate. A tub of ice-cream. Rainbow sprinkles. Crackers. Dips. Zoë grins and tosses four more blocks of chocolate into their shopping trolley, before swinging her leg over and clambering in.

Luca cheers and climbs in too, jostling and laughing as he and Zoë struggle for space.

'More dips, more chocolate, more crackers,' Zoë chants as Prakash pushes them along the confectionery aisle. 'This is unquestionably more fun than hanging with Darius.'

Luca laughs. 'Hell no, it's not. We're grocery shopping, he's throwing a party. Violet says there's a bottomless punch bar.'

'Damn it, man,' Prakash says. 'What are we doing, Zo?'

'I've got all I need here,' she grins, gesturing to the treats in their trolley.

'He's not that bad,' Luca says. 'You'll have us making voodoo dolls of the guy next! Just let him live!'

'Fine, don't listen to me,' Zoë says. 'But you're as indoctrinated as Violet.'

'Wait, I need a photo,' Prakash says, stopping the trolley in front of an assortment of lollies. Zoë and Luca wave the rainbow sprinkles and cheese at the camera as he snaps a few shots. 'If our arteries survive this week, we need to remember the most amazing shop of our lives.'

'And the time Zoë forced us to miss the party of the year to stock up on toilet paper,' adds Luca.

At the checkout, Zoë puts the groceries on her card and the others promise to transfer money later. The receipt is so long she wraps it around her neck like a scarf.

They lug their shopping bags along the street, stopping every few metres to readjust their grip.

'Half-price drinks,' Luca announces, nodding towards a sign out the front of a bar. 'Should we have a little celebration before we meet the others?'

'Celebrating what?' asks Prakash with a grin.

'Our pure awesomeness. Look, even their buffalo wings are half-price. It's meant to be.'

Zoë's phone beeps. A new email.

She swears. 'It's from Number Three.'

Prakash and Luca exchange looks as she opens the email and scans for information, swearing again when the instructions tell her to log into the university's portal to view her status. After endless scrolling through her inbox, she unearths her username and password.

Once she's in the portal, she clicks for the answer. Her hand covers her mouth.

'Well?' Luca prompts her. 'You're in, right?'

Zoë hangs her head. 'Better make them commiseration buffalo wings.'

Prakash swears. 'You're kidding? There's still two more though — don't give up.'

She nods, deflated. 'Maybe I should head back to the resort. Have a lie-down.'

'First, a drink on me,' Luca says, opening the door and waving them in. 'We'll dazzle you with our wit and make everything okay.'

'Either that or the blue cheese sauce will,' Prakash says, and Zoë manages a small smile.

Inside the bar, they slide into a booth and order drinks, seasoned fries and a bowl of wings. Luca twirls the paper umbrella around in his glass before tucking it behind Zoë's ear. By the time the food arrives, he's talking to a boy with a bun and a leather jacket three booths over.

'Leather? That guy must be on fire,' Prakash says. 'I'm hot in shorts.'

Zoë laughs, then clashes hands with Prakash as they reach for the same buffalo wing.

'Yours,' he says, nudging it towards her. 'How's your head after yesterday?'

'I got lucky, it's fine.' She dunks the wing into the sauce. 'But can I tell you something that I know the others won't get, not even Luca?'

Prakash nods. 'Course.'

'Last night's little fainting adventure wasn't great, but after meeting the doctor I couldn't stop thinking, *I want what this person has. I need it. She's helping people! She's helping me!* It was so amazing.'

'Does your brain ever stop?' he asks.

'Never.' She lets out a groan. 'P, I've been working towards this one thing, and I'm so, so scared it will be for nothing.'

'You're letting all kinds of thoughts take over now. You've got a week off from worrying about it, okay?'

Zoë's phone buzzes. A text from Greta.

Hi Zoë, how are things going? Gx

Zoë groans. 'Greta's spy school continues. It's like she's paranoid I'll ruin Mum and Dad's life. If she cared about me a speck of the amount she cares about impressing them …'

Prakash smirks. 'Admit one thing: it *was* cool how she helped your dad see the light about this week.'

'Fine.' Zoë smiles. 'True. But still, she's this perfect untouchable person in their eyes, and every time I screw up it only lifts her higher. How am I ever meant to keep up?' She looks around the bar. 'Everyone in here is so happy. Why am I the only one sweating over results and acceptance letters?'

'You've wanted to be a doctor forever,' Prakash says. 'Remember your little red stethoscope?'

Zoë sighs. 'What did I know? I was four! Maybe it's better if I don't get into medicine — I mean, someone's life in my hands. These hands!' She wiggles her fingers, which are stained with buffalo-wing seasoning.

Prakash shrugs. 'Deep down, everyone else in here is stressing too. They're just trying to block out the future for five seconds.' He points at a guy doing shots at the bar. 'He's petrified he didn't get into his course and he'll have to spend the next year living in his parents' basement.' He gestures at a girl nearby. 'She slept through her alarm on the final day and missed the entire exam, not only the final page. And him,' he signals a guy arguing with a bouncer by the pool table, 'he's the most stressed of them all. He's angry 'cos he wishes he'd tried harder, or 'cos his mates are headed to the other side of the country. Or maybe it's 'cos no-one's doing anything about climate change, or his girlfriend dumped him two weeks ago. Maybe all of the above.'

'That's quite the story,' Zoë says. 'Feel free to teach me your compartmentalising skills, Prakash Patel.'

He grins at her. 'You can't re-sit that exam or change what the email said, so you may as well have another buffalo wing.'

'Don't mind if I do,' Luca says, sliding back into the booth next to Zoë and picking up a wing. 'The boys here are so immature I could die. Now, who's up for Would You Rather?'

'No more games,' Prakash and Zoë cry out in unison.

A woman on rollerskates glides up holding a tray brimming with gifts and merchandise. 'Can I tempt you with a little memento, kids?' she asks in between chewing on gum. It snaps and clicks in her mouth. 'I've got roses, teddy bears, commemorative spoons and shot glasses.'

They decline, and Luca and Zoë lean over the table to admire her rollerskates.

'Hey Prakash, didn't you used to collect spoons?' Zoë asks. 'You had a little display on your desk?'

He grins. 'Shut up, but damn straight.'

The woman chuckles and tucks a pile of temporary tattoo stickers under their plate of wings. 'Here, knock yourselves out,' she says, before skating off to the next booth.

Luca picks up the tattoos and leafs through them. 'Seahorse, no. Dragonfly, as if. A dog's face? What? Its tongue is hanging out!'

'You should get that,' Prakash says with a wink.

'And you should get …' Luca sorts through the pile. 'This!' The design shows a smiling troll holding up a pint of beer.

Zoë flicks through the stack while Luca and Prakash joke around and tease each other. Prakash goes to get more drinks, dismissing their offers to take their wallets to pay at the bar. Then, Zoë sees it. The heartbeat. Small, fine, black in colour; a similar design to what she saw at the tattoo parlour.

She peels off the clear backing and places the tiny heartbeat ink-side down on the inside of her wrist, then dunks a serviette in her glass and presses it over her skin. She peels off the paper and admires the heartbeat zigzagging across her wrist.

'Thoughts?' She holds out her arm.

Luca claps. 'Adore! Why that design though?' His jaw drops. 'Are you in love? It's Prakash, isn't it? He's cute, I've always thought that.'

Zoë rolls her eyes. 'I just like it.'

She doesn't bother explaining that the heartbeat reminds her of what she wants and why she's pushed herself so hard. The study, the work experience, the sacrifice. She just gazes at the jagged black lines on her skin and smiles.

Prakash arrives back at the table with more drinks.

'Zoë got a tattoo!' announces Luca.

'She did what?'

'Temporary.' Zoë thrusts out her wrist. 'It's no little red stethoscope, but you like?'

'Love. Good one, Zo.'

Zoë sips her drink, feeling warm again. It's only then she notices how flushed the boys look too. She takes in the table cluttered with empty glasses and jugs, and for the first time since they arrived looks at the clock hanging above the bar.

'Hold up!' she gasps. 'We've been gone forever.'

Prakash looks up at the time and swears, before bursting into drunken giggles.

Zoë groans. 'Oh no, I just remembered ...' She reaches into a shopping bag and pulls out the ice-cream tub. 'In news that will be shocking to no-one, it's totally melted!'

'Well, it's as hot as a volcano in here,' Prakash says.

'It's still good,' Luca says, swirling his finger through the melted ice-cream. 'Dare you to drink it all.'

'No more dares,' Zoë says. 'I want chilled-out paradise.'

'Shots first.' Luca signals to the bartender. 'More drinks too.'

'No way,' Zoë says. 'Let's go back to the resort and binge something in our PJs.'

'First my thing, then your thing,' Luca says, gesturing to the bartender who's already making their drinks.

'Fine, but I'm picking what we watch.'

'Deal,' says Luca, leaning over to shake her hand. 'But it better not be one of those antiques shows.'

More time disappears before they remember they're supposed to be leaving. By now, Luca has ordered another round to celebrate Zoë's temporary tattoo, Prakash has fallen asleep in the corner of the booth, and Zoë's hugged the waiter who brought over their salt and pepper calamari.

The music suddenly kicks up in volume. Cheering with excitement, Zoë climbs onto their table and struggles to her feet, swaying along to the music with her arms stretched high.

Luca leaps up to join her. He takes Zoë's hand and twirls her around, dipping her backwards until her head almost grazes the cluttered table. They laugh, Luca's hands slip and they crash down onto the tabletop.

'Time to leave, you two,' a man bellows. 'And wake up Sleeping Beauty while you're at it.'

They clamber down, grab the bags and shake Prakash on the shoulder.

'I need to pee,' he yawns. 'Meet you outside soon.'

Zoë picks up her drink, which miraculously wasn't knocked over in the chaos, and finishes it. She takes Luca's hand and spins him around on the wet carpet, then they fan out into a line and do the can-can.

'Kick 'em higher! Higher! Higher!' Luca yells.

A nearby waiter looks over at his boss for help.

Suddenly the bouncer's there again. 'Listen, I said get out. That means now.'

'Yes, sir, right away, sir,' Zoë says, giving a quick salute.

Luca's eyes widen. 'Actually, right after I visit the bathroom too.' He leans in so close to Zoë that their noses bump. 'Your eyes are glassy.'

'I've never been better,' Zoë says, only now realising everything is spinning.

Luca thrusts his drink into her hands. 'Have this if you're thirsty. Back soon.'

Once alone, Zoë notices how loud and dark it is in the bar. Groups of people laugh and shout in booths, on stools, around the bar, and out in the beer garden. She feels outnumbered and impossibly small.

She sips Luca's drink but the feeling clings to her. There's a whiff of danger, like something might go wrong any second.

Zoë moves towards the bathrooms, but a group of boys barrel towards her, hollering at each other. Their hot bodies and sweaty T-shirts are too close, so she slips out of their web and heads for an exit. She spills outside and gulps in the fresh air. The sun is setting, its glow sinking lower in the sky, and Saldana Strip is flooded with people singing and shouting.

She watches the bar's entrance, waiting for Prakash to hurry out with a sheepish smile on his face, or Luca to saunter out with a new friend hooked through his arm. But everyone is going in. The line snakes around the building and down the street.

Zoë fishes her phone out of her bag to text the others. Flat battery. She swears.

She walks up to the bar's entrance but a bouncer steps in front of her. 'Back of the line,' he says, arms folded over his chest.

'I just came out,' she says, hiding Luca's glass behind her back. 'I'm looking for my friends. Can I go in to find them and we'll leave straight away?'

'Sounds likely.' The bouncer puffs out his chest.

'I'll only be a second.'

'No-one jumps the queue.'

'Please!'

He ignores her, so she walks over to a nearby bench and sits down, staring at all the people milling around. She swallows, suddenly feeling the weight of being alone in a strange city.

Her eyes hurt from the pulsing neon lights all along the Strip, so she squeezes them shut and wills her friends to appear.

Samira

Day 4: 6.39pm

At the train station, Samira drags her suitcase to the ticket machines. She rereads the timetable: she's missed the evening train by fifteen minutes, and the overnight train doesn't leave for six hours.

An annoyed grunt sounds behind her. She turns to see an older woman wheeling a small suitcase. 'Are you buying a ticket, darl?' she asks.

'Ah … maybe, I …' Samira's knuckles whiten on her suitcase handle. 'Actually, you go ahead.'

She steps to the side and checks her phone again. No messages or missed calls.

She tries her mum again. Nothing.

A quick glance up reveals the ticket machine is free. She strides forward, jaw hardening, and buys a ticket for the overnight train before she changes her mind.

* * *

Samira's phone rings. It's a withheld number so she doesn't answer. She's sitting slumped against the brick wall at the train station. Its hard edges dig into her spine. Her stomach growls and she regrets not raiding the fridge before storming out of the house.

She glances up at the enormous Alotta Peach billboard that dominates the train station. Alotta is dressed as a glittery flamingo and holds a bunch of peach-coloured helium balloons. Moments later, Samira's phone beeps with a new message. She glances at the screen, expecting to see her mum's name appear. It's Tilly.

Late notice but wanna hang? We're bored! Feel free to bring your group

Samira's fingers hover over the keys. She's unsure how to tell her new friends she's leaving.

She tries her mum again. No answer.

Out of habit, her fingers go to text Anoush. She's halfway through writing her an emotional message when she remembers overhearing the conversation earlier. Her stomach lurches. But then she imagines Anoush arriving back to their room with no warning of Samira's departure. In her fantasy life, she stormed out like she's the star of a soap opera, determined to never look back. But as hurt as she feels, she can't leave without saying something.

She deletes her first message to Anoush and writes a new one.

A, things have got weird. Call me ASAP

Her phone rings again. Zain. So much for Tilly's exorcism.

Samira swallows. Zain never calls. Not even when they were together. She stares at his name on her screen, remembering him with the girl in the bathroom or running his hands over the redhead's hips at the foam party.

She wants to move on. But she also wants to know why the boy who never rings is calling her.

'Yeah?' she says, surprising herself with the sharpness of her tone.

'Are you okay, Samira? I'm worried.'

She can tell from the thumping music that he's at a bar. He can't be that worried if he's out partying.

'I'm fine. We're not together, remember?' She glances at the Alotta Peach billboard again and the lyrics to 'Live Your Way' dance through her mind. 'I've left.'

'As in, going home?'

'Yeah.'

'Come meet me, we'll talk.'

'I ... can't,' she says, twirling her Alotta Peach bangle. 'Please don't call me again.'

As she's slipping the phone into her handbag it rings again. She snatches it up. 'Zain, I said don't call me,' she snaps. 'I can't take any more!'

There's a silence so long that Samira worries she's on speakerphone to the group. She holds her breath, waiting for an inevitable eruption of laughter.

Instead, a man clears his throat. 'Samira Makhlouf?'

'Yes, that's me,' she stammers. She glances at the phone screen. Withheld number. 'Who's this?'

'It's Tony from Tony's Luxury Limousines. I'm your driver for the evening, ma'am.'

'Omigod, I completely forgot.'

'Is your party ready? I've been waiting out the front for a while and no-one seems to be home.'

Like everything this week, Samira had booked the limo in happier times. It was to take the group clubbing, but the girls had ditched the itinerary plan in favour of Dan's party.

'Should I knock on the door again?' Tony asks.

'Um ...' Samira glances at her train ticket. Maybe there's time. 'Tony, I'm so sorry for the confusion but there's been a change of plan. Any chance you can pick me up at the train station?'

'Yes, ma'am. The complimentary drinks and cheeses will be ready on arrival.'

'Thank you,' she says, getting to her feet. 'I'll be out the front by the gardens and fountain.'

Samira's eyes water as she takes in the colourful blooms and magnificent trees by the nearby lagoon. She'd originally planned for the group to have a photo shoot here later in the week before the Alotta Peach concert. It was supposed to be a keepsake before they all went in different directions because Anoush always complained they never had any pictures of everyone together.

When Samira slips into the back of the limo, she's hit with an overpowering loneliness. Where she'd imagined her friends, there are only empty seats. Instead of party music pumping and competing conversations, there's nothing but the sound of Tony huffing and grunting as he struggles to put her luggage into the boot of the limo.

She tries to call Anoush just in case. As predicted, it goes to voicemail.

Her phone beeps. A message from Zain.

can we talk?

Beep.

Pls

Another beep.

i made a mistake

Seconds later, a bubble with three dots appears on the screen. Zain is typing. Samira holds her breath and stares at the dancing dots. But then they disappear and no more messages come through.

Tony starts the limo. 'Where to, ma'am?'

Samira's stomach flutters with butterflies as she tells him the address.

As the limo drives along winding streets lined with palm trees Samira loses herself to the music on the radio. When they get to the beach house, she notes that it's dark inside and still picture-perfect, just like in the brochures. The limo edges past and pulls up in front of Tilly's house next door.

'Here, ma'am?' Tony asks.

'Here, thanks. Back in a sec.'

Samira gets out of the limo and pauses to take in the atmosphere. It's quiet on the street, almost eerily so compared to the chaos of Saldana Strip and the train station. But then she hears familiar laughter from inside.

She knocks and the door swings open to reveal Tilly.

'I love surprises,' Tilly cheers. 'The Warrior has come to save us from boredom and ourselves.' She waves Samira inside, then plucks a purple plastic sword and shield from the kitchen counter. 'For you. We found them at an op-shop today.'

'Omigod, too good.' Samira breaks into a grin as she strikes a pose with the armour.

'Now you look like a true Warrior,' Tilly says, waving her in. 'Sammy, I'm so relieved you're here. Kris and Harry are joking about leaving! At least I think they're joking. Turns out we should've made some plans beyond trailing Alotta Peach this week.'

Samira smirks at the irony. 'You need something to do? I might have an idea.'

'I like ideas.'

'I swear this isn't a regular activity for me, but … do you want to ride in a limo? As in, right now?'

Tilly's eyes light up. 'Absolutely!' She turns and shouts into the house: 'Bums off the couch and get fancy, you two! We're going in a limo!'

While Tilly rounds up Kris and Harry, Samira waits on the front lawn under the stars, twirling the shield in one hand and swishing the sword through the air. She stops, conscious that Tony might see her, then shrugs and gives the shield another spin.

Her phone beeps. It's her mum.

Sorry I missed you darling! Is it a good time to call? x

As the Peachies spill out of the house, Samira fires

off a text — *Just saying hi. Talk soon x* — then slips her phone into her bag.

Tilly leads the boys down the pathway towards Samira, her knee-high laced boots striding over the grass and cloak soaring behind, her long red hair in a high ponytail and adorned with a bejewelled plastic crown.

Kris hobbles along in a silver DIY robot costume. He bumps into the mailbox and an overgrown flower bush before he reaches Samira.

'Can you even sit in that?' she asks, admiring his handiwork.

'With great difficulty.'

Harry, who's wearing tattered trousers, a black bandanna and an eye patch, ties a purple cape around Samira's neck. 'Borrow this,' he says, stepping back in his heavy boots to admire it. 'It completes your look.'

Samira stands a little taller and leads the Peachies to the limo. They erupt with excitement when they see it.

'This is like a movie!' Tilly squeals.

'Living for this,' Kris says, opening the door and peering inside. 'There are teeny-tiny bottles in there.'

'Why are teeny-tiny bottles so much better?' Tilly asks. 'No-one even answer that! We just know they are.'

Harry cocks his head to one side. 'Sammy, your group's missing this? Are they out of their minds?'

Samira shrugs. 'I know. Should we do this or …?'

'We should. Their loss!' Harry cheers and crawls into the limo next to Kris, whose costume takes up half the back seat. 'Thanks, Sammy. Best surprise ever.'

Tilly and Samira pile in too, everyone's costumes squishing up against each other.

'Where to?' Tony asks from the driver's seat as the boys ferret through the smorgasbord of drinks and snacks.

Samira's phone buzzes, but it's slipped out of her bag and is trapped under Kris's costume. She lets it ring out and instructs Tony to head for Saldana Strip; they'll direct him from there. She doesn't want to stray too far from the train station, but she also wants to see where the night takes them.

As they drive along the Strip, Harry winds down a window. He pokes his head out. 'Best night ever!' he shouts as Tony honks the horn and the others whoop and cheer.

A bus goes past with an enormous Alotta Peach advertisement on the side of it. The Peachies scream. Tilly holds up her phone, blasting an Alotta song to the group. The familiar soaring strings kick off, followed by a vulnerable, almost whispering Alotta, but then the chorus fires up and she and the Peachies belt out the vocals.

Her phone buzzes again. Kris rescues it from beneath his leg and passes it over.

It's Zain. Another message.

have you rly left?

She stares at the message, then puts the phone away without answering.

Zoë

Day 4: 8.13pm

'You there! Wanna party? We've got something that'll wake you up.'

Zoë cringes at a group of strangers hollering at her as they meander along Saldana Strip.

'No,' she says. 'I'm fine.' And she folds her arms around herself, as though she's trying to hide away in the night. She's lost track of how long she's been waiting. One thing seems clear though: Luca and Prakash have disappeared.

She stands up, still holding Luca's drink, and attempts to recall the direction of their resort, but the beach and rows of shops stretch on. Her head buzzes so hard she can't remember their resort's name, let alone its address.

She walks left, desperately looking for a landmark beyond the swarming crowd to prove she's headed in the correct direction. But by night the high-rise buildings looming on Saldana Strip seem identical in size, height and colour. Everything mixes together and nothing seems familiar. Zoë wants to be home right now, in her bed, listening to the muffled noises of her parents pottering around the house.

She walks a bit further along the footpath, head pounding and swaying a little as she clings to her bag. When she looks over her shoulder for any sign of her friends, there's a guy leering at her. He's so close she can smell the rum on his breath.

'Hey cutie,' he says. 'I like your lips.'

Zoë grimaces. 'Leave me alone,' she snaps, picking up her pace to escape him. She weaves around parked cars to avoid the flow of people on the footpath. Many of them are waving glowsticks and smoking cigarettes. Streetlights blur her vision as she stumbles along, her hips occasionally knocking into cars' side mirrors.

SCREEEEEEECH. The squeal of brakes pierces the night as a moped swerves to miss hitting Zoë.

In shock, she steps backwards. Luca's drink slips from her grasp and shatters on the concrete, dusting glass over her toes. She hears muffled shouts behind her, but is fixated on the moped now pulling up at a red light. The rider turns around and swears, shaking her fist.

* * *

As two police officers ask Zoë questions, her mind won't stop replaying an incident from Year Eight. She'd been scribbling notes and talking with a friend in music class, so the teacher gave them a warning. They stopped momentarily, before changing to whispering behind their hands. The teacher stormed over and threatened them with detention if they spoke again while she was talking. That was the only time Zoë ever got in trouble at school.

The older of the two officers, Senior Constable Bette Kolovelonis, notices the shattered glass. 'How many drinks have you had?' she asks Zoë.

'I ... I don't know.'

'More than that one?' Constable Terri Inglis suggests. 'Is that alcohol spilled down the front of your dress?'

Zoë's chest tightens. She nods.

Kolovelonis clears her throat. 'You could have caused a pile-up tonight. Why were you on the street instead of the footpath?'

'I ... I was only walking,' Zoë stammers. 'Am I under arrest? Do I need a lawyer?'

'We're just asking a few questions and want to make sure you get back to your accommodation safely,' Kolovelonis says. 'We need to see some ID though.'

'Sure.' Zoë reaches into her bag and rifles around for her wallet. There's a long pause. 'I don't have it.'

'You don't have any ID?' Kolovelonis asks, eyebrow raised.

'My entire wallet. I had it at the supermarket because I paid, and I thought I had it in the bar ...' She shifts her weight from one foot to the other. 'My name is Zoë Rusho.'

Inglis smiles. 'Okay, Zoë Rusho, what are you—'

'I mean Russo,' Zoë interrupts, biting her lip at her mistake. 'Sorry, I'm nervous. It's definitely Russo.'

'Zoë, are you under the influence of any illicit substances?' Inglis asks.

'No! Never.'

Kolovelonis makes a note in her pad. 'This is serious, you get that right?'

'I'm fine, I promise.'

The officer's jaw hardens. 'Ms Russo, do you know what we've already seen this week?'

Zoë shakes her head.

'Drug-dealing. Ticket-scalping. Multiple overdoses. More arrests for drunken and disorderly behaviour than the last two years combined. One critical injury from balcony-hopping. One death: a drowning at an unpatrolled beach a few kilometres away. All because someone made a choice they shouldn't have.'

'Am I under arrest?' Zoë asks again, tears spilling down her cheeks.

'No, Ms Russo, Senior Constable Kolovelonis is just laying out the facts,' Inglis explains.

'It's clear you've been drinking alcohol — some of it in a public space,' Kolovelonis goes on. 'And you almost caused a potentially fatal crash on the main street. Plus, you have no ID, no friends around, and it's night-time.'

Zoë hangs her head in shame.

'Based on all that, we're going to give you a lift back to your accommodation,' Inglis adds. 'We can't have you wandering around Saldana Strip by yourself.'

Zoë glances at the police car and imagines having to

sit in it like a criminal. 'I'm meeting my friends,' she says. 'I'll call them right now.'

She reaches for her phone and remembers the battery is flat. It lies in her hand, useless.

'Where are you staying, Ms Russo?' asks Kolovelonis.

Zoë catches her breath. Her mind is blank. She can picture the resort's lush greenery, sweeping landscapes and ocean views. But she still can't remember its name.

'It's not far from here,' she says. 'Maybe the Seaside on the Strip? No, that's not it. But it's big, really really big, and has palm trees and a pool.'

Kolovelonis raises an eyebrow. 'A pool? That doesn't narrow it down.'

'The Ella Suites?' Inglis suggests.

'No, I don't think so,' Zoë says. 'I'll get myself there. I promise.'

'You don't know where you're staying or where your friends are, or even how to reach them,' Kolovelonis says. 'We're sticking with Plan A: you'll come to the station and hang out until you sober up, then we'll get you back to your friends. Deal?'

Zoë's cheeks burn bright.

She climbs into the back of the police car and slumps down as low as she can while Kolovelonis and Inglis trade stories about their upcoming days off. Kolovelonis has a friend's birthday party, while Inglis is going for a drink with someone she met on a dating app. For the officers, this is just another shift at work. For Zoë, it feels like one of the most humiliating moments of her life.

They arrive at the police station and Inglis offers Zoë a drink of water and a bathroom break. She accepts both, then splashes her face in the sink. As she washes her hands, she glares at her reflection in the mirror, stunned by her reddened eyes.

Then the officers take her to a cell.

Zoë freezes, staring at the tiny metal bench with a thin mattress in one corner, and the toilet and sink in the other. 'In here?'

'You're not arrested,' Inglis says. 'We're getting you sobered up and it's safe here. Or you're free to go if we can release you to a responsible, sober adult now. Would any of your friends fit the bill?'

'I doubt it.' Zoë pauses. 'Definitely not.'

Kolovelonis steps in. 'Anyone we can call for you?'

'I don't know anyone's number off the top of my head except my parents'.'

'We can try them?' Inglis suggests.

Zoë's eyes widen. 'I'd rather die!'

The officers try not to smile and offer to charge her phone so she can get in contact with her friends later.

'Rest up and count some sheep,' Inglis says.

Her radio goes off and she says something into it that Zoë can't make out. Inglis turns to Kolovelonis, who gives her a nod.

'We'll check on you soon,' Kolovelonis tells Zoë.

As they walk away, Zoë feels like the last person left on earth. She sinks onto the bench, fingernails tracing over the jagged lines of the heartbeat tattoo on her wrist.

Dahlia

Day 4: 9.41pm

Dahlia sits near the edge of the cliff, glaring at the darkened ocean and twirling a blade of grass around her finger. In the quiet, it's even more obvious Stevie isn't here.

Her stomach grumbles, snapping her back into the moment. She reaches into her bag for her phone. It's a black screen. She groans, remembering she turned it off earlier before she stormed away from Kiko and Florence. When she turns it on, the screen glows yellow. It's 9.44pm.

'What?' She sits up, scrambling to piece together how so much time has slipped away. But she can't remember. Her mind is too crowded.

It's not the first time Dahlia has lost herself. Sometimes she feels so frustrated with her foggy brain that she daydreams of waking up as another person for a day, just to experience a different type of life. Or hurling herself beneath rolling waves and emerging feeling whole again. Or casting a magic spell to help her outrun the prison of her mind.

But wherever you go, there you are. Dahlia hears the echo of Stevie's voice reminding her there's no escaping yourself. *I'll believe in you for as long as it takes for you to believe in yourself, Dahlia Raine Valour, and then I'll believe in you for a thousand more years.*

Her inbox fills with notifications, missed calls and messages from Kiko and Florence. She replies with shaking fingers.

At beach, coming back now xx

She staggers through the sand, desperate to feel anything other than sadness and guilt for losing the list.

As she reaches the raging party, the flashing strobe lights and confetti and the sweaty mass of people dancing and screaming lyrics, she keeps her head down. Suddenly, a microphone is shoved in her face.

'Want to win an amazing prize?' a voice booms.

Dahlia looks up into the eyes of a man wearing a tie-dyed T-shirt. 'I'm leaving.'

'Why?' the man laughs. 'The night's just beginning.'

Dahlia bites her lower lip as she sees a crowd surrounding them, hanging onto every word.

'Who doesn't want to win something?' the man goes on. 'You look like you could use a pep-up.'

Dahlia scowls at him.

'All you have to do is compete in three simple challenges and the prize of tickets to the Alotta Peach concert could be yours.'

'Alotta *who*? And this isn't my thing.' She gestures to the crowd. 'I'm not a competitive person.'

'An underdog — love it,' he says, slapping a wristband on her arm. 'Head past that barricade and up to the stage.'

Dahlia imagines Stevie at her side, nudging her, cheering her on. *I'll believe in you for as long as it takes for you to believe in yourself.*

Swallowing hard, she moves through the crowd and climbs the steps like there's a mysterious force pushing her from behind. On stage, she joins a line-up of people in swimsuits, board shorts, even a feathery chicken suit. Everyone except Dahlia is screaming with excitement.

The challenges are revealed. Round one: an eating competition. The referee — the pushy guy with the microphone — spells out the rules. There's one goal: eat as many hot dogs as you can in five minutes.

Dahlia's mind feels fuzzy as she ties the bib around her neck. The horn goes off and she lurches towards the plate. She stuffs the first hot dog in her mouth and crumbs from the bun spray everywhere. She keeps munching, slower now, but more focused. There's cheering from the crowd but no-one chants her name so she thinks of Stevie instead. A small smile pulses at the side of her mouth as she imagines Stevie screaming, 'Go, Dahlia!' on repeat.

Tomato sauce is smeared all over her lips and chin and cheeks, but she pushes on, shoving another hot dog into her mouth. When the horn sounds to finish, Dahlia has managed almost two hot dogs. The girls next to her are still chewing their first, and two boys on her other side ate two and a half each.

The winner is a girl who ate three hot dogs in five minutes. She burps then rushes offstage holding her stomach.

The people in the crowd toss giant beach balls around while the contestants are ushered to the next obstacle. Round two: jelly wrestling.

Everyone is split into pairs and arranged either side of a row of small plastic pools filled with orange jelly. Dahlia's opponent is the girl in the chicken suit.

Dahlia's jaw drops as the referee rattles off the rules: no shoes, no kicking, punching, biting, choking, headbutting or hair-pulling. Winners proceed to the next round, losers are out.

Another horn sounds, then a voice shouts, 'Get in there, underdog!'

Swearing, Dahlia kicks off her shoes and steps into the pool. The jelly squishes between her toes.

The girl in the chicken suit grins, like she's been preparing for this moment.

'What happens next?' Dahlia asks, just before the girl charges at her and knocks her onto her back in the pool.

Her breath catches as the girl sits on top of her and pins her down. Jelly squelches everywhere. Its sweet stench is overpowering. For once Dahlia can't think about the future or dwell in the past.

The referee's commentary is muffled by the jelly squished in her ears, but she can still hear the crowd laughing and cheering. Dahlia wants to give up. But then she imagines Stevie beside her, loving the madness of it all. Stevie would have given anything to be alive right now, wrestling a girl in a chicken suit.

As the girl pushes down harder, a fire lights within Dahlia. She releases a guttural moan and drags the girl off her, flipping her onto her back. The girl bucks beneath her but Dahlia grips handfuls of feathers. Wriggling and jostling, they ram against the edge of the pool. Jelly flies out over the side.

The girl breaks away and lunges at Dahlia, who rolls to one side into the soft, sticky jelly. Gasping for breath, she struggles to her feet, but the girl tackles her around the waist. They slip and struggle in the pool, jelly crushing against their skin.

Straining, Dahlia manages to flip the girl over. This time, she stays on top. The referee counts down while Dahlia keeps the girl pinned. The girl protests, arching and writhing. Every muscle in Dahlia's body burns and orange gunk coats her face.

Dahlia feels a tap on her shoulder, then she's pulled to her feet. She can barely see through jelly-caked eyelashes. The referee holds her right arm high, pumping it and screaming 'Winner!' on repeat while the crowd roars. The girl in the chicken suit shakes her head in defeat and climbs out of the pool.

Dahlia tries to scoop jelly out of her ears while the referee nudges her along the stage for round three: podium dancing.

Dahlia calls to the referee that she can't dance, but the music pounds so hard that it drowns her out. Swearing, she clambers onto her podium, her feet sticking and squelching from the jelly. There's a girl in a retro one-piece to her left, and a guy with a jelly-stained singlet and board shorts to her right.

The music kicks up a gear but Dahlia is frozen on the spot. The girl next to her drops down, arching and popping her body like they do in music clips. The guy drags off his singlet and everyone cheers. He circles it in the air and tosses it to a girl bouncing on someone's shoulders in the mosh pit.

Dahlia's heart pounds as she runs her hands over her pink pixie cut. Her feet feel like they're trapped in wet cement but she forces them to move, edging them side to side. This time, she hears people cheering for her.

'Get it, Pink Girl! Do it, Bubblegum!'

'Yo! Bubblegum! Move it, Bubblegum! You got this!'

'Bubblegum! Bubblegum! Bubblegum!'

The chanting buoys her and, as the music pulses, her feet move faster. Her arms and shoulders relax as she whirls and twists and twirls. The crowd shout their support so loudly that she can't hear the beat any more, but Stevie's favourite dance track plays in her mind just for her. Dahlia's smile stretches wide as she struggles to stay balanced on the podium while doing the lawnmower, the sprinkler, the chicken dance, the shopping trolley, the dice roll.

The referee screams that there's only thirty seconds left. With the crowd's chanting in her ears, Dahlia high-kicks then slides into a half-split. But she gets stuck halfway down, wobbles and slips off the podium, landing in a huge pit of foam blocks below.

Everyone roars.

Hiding her reddened face, Dahlia splays like a starfish in the blocks and imagines Stevie cracking up at her fall. A grin sneaks out the side of her mouth and she breaks into embarrassed laughter.

Moments later, strangers from the crowd pull her from the pit and direct her back to the stage. She joins the other contestants in line, and they give her encouraging high-fives while the referee announces the competition winner is decided by the crowd.

A wave of clapping rises as the referee passes the girl in the one-piece and the guy in the board shorts, and swells into an overwhelming rush of cheering and shouting when he reaches Dahlia.

He takes her hand and thrusts it into the air. 'Your winner, everyone! Bubblegum! And if you missed the rest of the competition, snippets will be aired on the late-night news.'

Dahlia's jaw drops. 'This will be on TV?'

He thrusts an envelope into her hand. 'Enjoy yourself.'

Dahlia is surrounded by cheering as she walks in a daze back into the party. People swarm her, asking for hugs and selfies. Some challenge her to a dance-off. Still stunned, she poses for a few photos with sunburnt strangers before she breaks away and squeezes through the crowd in search of the nearest exit.

She whips around when she hears her name cutting through it all. Kiko and Florence sprint towards her and she charges at them, collapsing into their arms. They hold each other tight, arms and bodies entangled, as the party rages around them.

Eventually, Kiko pulls back. 'Where were you?' she asks. 'We've been stressing.'

'It's been hours,' Florence adds gently.

'I'm sorry,' whispers Dahlia, bottom lip trembling. 'I'm sorry, I'm sorry, I'm sorry, I'm sorry.'

Kiko exhales and pulls both girls closer again. They sink into each other's arms, buried in necks and hair and breath, ignoring everything and everyone else.

Dahlia doesn't know how long they stand there. She's the first to break away. 'I love you both, but can we go?' she asks.

They surge through the crowd, ducking and dodging flailing arms and elbows on the dance floor. Eventually they spill out the other side where the sand meets the grass. Florence gestures to an empty space beneath a tree, and they sink down onto it.

Kiko turns to Dahlia. 'Are you okay? *Really*?'

'I think so,' Dahlia says, her gaze drifting to the stars.

Kiko gives her arm a little squeeze.

'Now we know that Dahlia's safe and everything's going to be alright,' Florence says, 'can we talk about the thing that no-one is talking about? I mean, how are we not talking about it?'

Dahlia raises an eyebrow. 'What thing?'

'You were dancing on a podium,' Florence hoots. 'You!'

'Don't forget the hot-dog-eating and jelly-wrestling,' Kiko adds, leaning in to wipe jelly off Dahlia's jaw.

Dahlia cringes. 'You saw all that?'

'It was hard to miss ... *Bubblegum*,' Kiko says.

'We'd been looking for you everywhere for hours, literally hours and hours,' Florence adds. 'And next minute, look who's on stage: the dancing queen herself!'

Kiko laughs. 'The winner!'

'Dahlia won a jelly-wrestling competition,' Florence says. 'Now there's a sentence I didn't think would ever come out of my mouth.'

'I don't know what came over me,' Dahlia admits. 'Everything was a blur. But I felt Stevie with me.'

'I don't doubt it. I mean ... jelly-wrestling? Doing the splits on a podium?' Kiko exclaims. 'Stevie wouldn't miss that for the world.'

'I still feel like I've let her down,' Dahlia whispers. 'The Too Late List meant so much to her.' Her fingers nervously rake her hair.

'You could never let any of us down,' Kiko says. 'Stevie's nothing but proud.'

'She's looking down from her podium in the sky and shaking her bum with you,' adds Florence. 'Probably while eating a hot dog.'

The girls fall quiet against the background thumping of the party.

Florence looks up and traces the outline of the moon with her fingertips, while Kiko gently wipes jelly from Dahlia's shoulder and points out a group of stars glittering above them.

Suddenly there's a pop, and a fizz, and a shower of colour erupts and rains down. And another. And another. The girls cuddle in close as the fireworks crack open the sky, painting an effervescent rainbow across the night.

Samira

Day 4: 11.01pm

The limo follows the twists and turns of the highway as it wraps around the rugged mountainside looming above the beach. Samira rolls down a window, enjoying the feeling of the wind through her hair. With nothing but mountains and an endless ocean extending before them, Saldana Strip feels worlds away.

In the near distance on a hill stands the snowy lighthouse with red trimming that she and Anoush had planned to visit on what turned out to be their unsuccessful girls' day. Its radiance cuts through the darkness, calling them in closer. Tony parks the limo on the grass at its base. They all tumble out and kick off their shoes to feel the grass beneath them.

Samira and Tilly cartwheel in sync before flopping onto their backs and contemplating the sky. As the minutes melt into each other, everyone lets slip little things about themselves; morsels that stretch a friendship into deeper territory. Samira's love of watching kids' cartoons in nothing but a T-shirt, undies and her mum's old socks. Kris's debilitating fear of snakes that left him shaking during a school excursion to the zoo. Tilly's admission that she likes being an only child and gets sick of people asking if she wishes she had a brother or sister. Harry's first crush on the girl who lived around the corner, who rejected him then kissed the school bully in Year Five. Samira overhearing Anoush, Claire and Rashida bitching about her. Tilly breaking down in tears because she knows how it feels to be excluded from a group too. They drain themselves of these little confessions, speaking until their throats ache.

There's a lightness to getting lost in time with the Peachies that Samira isn't ready to let go of yet. So when they beg her to stay on their couch for the night, she calls the rail company and swaps her ticket for credit.

Afterwards, she jumps to her feet. 'I need a reset. Thinking what I'm thinking?' she asks Tilly with a wink, gesturing at the wide-open area before them.

Samira drives her sword high, releasing an ear-splitting war cry into the night then she and Tilly run barefoot on the grass towards the lighthouse.

Day 5

Zoë

Day 5: 12.06am

Shouting from a nearby cell wakes Zoë up. She opens bleary eyes and rubs her aching neck. Another voice cries out, followed by the banging of a fist against a wall. Zoë shrinks into herself, bringing her knees up to her chest, and spots the heartbeat design on her wrist. It's half-scratched off.

Sighing, she stands up and walks to the bars. She strains forward and spots Kolovelonis drinking a cup of coffee in the hall.

'Hello?' she calls out, voice cracking. 'Officer?'

Kolovelonis walks over. 'You're up,' she says. 'Good sleep?'

Zoë nods. 'Am I allowed to go?'

'Remind me: are we waiting for your parents?'

'No!' Her heart rate quickens. 'I need my phone back to call my friends. It was charging ages ago. What time is it?'

'Past midnight,' Kolovelonis says. 'Big night, huh?'

'Big year.'

Kolovelonis takes Zoë's phone off the charger and passes it through the bars. 'Well, if your friends are of-age they can come and collect you — but only if they're sober. Otherwise we'll drive you back to your accommodation. Remembered where it is?'

Zoë blushes. 'Still working on it.'

She calls Prakash who answers with, 'Where have you been? We've been calling and messaging all night!'

As she tries to explain, he excitedly talks over her, telling everyone in the suite to do another shot because Zoë's ready to party again. She hopes Kolovelonis can't hear him.

'Prakash, listen,' she says, cutting off his animated rant. 'This is important. I need you to tell me our resort address.'

He laughs. 'Paradise Road, Paradise, baby!'

'No, I'm serious,' she hisses. 'What's the name of our resort? I need your help!'

There's crackling and heavy breathing followed by raucous laughter.

'Prakash,' Zoë begs. 'I need the name or number. Now!'

'It's me!' Luca's voice rings down the line. 'Where'd you go? Prakash and I waited by the back exit forever.'

'Back exit? Why were you ...' Zoë rolls her eyes at the miscommunication. 'I'll explain everything later, but I need the—'

The phone cuts out. Zoë's chest pounds as she imagines having to spend the rest of the night in the cell.

Kolovelonis raises an eyebrow. 'Get it?'

'They're checking,' she fibs. 'I feel fine again so I'm happy to get myself there.'

'Sorry, house rules,' Kolovelonis says with a shrug.

'Maybe I can get them to come here?'

'Sure. But if they show up over the limit, then no luck. If you get the address, we'll organise a lift for you, okay?'

Zoë nods. When Kolovelonis's back is turned, she calls Prakash again. It goes straight to voicemail. She swears under her breath.

Suddenly her phone bursts to life.

'Tiny Sloth!' Luca announces. 'Prakash's battery died. Where are you by the way? I've got a drink with your name on it. Wait, no, I'm mad at you. You ditched us!'

'I didn't!' Zoë sighs. 'Luca, I need the name of the resort.'

'Huh? It's the Grand Southwell on Saldana Strip. Oh, guess what — Akito saw Darius earlier and someone stole the couch from his suite! It just disappeared! They graffitied all this hardcore stuff on the living room wall too. Isn't that intense? Can you imagine the damage bill?'

Zoë rolls her eyes. 'Akito's still hanging with him?' She lowers her voice. 'What about the shoplifting?' She glances around the cell, cheeks flushing at the irony. 'Whatever, I'll see you soon.'

Forty-five minutes pass before there's a free car to drive Zoë back to the Grand Southwell. Her head pounds, but this time it's from exhaustion. Constable Inglis is driving; Zoë doesn't catch the older police officer's name. She slouches in the back seat, staring at the dazzling lights of Saldana Strip flying by. Unable to resist, she reaches for her phone. She scrolls through her unread mail but there's only a flood of newsletters she doesn't remember signing up for.

She sinks even lower as the police car pulls into the resort driveway. When she reaches into her bag for the card to let her into the resort and suite, she swears out loud. It's in her wallet, and she has no idea where that is. She texts Luca to meet her in the lobby.

Inglis flashes Zoë a kind smile. 'You've had quite the night. I'll walk you in.'

The other police officer steps out of the car and lights up a cigarette.

'Don't get too comfy,' Inglis says. 'We're heading back to the Strip after this.'

In the lobby, the man working the front desk glares at Zoë. She sinks onto the couch, wishing she could disappear into its soft folds. Inglis makes small talk with Zoë about the weather while checking out the resort brochures and the fish in the oversized glass tank.

When Luca dances out of the lift holding a beer, his eyes widen at the sight of Zoë with a police officer.

'Ah, hello, what's going on here?' he asks, slipping the drink behind his back as he sidles up to her.

'Long story,' Zoë mumbles. 'Thanks for the lift, Constable.'

'You bet, now get some sleep and look after each other,' Inglis says, before walking off.

Luca leans in close. 'The police? What's going on? Tell me everything.'

'It's simple. I lost you two, and couldn't find my wallet and—'

'Prakash has it. You left it on the table at the bar.'

Zoë sighs with relief. 'Finally a win.'

'Now back it up and fill me in, Zo. I'm dying here.'

The sound of laughter echoes through the lobby and they turn to see Darius and two guys amble out of the lift. As they walk to the vending machine around the corner, Darius nods hello in Luca's direction.

'Hey, man!' Luca calls out to him. 'Just a heads-up — there's a cop outside. You should tell her about the couch and graffiti.'

Darius's mouth widens. 'The cops? You lost your mind, bro?' He gestures to his pockets. 'I'll get a new couch.'

'Is he joking?' one of the other guys asks. 'Mate, are the cops really here?'

'Chill, just come hang at mine for a bit, we're sweet,' Darius tells them, shoving soft drink cans at their chests and heading back to the lift.

Zoë crinkles her nose, waiting until they've disappeared before speaking. 'That was shady.'

'Says the girl kicking it with the cops,' Luca scoffs.

'Nothing happened!'

Luca's and Zoë's phones repeatedly beep so they both glance down. It's a string of phone messages from Violet dropped into their group chat.

Zoë looks closer: they're pictures of her taken moments earlier from their suite's balcony. Stepping out of the police car. Standing with the police officers. Walking into the resort, head and shoulders slumped, with Inglis at her side.

Underneath there's a message in the group chat from Violet.

WTF Zo????

The chat lights up with comments from the others within seconds.

What is happening?????

Fake as

When good girls go bad

Law and Order: Zoë Russo Unit

Can someone explain what I'm looking at

where are your cuffs?

Someone handcuff me

lol, ew

Framing these

'This isn't funny,' Zoë says as more photos of her climbing out of the police car flood in from Violet. 'I'm going to kill her.'

Samira

Day 5: 7.56am

The morning sun beats through the bathroom window as Samira splashes her face at the sink. She dares to look next door at the beach house she hired: the bright blooms decorating the courtyard; the open balcony; the ceiling-to-floor windows. She sighs. From the outside, things look as perfect as she'd dreamt.

Her phone rings. There's no avoiding this call.

She puts it on speaker, lowers the volume and whispers, 'Hi Mum, hi Teta', before they launch into a loud wobbly rendition of 'Happy Birthday'. It's not until this moment that Samira realises how much she misses them.

Her mother's voice is wispier than usual and Samira knows that means she's stopping herself from crying.

'Is it everything you wanted, my darling?' her mum asks.

'It's been memorable.'

Samira hates keeping secrets from her family, but she doesn't dare tell them about the messiness of the week. Instead, she lets their love fill her to the brim.

'Oh good! And how are you, darling? How's Zain? And Anoush?'

Samira dries her face, puts in her earbuds and lies down on the couch. 'They're …' she begins, skipping over the first question, 'they're doing everything they want.'

'Wonderful. Well, I hope you're all taking care of each other.' Her mother's voice cracks. 'You're a long way from home.'

In that second, Samira's mind races over everything that's happened. Anoush bitching about her with the girls. Zain breaking up with her at the train station. Feeling lonely in a house full of people.

But then she looks around the Peachies' living room, at their colourful outfits strewn about, the half-empty bowls of snacks from staying up late chatting, her very own sword and shield, and she smiles.

'I'm with good people,' she says. 'I'm okay.'

'Oh Sammy, that makes me so happy. That's all I've ever wanted for you.'

'That and having you home under her watchful eye,' Teta interrupts.

'Quiet down, Mum,' her mother says. 'But it's true, it's not the same without you here, darling. The bakery, the house. We miss you.'

In the background, Teta scolds her. 'You promised you wouldn't guilt-trip her! It's only a few more days.'

'Mum, let me feel my feelings.'

A deep laugh bubbles up within Samira. 'I'll allow it all,' she says. 'The truth is, I miss you too.'

Her mother sniffs. 'No, no, forget that. We'll be here waiting for you. Go have fun! We're proud of you, darling.'

'*Mum.*'

'We are. You planned this week and made your dreams come true.'

'Yeah.' Samira glances next door again. 'Love love love you.'

'Love you more.'

She hangs up, heart a little sore, then wheels her suitcase towards the front door.

'Happy birthday to you, happy birthday to you, happy birthday dear Warrior, happy birthday to you!' a chorus of voices sing.

Samira turns to see Tilly, Harry and Kris waving a half-deflated balloon and one of the glass candles from the bathroom.

Tilly grins. 'Sorry for the pathetic effort, we only learnt it was your birthday a few minutes ago. Your mum has some serious pipes on her!' She passes Samira a cereal box. 'Happy birthday! Look inside!'

'I ... I'm speechless,' Samira stammers, cheeks burning red. She sets her suitcase aside and peeks inside the box to see a chocolate bar, a handful of lollies, and a notepad and pen from the house.

'Also, this,' Harry says, passing her a small bunch of flowers. 'They're from the tree hanging by the balcony.'

'He picked them himself,' Kris teases in a singsong voice.

'I ... I don't know what to say. You didn't have to do this ... but thank you for doing this.'

'We're going to miss you,' Tilly says, pushing out her bottom lip. 'I wish you could stay for longer!'

Samira pauses. 'Well ...'

'Are you staying? Tell me everything you're thinking at this exact moment.'

Harry laughs. 'Let her talk, Tilly.'

'The house I booked is so beautiful. It would be a shame not to get to enjoy it, right?'

'I like where this is going,' Tilly says.

'But maybe it's too awkward.'

'At least you'd be feeling awkward in a sweet-as beach house,' offers Kris.

'True.' Samira picks up the plastic sword and twirls it around. 'I don't know what to do.'

'Want a bodyguard?' Harry asks.

Samira grins. 'Tempting. Actually, why don't you all come with me for a visit? Check it out?'

'For real?' Tilly asks, eyes widening. 'So you'll stay?'

'Maybe.' Samira reaches for her suitcase. 'Let's see.'

When they arrive next door, sunlight is drenching the lounge room. No-one is up yet so Kris and Harry stretch out across the couches, while Tilly checks out the balcony to admire the view of the Peachies' courtyard.

Samira plucks a stray piece of broken vase from behind a pot plant in the corner and pops it in the bin, before turning to the fridge. Her itinerary is still stuck behind the flyers and notes. She slides it out and reads it, shaking her head at all the broken plans.

'You okay, Sammy? Your face looks sad.'

She turns to see Tilly standing by her side.

'I'm good.' She offers a small smile. 'Just didn't think I'd be back here.'

'Yet you are. May I?' Tilly extends her hand towards the itinerary. She scans it then lets out a long whistle. 'When you said colour-coded, you *meant* colour-coded. Look at this rainbow!'

'I never joke about colour-coding,' Samira says with a wink.

Tilly's eyebrows narrow as she absorbs the itinerary. 'Foam party, tick. Limo ride, we got that. Snorkelling?'

'Cancelled. Meant to be yesterday.'

'Oh. Sorry.' She keeps reading. 'Hotel tonight?'

'It's nothing.'

'There's a love heart around it.'

Samira cringes. 'I thought it was going to be a special night, but I was clearly delusional.'

'Having hope isn't delusional. You should still go. Pamper yourself! It's your birthday.'

'Might be weird.'

'Nothing wrong with weird. Ooh, there's Alotta's concert for tomorrow night.' Tilly points at the schedule. 'Will you be here for it? Say yes and come with us.'

'I don't have VIP tickets.'

'I've got the perfect wig you could borrow, Sammy,' Kris pipes up from the couch. 'It's red, powerful and peak Warrior.'

'I don't know,' Samira says. 'That sounds fun, but I should try to talk things out with the girls. Things have turned pretty messy.' She looks around, sighing when she sees one of Anoush's bikinis drying on a door handle. 'Maybe it was a bad idea coming back here.'

'What's up? Is that your friend's?' Tilly asks, pointing at the swimsuit. 'Want me to take it for our next exorcism?'

'Stay away from the bikini, firebug,' Samira says with a laugh.

Someone says her name and she looks up to see Zain walking into the room.

'Ah, hey,' she manages, heart racing.

'About that girl you saw, I …' His voice peters out when he notices the others. 'Anyway, I heard voices so thought everyone was here.' His gaze finds Harry and Kris, before he returns to Samira. 'You said you were leaving. Are you back for good?'

She swallows. 'Maybe. I'm not sure. Have you seen Anoush?'

'The girls are still out.' He notices her luggage on the carpet. 'Did you, ah, did you get my text?'

'I saw it.'

He waits for her to elaborate but she doesn't. 'Okay. Cool. I … I guess I'll leave you to it then,' he says, before disappearing into the hallway.

Tilly scowls. 'The audacity. He didn't even say happy birthday. Next time we see him, I'm telling him that I hope he's destroyed by a flesh-eating parasite.' There's a sparkle in her eyes. 'Still plenty of time left for that though.'

Samira grins. 'You're out of control. Do you have plans right now, dear Queen?'

'If only we were that organised.'

'Cross everything and pass me that itinerary,' Samira says. 'I'm making a call.'

* * *

The boat cuts through crystal-blue water towards a secluded island. It's packed with people, but Samira is only aware of the Peachies. Heavy droplets spray over the boat's sides and they all shriek with laughter.

On one set of seats, Tilly and Kris are fake-reading each other's palms. Tilly's eyes widen as she predicts Kris will come into a huge sum of money soon. He pulls her hand closer and tells her she's going to have the most successful year of her life.

Behind them, Samira and Harry wring out their clothes and exchange wry looks.

'This is amazing,' Harry says, gesturing around the boat. 'Thanks heaps.'

Samira plays with the wet edges of her sarong. 'Pleasure. Luck was on our side.'

The phone operator at the snorkelling company had recognised Samira from her profuse teary apology the day before and said she and three friends could fit onto a tour if they made it to the wharf within the hour.

Harry passes her a fresh coconut and a plate of fruit. 'So you organised this for your mates and they bailed?' he asks. 'What's up with that?'

'No clue,' Samira says, clinking their coconuts together. 'Pretty silly on my part, huh?'

'More like pretty rubbish friends.'

'Yeah, maybe.' She gives Harry a sheepish smile. 'It's especially embarrassing because I'd worked on organising this week for us for, like, months.'

'That's not embarrassing. You care.'

She shrugs. 'I guess it isn't as important to them.' She pauses. 'Or it isn't important if *I'm* part of their week or not. They're all having a brilliant time without me and my itinerary.'

'Stuff them,' he says, offering her a chocolate that's already half-melted by the heat. 'We're enjoying it.'

'I'm glad someone is.' Samira sighs and turns to face him, one leg tucked beneath her. 'A thing about me is I changed schools this year, and I think I was so busy trying to keep these friends that I missed the fact that maybe we weren't even friends at all.' She laughs. 'I might need a class on friendship. Maybe a tutor. I clearly suck at it.'

Harry grins. 'You don't. The opposite.'

'Thanks,' she says, bumping their shoulders together.

'So what else was on your perfect itinerary?'

'Um, ziplining in the mountains.' She shrugs. 'I'll try to do it another time. Maybe with Mum.'

'You should. You really should.'

The boat pulls up at the secluded island and everyone rushes to the side for a better look at the sweeping beach dotted with palm trees.

Once their feet hit the white sand, the group scatters. Tilly and Harry strip down to swimsuits and sprint towards the waves. They shout about the chilly temperature but still plunge in. Kris hangs back under a palm tree, rifling through the box of snorkelling gear and flippers. The salty breeze grazes Samira's skin as she dawdles down to the water's edge, unties her sarong and wades into the gentle waves.

The afternoon drifts away in a blur of swimming, sunbaking and water fights. Hair sticky with sand and salt, they all curl up on the beach together.

Tilly's legs lie over Kris's knees while they apply aloe vera to his sunburnt shoulders and discuss which colour to paint their nails for the Alotta Peach concert. Unable to sit still for too long, Tilly pulls on a pair of flippers, drags Kris to his feet and they lumber towards the water.

Samira stays with Harry, who's humming to himself and lost in a daydream. Their knees touch, but they don't make eye contact. It suddenly clicks that she's in nothing but a wet bikini and sarong. She pulls the material a little tighter around her waist.

'So, um, thanks again for the flowers,' she says. 'They added to the day's overall loveliness.'

Harry shrugs. 'All good. You deserved them.'

'I don't know about that, but today turned out kinda great.'

'So great,' he says with a smile.

They're closer now and Samira fights the urge to sweep his wet curls off his face.

'Guess I'd been dreading it for nothing,' she says.

'Guess so.'

'Um …' Samira hesitates, breath quickening as she searches for something to say. Without thinking, she leans towards Harry and brushes her lips against his.

He kisses her back, fingers grazing the back of her neck, and she sinks into it for a moment, before pulling away, cheeks reddened.

'Omigod, sorry,' she whispers. 'I don't know why I did that.'

'Obviously my raw magnetism and charm,' he jokes in an attempt to lighten the mood. 'Impossible to resist.'

'Apparently,' she confesses with a smile. 'Probably best not to. I'm still a bit of a mess.' Her mouth stretches into a grin. 'That kiss *was* good though.'

'Agree,' he says, settling back onto the sand.

'I've made things awkward, haven't I?'

'Nah.' He tucks a loose strand of her hair behind her ear. 'We're friends. It's cool.'

Samira blushes. 'Thanks.'

'Hey Peachies, get in here!' Tilly calls from the water's edge, oblivious to what just happened. 'Last chance for a dip!'

Samira and Harry swap smiles as they join the others.

Samira stares at the shimmering ocean, realising it's the first time she's stopped to savour the view since they arrived on the island. Her shoulders soften as she breathes in the infinite blue.

Tilly splashes water in her direction. 'So what were you two secret squirrels whispering and plotting up there?'

Samira's and Harry's voices overlap in their hurry to speak. '*Nothing.*'

Zoë

Day 5: 5.20pm

Zoë checks her phone. There's the usual flood of notifications from the group chat, plus two missed calls and three unread text messages from Greta. She glares at her bowl of gnocchi with enough intensity she could shoot laser beams through it, then glances up and notices the group trading looks.

Violet groans. 'You already hate me so I'll be that person,' she blurts out, while the others stifle sniggers. 'What happened, Zo? The police? We're dying over here! You've been hiding in your room all day.'

Zoë rolls her eyes. 'I lost my wallet. I got a lift back. The end.'

'She speaks! But that summary skips over the power-nap in jail,' Luca says, a cheeky grin spreading across his face. 'You had to sleep it off in a cell block.'

'Shut it, Luca.'

'See anyone get arrested, Zo?' Akito asks with wide eyes. 'A drug bust? A sniffer dog?'

'Or any hot cops?' Violet asks. 'We need details! Paint us a picture.'

Prakash stretches across the table for a piece of garlic bread. 'Everyone give her a break. No more questions.'

'What are you, her publicist?' Luca teases.

'Manager,' Prakash says with a smirk.

'He wishes,' Zoë says. 'Look, it was nothing. Seriously nothing.' She pauses. 'But everyone taking and sharing pictures of me like the paparazzi was messed up. I want to forget about last night and move on.'

'That was Violet with the photos and social media stuff,' Akito chimes in. 'Don't blame the rest of us.'

Zoë raises an eyebrow. 'Social media?' She turns to Violet, whose head is lowered. 'Did you put those photos online? Tell me you didn't. I didn't say you could!'

Violet sighs. 'Calm down, Zo. I put everything online, I always have.'

'That doesn't make it better.'

'You with the cops was a tiny speck in my night! I put a hundred things up. Maybe more. People scroll so hard they barely take any notice, plus everything disappears in twenty-four hours.'

'Get rid of the photos now!' Zoë says.

Akito fake-coughs. 'Videos too.'

'I can't believe you did this, Violet.'

'You can't?' Luca asks. 'Remember when she saved all those not-safe-for-parents photos from my eighteenth on her laptop and the aunties saw everything? Believe it.'

Violet purses her lips. 'You two are so melodramatic. People love it.'

Zoë reaches for her phone and starts flicking through the apps. 'What people? What have you done?'

She finds Violet's profile and watches the first video. Instantly she's there, her face crumpled as Inglis opens the car door for her, head lowered as she walks alongside the police officer to the resort's entrance. Violet has added bright stickers and hashtags over the top to jazz up the clip: *OMG! WTF?* and #*badgirl* flash on screen.

'Delete it,' Zoë tells Violet. 'All of it. Now.'

'If you were more online and not so boring, you'd appreciate that you're getting in the way of me documenting a full and truthful story about the ups and downs of life,' Violet says. 'People are captivated.'

'Translation: she's getting loads of traction, likes and comments,' Luca adds. 'Not to mention more followers.'

'Fine, that too,' Violet says. 'But stop stirring the pot, Luca.'

'So much for people scrolling by and not taking any notice,' Zoë says. 'How would you feel if I posted terrible photos and videos of you? Where anyone can see?'

'The oldies follow my other squeaky-clean account,' Violet says with a shrug. 'They don't know about this one.'

'You're unbelievable.' Zoë shakes her head. 'Delete everything I'm in.'

'It's gone,' Violet sulks, tapping at her phone. 'Although I'm unclear about how *you* go to jail and I'm the bad one.'

'I didn't *go* to jail.'

'Anyway!' Prakash interrupts. 'Let's move on.'

'Good call,' Luca says, shovelling in a mouthful of gnocchi. 'Talk about a week you'll never forget though, right, Zo?'

'If only. Is it too much to ask for things to fall into place? Seriously, by this time of the year, Greta had been—'

'Accepted into the Gifted and Talented Program,' Prakash finishes. 'You're on a loop with this, Zo, and it's bumming you out. Forget her.'

Zoë's chest tightens as her brain fills with empty lined essay pages and imaginary red squiggles. 'You're right,' she says, trying to curb thoughts of Greta's overflowing collection of academic trophies. 'Guess my brain's fried.'

Violet raises her glass. 'Welcome to the club.'

'Cheers to that,' Akito says, clinking beers with Luca across the table.

Zoë groans as the others top up their glasses. 'Count me out, the last few days have trashed my liver. Let the record show: my relaxing week starts now.'

Dahlia

Day 5: 6.01pm

Dahlia's gaze locks on two men in tuxedos holding hands and smiling for photos on the boardwalk. Their beards glint with flecks of grey and gold.

She turns to Kiko, who's stretched out beside her on the bench in a wet bikini. 'Stevie wanted that, you know?'

Kiko leans over to squeeze out her hair. Droplets rain onto the grass. 'To be a silver fox?'

Dahlia snorts. 'No! Well, yes, probably, but I mean *that*. Love. Soulmate. Marriage.'

Kiko slips on her singlet. 'Marriage seems so non-Stevie. White picket fence, super traditional, kinda boring.'

Dahlia looks back at the men, who are laughing with their photographer as they look at the pictures on the camera. 'They don't look bored at all.' She shrugs. 'Getting hitched was on Stevie's list. I don't remember it all, but I remember that.'

'Are you a closet romantic?'

She scoffs. 'Nah.'

'Do you love love?' Kiko jokes in a breathy tone, flicking her black bob from side to side.

'Come on.'

There's a pause. Dahlia dares to look over. Kiko is watching her.

'So, have you ever been?' she asks.

'What?' asks Dahlia.

They both know but Kiko pushes on. 'Have you ever been in some kind of love?'

The weight of the question hangs in the air. Dahlia's words stay trapped in her mouth.

Kiko raises an eyebrow. 'Well?'

'Don't look at me like that,' Dahlia says with a smile, hoping her cheeks aren't as flushed as they feel. 'I can't bear it.'

'My face is that hard to look at, huh?' Kiko winks. 'It was just a little, tiny, minuscule question.'

'Don't,' Dahlia repeats, pretending to hide behind her fingers. 'It's a big, huge, enormous question. Colossal.'

The truth is Dahlia doesn't know what she thinks about love. The other girls have a full history of crushes, relationships and somethings-in-between. But Dahlia rarely dates. She's kissed five people — a convenient number to fit into her ready-made list template. While the bottom four names switch places depending on her mood, she's locked the latest addition into the top spot.

Top 5 Kisses of All Time
Kiko (under the stars at the beach)
Lulu (waiting for a train)
Jon (at his house)

Dahlia doesn't know how many people Kiko's kissed, but she knows it's more than she has. Kiko isn't into labels either, but she's only dated and hooked up with girls, even counting a few of them as girlfriends. But no matter how deeply a girl falls for her, Kiko ultimately ricochets away from them and prioritises Florence and Dahlia. For Kiko, friendship comes first.

The tension is thick in the air as Kiko waits for an answer. Dahlia peeks through her fingers and sees that Kiko hasn't taken her eyes off her.

She lowers her hands and says, 'Next question, lady.'

Kiko laughs. 'Noted.'

5 Things To Adore About Kiko
Her kindness
Her empathy
Her sense of humour
Her hair
Her smile

Dahlia looks again at the couple, now walking towards the beach. They each clutch their dress shoes in their spare hand while their fingers remain intertwined. The taller man stops to brush sand off his new husband's shoulders.

'If it makes me a romantic to think they're cute, then I'm a romantic,' Dahlia says. 'They look like they're meant to be.'

'I guess so,' Kiko says.

Her skin lightly grazes against Dahlia's as she readjusts her spot on the bench. A week ago, such a small gesture would mean nothing. Now, it means everything.

5 More Things To Adore About Kiko
Her skin against mine
Her positive outlook
Her curiosity
Her calming presence
Her honesty

'You can ask me the question again,' Dahlia says. 'The big one. If you want to, I mean.'

Kiko's mouth widens a little and she sits up straight. 'Have you ever been in some kind of love?'

Dahlia holds Kiko's gaze. 'Maybe.' A small smirk slips out. 'Some kind.'

'Interesting.'

'Have you?'

'Been in love?' She smiles at Dahlia. 'I think so.' There's a loud silence. 'Definitely.'

Dahlia's heart thumps. She wonders if that means what she thinks it does.

'Cool,' she murmurs. 'Another one to cross off Stevie's list.'

Kiko nods. 'A big one, some might say.'

'They might.' Dahlia glances up at the sky, which is blooming with fairy-floss pink and peach clouds. 'What should we do about the list? Time's running out on everything.'

'There's time,' Kiko assures her. 'We're still in the story. You're trying to fast-forward ahead, trying to peek at the ending.'

Dahlia knows Kiko is right, but her mind always looks for ways to brace against the worst possibilities. 'But there's this big clock ticking in my brain that reminds me this is all going to end soon.'

'Yeah?' Kiko replies. 'Then let's write up a new list. Make the time we have count. Skydiving, ziplining, all the things.'

Dahlia reaches up to her hair, fingers lingering over the strands. 'Can we do that? A new list? Will it be enough?'

'*Dahlia*. Yes.' Kiko's voice is almost a whisper. 'You live in your head so much! Be here with me now. It's why Stevie wanted us all to go away. Please try.'

'This is me trying.'

'Okay,' Kiko says, lowering her gaze. 'Okay.'

Dahlia looks back to the beach. The men have moved on. She cranes her neck until she spots them further along, pants rolled up to their calves and building a sandcastle.

She glances over her shoulder to see if Florence is on her way back with the fish and chips yet, but there's no sign of her. She and Kiko are still alone.

'Can I tell you something?'

Kiko sits up a little straighter. 'Go for it.'

'I think I lied before.'

'You did?' Kiko's voice catches in the back of her throat. 'About what?'

'When I said I was running out of time.'

'To do the new list?'

'Yeah. What I really mean is ...' Dahlia leans in so the tips of their noses touch, 'I hate that I'm running out of time with you.'

Kiko's mouth breaks into a grin.

'Why are you smiling?'

'Because I hate that too, and I'm glad you said it first.'

Kiko cups Dahlia's face in her palms and kisses her softly, tasting of sea salt and boysenberry ice-cream.

Samira

Day 5: 6.18pm

Everyone crosses paths in the beach-house driveway. Samira and Tilly are splayed out on the warm concrete as Claire and Rashida blow kisses to them and saunter towards the taxi waiting on the street. Mathieu trails behind the girls and grunts hello, while Harry and Kris stroll back inside their own house to play video games, apparently oblivious to the awkwardness.

Zain and Anoush are at the rear of the group. Zain, sunburnt, his nose red, shiny and angry-looking, spots Samira first while Anoush fiddles with locking the front door. It's impossible to miss the catch of his breath when he sees Samira wearing a bikini and sarong. He offers her a short, sharp nod, before disappearing into the back of the taxi.

Anoush struts down the driveway, fumbling with the tiny handbag bouncing off her hip. 'Samira!' she says. 'There you are! It feels like forever.'

'Were you looking for me? Did I miss a message?'

'No, I ...' Anoush breaks into laughter. 'It's the most boring story, girl, but we were at Dan's party yesterday —

which was off the hook by the way — and things got out of control, and I ended up dropping my phone in the pool. It's dead now. I've tried everything to fix it but nothing worked, so I'm, like, off the grid or whatever.'

'That sucks. Wait, so you never got my text?'

Anoush cocks her head to one side. 'I don't think so. What did it say?'

Samira pauses, then looks over at the taxi. Claire is leaning out the window, waving Anoush to hurry up.

'It's all good. No rush,' she fibs.

'Okay.' Anoush pauses. 'Do you want to come with us?'

Samira's heart stings at the offer. Anoush is saying the right words, but Samira can tell it's an afterthought.

'You go, I'm good. I … I think I'm going to stay at the hotel tonight. The one I booked for, um, you know.'

Anoush raises an eyebrow. 'By yourself?'

'Maybe. It's paid for so …' Samira shrugs, knowing it's impossible to forget what she originally hoped might happen there. 'Hey, are you still on for Alotta Peach tomorrow night?'

'Is that tomorrow? Shit.' Anoush bites her lip. 'I want to be free, but I don't think I am any more.' Her voice falters — a giveaway that she's lying about being disappointed. 'Dan and his friends are talking about us all going rollerskating, and you can totally come too of course. Anyone's welcome.' Anoush blushes. 'I mean, I'm not the biggest Alotta Peach fan so it's probably for the best, right?'

Samira nods. 'Sure.'

The taxi beeps and the others yell at Anoush to hurry up.

'I should …' she says.

'All good. Go.' Samira gives her a little wave and Anoush smiles and totters down the driveway.

Samira goes to call out to her to wait, then realises she doesn't know the right words to admit what's been weighing on her. She exhales, shoulders slumping.

Tilly stands up. 'It's Sammy's birthday, by the way,' she calls to Anoush. 'Just in case anyone forgot.'

Anoush's eyes widen. 'Of course it is,' she says, swearing under her breath with embarrassment as she teeters back to Samira. 'Happy birthday, girl.'

Samira feels Anoush's arms wrap around her but the distance between them has never been so wide.

After the taxi pulls away, Samira elbows Tilly in the side. 'Why'd you say that? It was so awkward.'

Tilly sniffs. 'I can't handle all the unsaid little *somethings*.'

'I hate conflict.'

'Fair. But there's nothing wrong with standing up for yourself.' Tilly pauses. 'She wasn't wrong about one thing though.'

'Anoush?'

'Yeah. That story about her phone *was* boring.'

Samira laughs. 'Hey, do you want to come to the hotel with me, Tilly?'

'A sleepover! I'm there.'

'There are only two rules: BYO PJs and no Zain talk. Like, zero.'

'Zain who?'

'Exactly.'

Samira's phone buzzes. It's a message from Zain. She groans.

i miss you

Another message comes through and her jaw tightens. She holds it out for Tilly to read.

i miss us

* * *

Zain is sitting hunched on a low brick wall in front of the hotel. Samira recognises him from a block away. As she strides closer, she notices his hands are shaking.

Behind her, Tilly calls out, 'Stay strong, Sammy. You're the Warrior. You've got this.'

Samira's stomach flutters with nerves. By the time she reaches him, she still hasn't decided how she'll cut through the silence.

He gets to his feet when he sees her, and passes her a long thin red rose in a plastic sleeve. It still has the price tag on it.

She mumbles thank you but wishes she'd said something stronger. Something true.

She tries to pull herself into the moment, but seeing him away from the others whisks her back to how it used to be. Her visiting his house on a Saturday afternoon.

Him sprawled on the bed. Sport blaring from the television. His phone would buzz with notifications from mates and he'd scroll through them, leaving her feeling like an afterthought.

'Samira,' he says, stepping in closer. 'Hi.'

She nods. 'Hey.'

'I ... I had to see you.'

Samira turns to Tilly, who's glaring at Zain. 'Why don't you go ahead and chill out in the hotel lobby?' Samira suggests.

'I can stay,' Tilly says, before leaning in to whisper, 'I'll take him out. Just say the word.'

Samira laughs. 'I'm good. Promise. I'll meet you there.'

'Call if you need reinforcements,' Tilly says as she walks towards the hotel, glancing over her shoulder to shoot Zain dirty looks.

'What's her deal?' Zain asks, his dark eyebrows narrowing with confusion. 'Who is she?'

'A friend, it's a long story.' Samira shrugs. 'I'm more interested in why you're here.'

'It's your birthday,' he attempts, gesturing to the rose. 'I didn't want you to spend it alone — although that's clearly not a problem.'

'I'm fine.'

'Well, we had a plan, right? It was on the itinerary.'

She rolls her eyes. 'No-one's been following the itinerary. And plans change. Look at this week.'

'But everyone told me you were still coming to the hotel. Doesn't that mean something?'

Samira twirls the rose around. 'It means I already paid for it and Anoush ran her mouth. Are you sick of hooking up with other girls already?'

'No. Wait, I mean, yes! They don't mean anything to me. And I know I stuffed up.'

'So we agree on something.'

'I thought you'd want this,' he says.

She stands taller, shrugs.

'Or not,' he flounders. 'Samira, I—'

'Zain, this is embarrassing for both of us. The awkward levels are, like, hazardous.'

He clenches his jaw. 'But you loved me.'

'I also thought the girls were my friends. What did I know?' She pauses, then admits, 'I did care for you though. Maybe too much.'

'Well, I still care,' he says. 'What's the problem?'

'You dumped me! And that was hard at first, but I realised something: we don't make each other laugh. So what's the point? Like, right now, there are zero feel-good vibes.'

A small grin slips out as she pictures Tilly giggling and pep-talking her by the fire pit.

Zain's face crumples. '*Huh*? Good vibes?'

'It's fine,' Samira says, shrugging. 'It doesn't matter. Thanks for the rose, but you shouldn't have come.'

'We can take it slow. Talk all night.'

'*I* paid for this,' she says, gesturing at the hotel, 'with extra shifts at Mum's bakery. And it was for *my* birthday. So *I'm* staying here.'

He shakes his head. 'Man, this isn't how I wanted it to end.'

'How then?' Samira can hear her voice getting stronger with every word. 'Would you have ended it after we'd ... *you know*? Or on the last day of the trip? Or before your apprenticeship starts? When?'

'I have no idea.' He leans closer and tries to take her hand.

She pulls back. 'Stop. You're lonely and that sucks, but it happens. Please go.'

'Are you into those random guys from next door?'

She pauses, remembering her kiss with Harry. 'It's none of your business.'

'Babe, that's not a no.'

'We're over. You said it. And, for the last time, don't call me babe.'

Zain swears. 'You've changed.'

'I hope so.'

He lingers, arms open, waiting for Samira to envelop him in a hug. When she doesn't, he glares at her and walks off without saying another word.

She watches him until he's a tiny figure in the distance.

Exhaling, she takes out her phone and blocks his number, and deletes him from her social media.

Zoë

Day 5: 7.01pm

Zoë pulls her hair into a tight bun and ties the shoelaces on her sneakers.

'Tell me you're joking with the activewear, Zo,' Prakash says, sitting down on the bed beside her. 'I ironed my shirt and everything. You're coming out with us, right?'

She shrugs. 'I need a break.'

'You do. A run can wait. Footy season's over.'

'No, a break from the others. Violet crossed a line with those photos and videos. She doesn't get it.'

Zoë's phone buzzes on the bedside table. She lunges for it and gasps when she sees the email notification. It's from Number One, her top preference. The news she's been waiting on.

'Is it your dad?' Prakash asks in a worried tone.

'No. It's not him.' Her grip tightens on the phone. 'I'll be back in a sec, P.'

She slips out into the hallway, takes a deep breath and psyches herself up to click on the email. This time, there's no portal or password needed.

Dear Ms Russo,

Thank you for your considered and impressive application for early acceptance at our institution. However, we received an unprecedented number of exceptional applicants this year and we regret to inform you that you have been unsuccessful in this round.

Zoë's hand presses to her collarbone. 'No,' she murmurs. 'No, no, no.'

She's fantasised about attending this university all year, even pinning photos of the campus to a vision board above her desk. It had been so clear in her mind that, until the biology exam, she hadn't dared to think it might go another way.

Her thoughts race as she replays the year, wondering what, apart from the exam, she could have done differently. She'd tried her best; she'd given it everything. She'd studied, she'd sacrificed, she'd pushed harder than she'd ever thought possible, yet it hadn't been enough. Will she ever reach the insufferably high bar that Greta set?

Her gaze returns to the email. *Unsuccessful.*

As she blinks back tears, Prakash suddenly appears by her side.

'Zo?'

'I didn't get in,' she manages, her thoughts still spinning from the rejection email. 'Number One doesn't want me. It's over.'

'Shit. I'm sorry.' He wraps his arms around her and she buries her face in his chest.

They lock in together, Zoë sniffling into Prakash's shirt, as the sound of the others laughing and getting ready to go out echoes through the suite.

'I know this meant everything to you,' he murmurs. 'Want to talk about it?'

'Not right now.'

She wipes at her wet cheeks and slowly pulls back, mouth widening in horror when she notices the mascara stains on his crisp white shirt.

'Oh, P,' she cringes. 'Take it off, I'll soak it for you in the laundry.'

'Any excuse to get my kit off,' Prakash jokes. 'It's all good, wait here,' he adds and dashes into his bedroom across the hall.

When he returns, he's in a pair of shorts, a loose singlet and running shoes. 'Let's go.'

She breaks into a watery smile. 'Now who's the gym bunny? What happened to going out?'

'Turns out I got a better offer.'

'You don't need to worry about me. Go have fun.'

'Exercising after gorging on an enormous Italian feast isn't fun? What could go wrong?'

Zoë giggles. 'Living on the edge, hey? I'll race you to the beach.'

'First one to get a stomach-ache loses,' Prakash says with a grin before sprinting past her and disappearing out the front door.

Samira

'You really know how to treat a gal,' Tilly says as Samira leads them inside the hotel room. Rose petals are scattered over the bed and carpet. 'Looks like the hotel staff have cranked the romance up to an eleven.'

'Omigod, hilarious,' Samira giggles, dropping her bags near the couches. 'I may have requested this when I booked a few months ago.'

'A brilliant decision,' Tilly says. 'Now, don't leave me waiting. Did my exorcism work?'

Samira smiles. 'Yeah, looks like it. He's gone for good this time.'

'Yes! It was the burnt sock at midnight that did it.'

'Not arguing with you,' Samira says with a snort. 'Thanks for everything, Tilly.'

'It was all you,' she says. 'So you told him where to go?'

'Pretty much. All these words were erupting out of my mouth! I couldn't stop them. I actually said what I was feeling, like, in the actual moment. It's happened a few times this week.'

'That's the best,' Tilly says. 'Now we can celebrate. Look at this place!'

'It is beautiful,' Samira murmurs, taking it all in. She looks around the living room, noting the sweeping city views, before disappearing into the bedroom. When she re-emerges, she's holding plush white bathrobes and fluffy hotel slippers. 'Look at these! We have to!'

Tilly cheers. 'If I have to pamper *myself* to ensure you receive maximum birthday pampering, that's a sacrifice I'm willing to make.'

Giggling, the girls put on the bathrobes and dance and strut around the hotel room like they're on a catwalk.

'Want to do a sheet mask?' Samira asks breathlessly as she stops to pour strawberry milk into two champagne flutes. 'There are heaps in the ensuite.'

The girls hurry into the bathroom, alternating between strutting and sliding in their fluffy slippers. They remove the masks from the packaging and gently press them onto their faces, cackling at their reflections in the mirror.

Afterwards, they flop onto the couch in their robes, masks and slippers. Tilly nibbles on a piece of chocolate while Samira turns on the TV. The news is showing a fast-paced montage of the events of the past few days. Blaring footage of sweaty, happy people on the beach. A pub brawl. A couple posing in front of a food truck. A jelly-wrestling competition between a girl with a fairy-floss-pink pixie cut and a girl in a chicken costume.

'There are so many feathers, I can't look away,' Samira says.

The montage cuts to footage of the jelly-covered pink-haired girl doing the sprinkler on a podium while the crowd roars, 'Bubblegum!'

'How hilarious. She's, like, my inspiration for the week,' Samira says, before gasping as the girl falls off the podium.

Tilly's jaw drops and her hands race to secure her mask. 'You might need a new hero.'

The girls stare at the TV, then leap onto the bed in celebration as the girl with pink hair is pulled onto the stage and declared the winner. Rose petals flutter everywhere as they jump up and down with glee.

Suddenly, there's a loud knock on the door.

'Could it be Zain?' Samira asks Tilly in horror. 'I was clear it's over.'

Another knock. 'Room service!' a man's voice calls out.

'Is this a trap?' Tilly whispers, tightening her bathrobe. 'We haven't ordered anything.'

'I remember! I pre-paid for it months ago.' Samira laughs, then winces as the sheet mask strains against her skin. 'Let him in.'

Tilly jumps from the bed and opens the door, beaming as the room service attendant wheels in a trolley. His mouth opens slightly when he sees their masks and fluffy robes.

'Your three-course dinner for two,' he manages, parking the trolley in the corner. 'Garlic prawns, fettuccine carbonara and gelato to finish.'

'Amazing,' Samira says. 'Hey Tilly, can you grab my wallet from my handbag so we can leave a tip?'

When Tilly reaches into the bag, out spills the unopened packet of condoms. Her eyes widen. 'Oh,' she says, before finding the wallet and passing it to Samira.

Blushing, Samira fishes out a few notes and passes them to the attendant. He wishes them a beautiful evening and excuses himself with a small nod.

'So much for no Zain reminders tonight,' Samira says, breaking into nervous laughter.

Tilly nods. 'Want to talk about it?'

'Nah.' She pauses. 'But is it weird to be disappointed and relieved at the same time? He was going to be my first.'

'Doesn't sound weird to me,' Tilly says, before breaking into a grin. 'But not much sounds weird to me.'

Samira smiles. 'I love that.'

'Now, did that waiter say three courses?' Tilly asks, lacing her long red hair into a thick ponytail. 'Sammy, this is luxury.'

'Who's living like a true Queen now?'

Tilly groans with pleasure as she lifts the lid on each dish and steam spirals towards the ceiling.

They peel off their sheet masks, gently massage the remaining serum into their skin, then each piles a plate high with carbonara and prawns. Strawberry milk in one hand, creamy pasta in the other, they curl up on the bed against a mountain of pillows.

'Birthday talk,' Tilly says through a mouthful of fettuccine. 'I know it hasn't been the easiest week and it's not exactly what you planned, or even *at all* what you planned, but has it been a good one?'

Samira smiles. 'Yeah,' she says, sipping her strawberry milk. 'Incredible, really, thanks to the Peachies.'

Tilly wrinkles her nose with joy. 'I feel bad saying this week has been amazing for me — with a capital A. We got to meet you! But I have to confess: this is my first sleepover.'

'No! Seriously?'

'Yeah, I've never been invited to one before. Well, except once and it turned out to be a prank. So, yeah, this is kinda special.'

'Hey, any time. And people like that don't deserve to have a spectacular human like you in their life anyway.' Samira squeezes Tilly's hand before squealing with laughter. 'Your hands are coated in garlic sauce!'

'Sorry! Those garlic prawns are so good they could solve the world's problems,' Tilly says with another cackle, wiggling her fingers before wiping them on a serviette. 'Hey, we really blasted into each other's lives and stirred them up, didn't we?'

'Good and proper.'

Tilly sets aside her plate. 'Hey, can I read your palm?'

'You really know how?'

'Does it matter?' Tilly extends her hand. 'Are you in?'

Samira grins. 'Garlic sauce and all.'

Tilly dims the lights to a soft glow, then takes Samira's hand and peers closely at her palm. 'I've never seen such perfectly created lines in my many, many years in this world,' she gushes.

Samira tries not to chuckle.

'I'm picking up something now … oh yes, I see it. Things are changing for you,' Tilly says, moving her finger over Samira's palm. 'And they're changing *fast*, which can feel scary. But in the long run, all this change might turn out to be the most magnificent and beautiful thing.'

'Which line on my hand reveals that?' Samira asks.

'Oh, all of them.'

A laugh erupts before Samira can stop it. 'I'm getting the gelato.'

Dahlia

Day 5: 9.09pm

Dahlia stares at the newspaper clipping on the hostel corkboard. The pink hair, the denim shorts, the jelly-coated skin — there's no denying it's her in the photo pinning down the girl in the chicken suit in a pool of orange jelly. She remembers the roar of the crowd counting her down. Stevie's voice cheering her on in her mind. The thrill of something taking over and pushing her to fight for herself.

When she steps back, she notices the Hall of Fame sign pinned to the top of the corkboard.

'Oh my ...' she says, shaking her head in disbelief.

Florence rests her chin on Dahlia's shoulder. 'You're famous, lady! That is one of the most hilarious things I've seen, probably ever.'

'It's like I'm someone else,' Dahlia says, staring at the photo.

'You look amazing,' Florence says. 'Kicking butt, super woman, strong as hell.'

'I wouldn't believe it happened if there wasn't photo evidence.'

'It happened.' Florence grins. 'You falling off the podium is burnt onto my retina for the rest of eternity. Hey, any word on your luggage?'

'Nope, the airline are clueless and the hostel haven't heard anything. My bag's disappeared.'

Florence furrows her brow, before perking up again. 'Well, we've got the hostel mixer to take your mind off things. The pamphlet said it's *musical chairs meets speed-dating, but for friends.*'

Dahlia nibbles her fingernail. 'Joy,' she says, chest tight at the thought of making small talk with strangers.

Florence's face softens. 'You were light years out of your comfort zone yesterday and survived,' she says, pointing at the newspaper clipping. 'But if you're not up for it, we'll stash some food for you.'

Dahlia watches as a stream of people storm through the hostel towards the mixer. Stevie would have been the first one there, probably introducing herself to people before the music even started.

'I'm coming,' she says, 'but I'm freaked about the interrogation. All those questions — Where are you from? Who are you here with? What are you doing next year?' She twists her hair around her fingertips. 'It's a lot. I don't have all the answers.'

'Who does?'

'You. Kiko.' Dahlia shrugs. 'You've got the hairdressing traineeship, she's got computer programming.'

'And you'll be an au pair.' Florence crinkles her nose, highlighting the soft smattering of freckles. 'It's a start.

And it's okay not to know past that,' she adds, giving Dahlia's shoulder a little squeeze. 'Take your time, lady.'

Dahlia exhales. 'I'll try.'

'So, as someone who *does* have some of the answers, I'm begging you to let me run a conditioning treatment through this cute little mop when we get home,' Florence says with a grin, playing with Dahlia's pixie cut. 'It's crying out for TLC.' She peers at the back of Dahlia's head. 'Lady, I'm not coping — you have knots within knots!'

Dahlia laughs. 'Fine, deal. And hey, can you maybe *not* tell Kiko I was freaking out again? I don't want to scare her away before we even know what we are.'

'As if you could. Look, I'll do whatever you want, but our girl likes you — *all* of you — and she has forever. The worst-kept secret is out of the box.'

Dahlia lowers her head, blushing. 'It blows my mind. She's *Kiko*. Everyone loves her. Why me?'

'No idea, but like I said, it's been *forever*,' Florence repeats. 'Come on, let's find her.'

Inside the mixer, music pounds and lights sparkle. Dahlia tells herself that one day she'll enter a room without wishing Stevie was there to egg her on and drag her onto the dance floor, but today isn't that day. She rolls her shoulders down and walks in anyway, smiling as Kiko greets her with a kiss on the cheek.

A loud horn goes off, creating screams of excitement, and the mixer begins. The music only plays for thirty seconds before a boy with dyed orange hair sits down in front of Dahlia and starts talking. He tells her he recognises her as Bubblegum from the beach party competition and wouldn't have been caught dead on stage himself. How he's staying in a five-star resort on the other side of Saldana Strip but wants to experience another side of life tonight. He's halfway through a story about why everything would be easier if he was an Aries when the horn rings out again. He waves goodbye despite never saying hello and dances off into the middle of the room.

Dahlia swears. 'That was exhausting.'

'Did you even get a word in?' Florence asks with a giggle.

'Nah, he was the worst. But on the plus side, I didn't have to answer any questions.'

'I could hear his voice yapping over my guy, who thinks he aced his modern history exam by the way,' Kiko adds with a grin, raising a glass in his honour. 'Good one, Johnno.'

The horn sounds for the next round.

A girl slides in opposite Dahlia with a nose so sunburnt that the skin is peeling off. She talks quickly and Dahlia misses her name twice, but hears that she's heading further up the coast to pick fruit until she works out what's next. Her plan is to spend her spare time writing songs. She sings a few lines out of tune and with sappy lyrics, but Dahlia flashes her an encouraging smile. When the horn sounds, the girl asks to swap social media details but Dahlia fibs and says she isn't online.

The girl walks away and Dahlia slumps down in her seat, sipping her drink. She watches Kiko and Florence locked into chats with strangers, smiling and nodding and asking questions with such ease. Stevie had been the same. No topic was off limits. Dahlia had once watched her discuss the pros and cons of picking a pimple with a plumber who was trying to fix the taps in her parents' ensuite.

'Hating this too?'

Dahlia looks up to see a boy with long hair and a bold Hawaiian shirt grinning at her from a wheelchair.

'Only with my entire being,' she says. 'How about you?'

'A guy just ranted at me about the time he got food poisoning and now I want my memory erased.'

'A reasonable response.'

He laughs. 'I'm Steve. You?'

Dahlia freezes. 'Hi,' she says, breath catching. 'Sorry, what was your name?'

'Steve. Or Stevie. Stevo. Stephen if I'm in trouble with Dad. And yours?'

'Just Dahlia,' she manages, still stuck on his name being so similar to Stevie's. 'So … are you having fun?'

'We covered that. *No.* You?'

'Also no.'

Dahlia tries to think of something to ask, but she's lost for words. If Stevie was here instead, she'd be leaning forward and firing questions, and answering them too, probably landing herself an invite to hang out with Steve another time.

'You alright, mate?' Steve raises an eyebrow.

'Of course,' she lies. 'So, ah, tell me about yourself. I like your shirt, by the way.'

'Thanks. You go first though.' There's a gentleness to the way he smiles and nods for her to go on, his eyes crinkling at the edges. 'Something up?' he asks when she doesn't speak.

The tightness gripping her chest relaxes. 'I miss my friend,' she admits. 'A lot.'

'They couldn't make it?'

'No.'

'That's a bummer.'

'Yeah. She was meant to be here and, not to get too deep, I still can't believe she's going to miss a lot of stuff. Everything else that there is actually.' She pauses. 'Sorry, that didn't mean to come out. I'm a real emotional vampire tonight.'

Steve's expression softens. 'Nah, not at all. You mean your friend ...?'

'Cancer. It's shit.' She nibbles at the edge of her thumbnail. 'I bet food-poisoning dude doesn't seem so bad now, huh?'

He clears his throat. 'I obviously don't have a clue how you feel but ... I'm sorry for your loss.'

'That's really kind.'

Dahlia is impressed by his empathetic words. If she mentions Stevie's death, people are often stunned into awkward silence or say something misguided and tactless like, 'Everything happens for a reason' or, 'It must have been her time to go'. But not Steve. He stays quiet, nodding for her to continue.

She swallows. 'It's been a year. I keep thinking it'll get easier, but then this week hits, when she should have been here, and it's like finding out she's gone all over again.'

He swears and shakes his head. 'That's rough, mate. She clearly meant heaps to you.'

'She was my best friend,' Dahlia whispers, then gestures to Florence and Kiko. 'They loved her too, but they're strong, resilient. They slipped back into their real lives so much easier than I've been able to. I feel out of my body almost all the time.' She clasps her hand over her mouth. 'Why am I telling you all this? We're at a party! What a downer.'

'Nah,' Steve says. 'You're all good. Sometimes it's easier to chat with strangers, right? And your mates would be missing her heaps too, I bet, just in their own way. When my pop died, I was blubbering like a water fountain but my sister didn't cry for months. Grief hits everyone differently.'

'I never thought of it like that.' Dahlia glances at the girls, wondering if they're struggling beneath the lightness shimmering on the surface. 'Steve, you're one wise dude. You must hear that all the time.'

He grins. 'Never. But I'll take it.'

The horn sounds.

'Time's up, mate,' he says. 'That completes our therapy session, please see the receptionist on the way out to pay your bill.'

Dahlia smiles but tears spring to her eyes. It's something Stevie would say. For a moment, as she dabs her eyes with a serviette, it's almost like Stevie is there with her, filling the room with light.

5 Ways Stevie Lives On (Right Now)
Steve's humour
Florence's untamable spirit
Kiko's compassion
My sensitivity

She pauses, struggling to think of a fifth addition to the list. Her lips crack into a smile as she remembers the jelly-wrestling photo and article displayed under the Hall of Fame sign.

My courage

'So Steve, what do you like to do when you don't have strangers emotionally dumping on you?' she asks.

He laughs. 'Nah, horn's gone, I'm off the hook with the questions. But do you fancy a dance? I've been taking lessons.'

'Oh yeah? You should know, I suck.'

'Perfect,' he grins, reversing the wheelchair towards the dance floor. 'Leaves more of the limelight for me.'

They twirl and twist on the spot, succumbing to the disco lights and retro pop music.

'This is so embarrassing!' Dahlia shouts over the music, but she doesn't stop moving to the beat.

Kiko and Florence salsa towards Dahlia and Steve, waving over a handful of strangers to join them. Kiko's hands find Dahlia's hips and a conga line quickly forms behind Steve, who sings at the top of his lungs and snakes them around the room.

Day 6

Dahlia

Day 6: 9.01am

Kiko's panicked words wake Dahlia. 'It's gone! It's gone!'

'Huh?' Florence groans, dragging the sheet over her head.

Dahlia rolls onto her side. 'What's wrong, lady?'

'The envelope of cash, our emergency credit card ...' Kiko says, rummaging through her luggage. She throws her bag back on the ground. 'Even the coins in my spare socks. It's all gone!'

Dahlia crawls out of bed and rifles through her tote bag, which is strewn over a chair in the corner. 'Shit! They took my purse of cash. Who would do this?' She looks around the room. 'And they trashed the place!'

'No, that's all us,' Kiko says, not joking.

Florence, still in bed, laughs. 'Room 22 has seen better days! But the door is locked. Dahlia made a big circus about locking it when we got back from the mixer.'

Dahlia yawns. 'Did I?'

Last night is a haze of conversations, dancing and pastry pinwheels. She recalls seeing Florence and Steve flirting in a corner before he left for his hotel, while she and Kiko danced in a circle of people whose names she'll never know.

'You were nagging us hard,' Florence says. 'Not that I remember much about the end of the night.'

'Other than Steve's tongue down your throat,' Kiko says.

'That I remember fondly, *mate*.' Florence grins, impersonating Steve's charming drawl. 'Nicest guy.'

'Can you focus for a second?' Kiko asks her. 'Our stuff is gone, this isn't a joke.' Sighing, she inspects the door. 'It's unlocked. Wait, that means ...' She shudders. 'They broke in here while we were sleeping?'

She spots a bottle of lemonade by Florence's bed. 'Where did you get that drink?'

'Vending machine in the hallway. Middle-of-the-night craving. All that dancing left me wiped.'

'As in you left our room and maybe didn't lock it when you got back?'

Florence cringes. 'I thought I did!'

Dahlia holds up her hands. 'This is no-one's fault.'

Kiko's jaw tightens. 'It's kind of someone's fault.'

'Let's focus on the prick who snuck in here while we were asleep and stole our stuff,' Florence insists, jumping down from the top bunk to pick up her bag from the floor. She rifles through it then swears. 'My wallet's gone too.'

'We have no money,' Kiko says. 'No cash, no cards. Literally nothing. We'll have to cancel everything.'

Dahlia gasps. 'My money belt!' She lifts up her

T-shirt. Her mum's money belt encases her waist like a sausage skin.

Florence laughs. 'Did you sleep in that heinous thing?'

'Twelve dollars, my ID and my juice bar card,' Dahlia announces, scooping them into her palm. 'Only one more stamp before a free mango crush.'

Kiko nods. 'It's better than nothing if we're smart about it.'

'That heinous thing is amazing and wonderful and we love you for wearing it, even when you're asleep and it seems unnecessary,' Florence adds with a grin, batting her eyelashes.

'I'm sure,' Dahlia says. 'So ... twelve dollars. How are we meant to do Stevie's list now? Skydiving and ziplining cost money. Like serious money.' Her hands reach up to tug at her hair. She stops herself and draws in a deep breath. 'We can't afford anything.'

Florence sighs. 'We all love Stevie, but isn't the more relevant question: how are we meant to eat?'

Dahlia shrugs. 'No idea. And we've still got days here. *Days.*'

'Breakfast today is covered in last night's mixer ticket, so let's start there,' Kiko says.

'Good plan. Drink?' Florence asks, offering the girls the suspect lemonade.

Kiko rolls her eyes, while Dahlia tries not to laugh.

On the way to breakfast, Kiko reports the theft to the hostel staff, who appear less than worried as they write down details in a puckered old notebook. They tell the girls they'll keep an eye out for any suspicious activity and confirm there's still no word on Dahlia's luggage.

'Twelve dollars.' Dahlia shakes her head as they file down to the dining hall. 'Should we call the police?'

'I thought about that, but what could they even do?' Kiko replies. 'There's no surveillance footage and the hostel staff are hopeless.'

'Dust for fingerprints? Is that a thing?' Dahlia shudders. 'Imagine how many grimy prints are in a hostel room. I bet stuff is stolen all the time.'

Florence groans. 'I really am sorry, you two, but you know how thirsty I get at night — especially after a dance-off like that, which I think we can all agree was an extravaganza.'

That earns a grin from the others as they line up at the buffet and fill their plates high with soggy scrambled eggs, burnt toast, roasted tomato, button mushrooms and wilted spinach.

'Grab some of those little yoghurts,' Florence hisses as they make their way to a table. 'And choc-chip cookies. We've got bellies to fill.'

They sit down with their food and Dahlia lines the coins in front of her on the table.

Florence gazes around the dining hall. 'Who looks guilty? Imagine if the Hostel Bandit's in here scoffing eggs with us.'

Kiko gestures to a girl with her hair in high pigtails and an even higher, ear-piercing giggle. 'What if it's her?'

'Don't let that hair fool you, she's hiding a dangerous secret,' Florence whispers and the other two suppress laughter behind serviettes.

Dahlia points out a guy they guess is about ten years too old to be attending this week.

'Arrest him for all the crimes,' Florence says.

Kiko spots a couple with matching sneakers and backpacks who've put nothing on their plates except boiled eggs and apples.

'Guilty as,' Florence says, using a piece of bacon to mop up what's left of her eggs. 'Now, if you'll excuse me, I'm going to stake out our room in case the thief returns.'

'Translation: you're going back to bed,' Kiko says.

Yawning, Florence stands up and kisses the girls on the cheek. 'We're out of money and it's free, right? Just doing my bit to help.'

Florence leaves, and Kiko plays with the coins on the table, rolling them around, piling them up, knocking them down.

'This meeting of minds is now in session,' she says to Dahlia. 'How *do* we survive on twelve dollars and no credit card?' She stamps the ground with her heel in frustration. 'Argh, the credit card! We need to cancel it. I better make the call before I forget again.'

'Can I help?' Dahlia asks, spinning one of the coins on its side.

'All good.' Kiko's fingers find Dahlia's. 'By the way, I know this changes the plan for Stevie's list. Are you okay?'

Dahlia shrugs. 'The only thing I know is that I don't know.'

'I hear you,' Kiko says.

Dahlia remembers what Steve said the previous night about the girls grieving and struggling in their own way. 'You … you know I'm here for you too, right?' she adds, giving Kiko's hand a squeeze. 'Whatever you need.'

Kiko's eyes widen, then get watery. 'Oh. Thanks lady. I, ah, I better call the bank,' she says.

With both girls gone, Dahlia picks up her phone. Her mind races and she wills herself to resist opening the album of Stevie videos.

5 Things To Do Instead of Watching
A Video of Stevie
Eat more scrambled eggs
Journal on a serviette
Have a shower
Meditate
Literally anything, anything, ANYTHING

But her fingertips do their usual dance and she opens the album and presses play on the first video.

It's from four years ago. Stevie is skateboarding down the alleyway behind her house. Her eyes are tinged purple with coloured contact lenses because she loved experimenting with different looks. Dahlia is behind the camera, but the focus cuts to her occasionally as she makes sarcastic comments and tries to hide her giggling.

She's softer in the face and sports a high white-blonde ponytail with a shaved zigzag pattern at the bottom of her nape that she'd regretted immediately. The hairdresser had told her it made her look edgy, which he meant as a compliment, but Dahlia worried people would confuse her for someone with a tough skin when she actually felt soft on the inside. Stevie slips off the skateboard, grazing her hands and knees on the concrete, and rushes to show Dahlia the blood. Dahlia squeals and the camera cuts out.

Kiko is still pacing up and down on the phone to the bank. Dahlia finds the play button again.

This time Stevie's wearing a broad-brimmed hat and has dirt smudges on her cheeks. She's spraying her parents' roses and pretending she's hosting a gardening show. She teases Dahlia, who's behind the camera again, then squats down to pull out some weeds, deliberately leaning too far over to reveal a hint of her bottom. She glances over her shoulder, grinning, before belly-flopping onto the grass. This was how Dahlia saw Stevie: her friend, the clown, the soft landing.

She presses play on another clip.

Zoë

'Where are your fairy wings, Zoë?' Luca pauses from combing gel through his hair. 'And why are you in shorts?'

Zoë sizes up her reflection in the bathroom mirror while Luca returns to humming along to the Alotta Peach song blasting from his phone. 'What's the problem?' she asks. 'They're comfortable.'

'No more bailing on your favourite cousin. We're doing this concert properly.' He peers out the doorway. 'Violet, we need another set of wings in here!'

Violet hurls a set of rainbow wings through the open door.

'Do we though?' Zoë asks. 'Aren't we going to the Strip?'

Luca groans. 'Keep up. Darius scored a stack of last-minute Alotta Peach tickets so we'll have pre-drinks this afternoon, then head to the concert tonight. I've covered yours 'cos he wanted cash.'

Akito walks in with a towel wrapped around his waist, and sprays so much cologne over his half-naked body that it fogs up the mirror.

'Are you trying to kill us?' Zoë splutters, flapping her arms. 'You've put on enough for three weeks!'

Luca grimaces. 'How are you not ready yet, Akito?'

'Forget the concert, Luca, I'm out,' Zoë says, shooing Akito out of the bathroom. 'Seeing Darius again is the last thing I need.'

'Zo, pull it together. He's done us a big favour. The concert was sold out.'

'And what does he expect in return?'

'We've paid him, so nothing,' Luca says. 'Now put on your wings.'

Zoë slips the wings over her shoulders. 'Glittery,' she says. 'Fine. I'll come, but I'm staying away from him. Happy?'

'I will be once we get there,' Luca says. 'From what I read online, Alotta Peach fans go all out. Big costumes, bold make-up, even props. We'll be the most boring people there.'

'You, boring? Never,' Zoë teases him.

The suite phone rings. No-one answers it and it eventually rings out. Moments later, it kicks off again.

'Someone!' Luca calls out from the bathroom. 'Zo? Can you deal with the phone? I'm covered in gel.'

Zoë groans and hurries towards the phone, slipping in her socks on the floorboards. 'Yeah?' she mumbles.

'Good afternoon, I'm calling from the front desk downstairs. Is a Miss Zoë Russo there?' a woman asks.

Zoë stands up a little straighter. 'That's me.'

'I have a Greta Russo here. She's insisting on seeing you, but she's not on your group's approved visitors' list.'

'Greta?' Zoë's breath catches. She'd rather see anyone else on the planet right now than her sister. 'Sorry, Greta's *here*? In the hotel?'

'Yes, and she's refusing to leave the premises,' the woman says. 'I should point out that security are on alert if she needs to be escorted out.'

Zoë swears under her breath. 'No, it's fine, she's an approved visitor,' she fibs. 'It must have slipped my mind.'

'We'll need you to come and collect her immediately.'

'On my way,' she says, hanging up.

When she gets to the lobby, Greta is sitting on a chair with a backpack in her lap, a security guard next to her. Jaw tightening, Zoë recognises him from the night Constable Inglis escorted her back to the resort. Keeping her head down, she rushes to Greta's side.

'Come with me,' Zoë hisses, leading her sister by the hand out the door and down the wide sweeping path towards the gardens. She storms along in silence before pulling Greta into a private garden with a tree standing over a sweetheart bench.

Zoë turns to her. 'This is so embarrassing. *What* are you doing here?'

'Hello to you too,' Greta says, placing her backpack on the bench. 'I could ask you the same thing.'

'Everything is fine,' Zoë says. 'I've spoken to Dad.'

'You're welcome by the way. They were ready to disown you.' Greta folds her arms over her chest. 'But that's not the problem. I saw Violet's photos and videos.'

It feels like a punch to the stomach. 'What?'

'On her profile. The *police*, Zoë? I messaged you, no reply. I called you, no answer. So *that's* what I'm doing here.'

Zoë groans. 'It's nothing,' she says, mentally berating herself for getting stuck in the whole mess to begin with; for not being more responsible, like she'd promised their dad. 'It's a misunderstanding.'

'Help me understand what's going on then.'

Zoë holds her hand up. 'You've crashed my week, Greta. You don't need to come to the rescue again. And since when were you ever online and stalking everyone's profiles?'

'Violet's my cousin too. I was worried!'

'More like you were worried I'd bring more shame on our family. You think you're so much better than me and you *always* take Mum and Dad's side.'

Tension hangs in the air.

Greta takes a deep breath, then exhales. 'That's not true or fair. I know you don't believe me, but I'm here because I'm your big sister and I feel like something's up. Are you okay, Zo?'

Zoë freezes. Greta rarely calls her Zo.

'Did you hear me?' Greta asks. 'Zo?'

'I'm fine,' Zoë manages, but her voice cracks. 'One hundred per cent fine.'

271

'I wish I believed you.' Greta's gaze softens. 'I think Mrs Pepper's lemon tree needs pruning,' she says, slowly, deliberately.

Eight words that press pause on everything.

A small smile slips out of Zoë's mouth. 'Don't.'

They'd first used the phrase when Zoë was six and Greta was eleven, but Zoë couldn't remember the last time they'd said the words. It was a childhood secret SOS call; a circuit-breaker to let the other one know they were in it together. Whenever their parents had friends or relatives over — which was often in their family — one of the sisters would inevitably hit a point when she couldn't handle another second of hearing Great-Aunty Martina, who wasn't their aunty at all, talk about her painful bunions. She'd utter the phrase 'I think Mrs Pepper's lemon tree needs pruning' to loop in the other so they could make their escape together. There were always confused looks from the adults, but no-one ever questioned it.

Greta takes a step closer. 'I think Mrs Pepper's lemon tree needs pruning,' she repeats.

Zoë sighs. 'We were kids. It's silly.'

Greta shrugs. 'Fine. But what's going on, Zo? I'm not a rat. I haven't told Mum and Dad about the police. They don't even know I'm here — they think I'm driving back to campus. I came as soon as I saw what Violet posted.'

'Why though?' Zoë's voice is barely a whisper.

'Because I care.'

'Since when?'

'Since always.'

Zoë sinks down onto the bench, unsure what to say next. Her life feels messy and smudged over the edges, while her sister's always seems perfectly within the lines.

'I feel like a failure,' she blurts out, brushing away tears with the back of her hand.

Greta sits down next to her, their shoulders pressing together. 'That couldn't be further from the truth. What's happened?'

Everything spills out. The final biology exam, the two rejection emails, the night in the cell.

'This year was so challenging, but I can picture what I want for my future so clearly it hurts,' Zoë continues with a sniff. 'I've worked so hard and sacrificed so much. I want to help people, but I've never been so scared that it won't happen.'

'I know how hard you work,' Greta says. 'You put too much pressure on yourself, but it's all going to come together somehow. I promise.'

Zoë groans. 'Don't say that — you don't know. Everyone expects so much of me because I'm *your* sister. You're the perfect daughter, student, all of it. You've never let Mum and Dad down — not once.' She pauses. 'Your achievements are gargantuan, and they hover over everything. Now I'm going to fail and disappoint everyone.'

Greta nibbles her fingernail. 'I hate that you feel that way. No-one is perfect. You know that, right?'

Zoë thinks of Greta's trophies, the smiling photos of her at graduation, the way their parents gush whenever a relative asks how she's doing. 'I think your grades, teachers and our parents would disagree.'

'You're wrong. Perfect doesn't exist.'

'Maybe not for me, but things seem perfect for you.'

Greta turns to face her. 'You play sport, you're in musicals ... you're school captain! You have brilliant grades *and* friends. I just had school ... a haven and a prison.' Her bottom lip trembles. 'That's it.'

'Greta, come on.'

'It's true. People like you, Zo. They have fun with you; they miss you when you're not around.' Greta's voice shakes a little. 'There were years when you were my only friend, and I was never that for you. I didn't have friends, not really. Everyone in class saw me as competition. A girl even told me she was sick of coming second to me and stopped inviting me to sit with her at lunch.'

Zoë wraps an arm around her older sister's shoulder. 'That's awful,' she murmurs, feeling guilty because that's how she felt for years. She'd always seen Greta as a genius who has everything worked out. The bar to meet if she ever wants to be a success. But here, on the bench in the gardens, she looks small, like her natural gifts could be crushed to dust.

'And I do miss you at home,' Zoë continues. 'The house feels so empty.' It's the first time she's said those words, but she means it.

'Really?' Greta replies. 'Because I miss you terribly. I don't want to be someone you compare yourself to. Dad always says that when it comes down to it, we're all we have. It's why I'm here.'

'Stop it, you'll make me lose it,' Zoë says, wiping away a tear.

Her phone buzzes. It's Luca in the group chat.

Where are you?!!!!

'Look, I should head up and meet the others,' she says, 'but why don't you come with me? You can stay with us, there's loads of space.' She gestures to her rainbow wings. 'You'd make a fine fairy too.'

Greta shakes her head. 'I'll leave you and the cousins to it. I don't want to embarrass you any more than I already have.'

'Come! You're their cousin too. Plus, I can introduce you to Prakash and Akito.'

'Prakash? The little boy who weed on our kitchen tiles?'

'That's him,' Zoë says with a laugh. 'It'll be fun. And if it's not, we can whinge about it together.'

'Okay.' Greta's mouth stretches into a smile. 'But I don't have any nice clothes with me.'

'We'll find you something. Violet brought two suitcases.'

Greta's phone suddenly bursts to life. She holds it out: their parents are video-calling. 'Should I answer? They're calling to check I've made it back to campus safely.'

'Alright,' Zoë says, drawing in a deep breath. 'But don't say a word about … well, any of it.'

Greta takes the call and their parents' faces fill the screen.

'Hold it out further, Dad,' Greta says. 'I can't see you properly. I swear they should teach phone courses for adults.'

Zoë leans in over Greta's shoulder. 'Surprise.'

Mrs Russo moves even closer to the screen. '*Zoë?*'

'Chickpea!' Mr Russo beams. 'You're together? I don't understand.'

'Greta's passing through,' Zoë says, voice cracking at the sight of her parents. Despite everything, she wishes they could all be together right now. 'How ... how are you two?'

'I'm turning your bedroom into a gym as we speak,' Mrs Russo jokes dryly.

Zoë giggles. Teasing from her mother is a good sign. 'Don't forget to add an elliptical,' she says.

Her dad hasn't stopped smiling. 'What's happening with you? It's good to see your face.'

'Not much, Dad, just ...' She notices the cabinet full of trophies and certificates behind them and her body stiffens. 'Well ...' The truth tumbles out about the two rejection emails. 'I'm so sorry I've let you down,' she whispers. 'I'll work twice as hard to make up for it if I have to. I'll do whatever it takes to make you proud.'

There's a pause so long that Zoë wonders if their connection has stalled.

Then Mr Russo breaks the silence. 'I know you're upset and we hate to see that, but we are proud of the person you are, medicine or no medicine. You've worked so hard, Chickpea. Put so much pressure on yourself. Too much, I'm starting to see. I only wish we'd understood that sooner.'

Mrs Russo nods. 'Your father's right. Life will go on and on, after all.'

'Who brainwashed you?' Zoë teases. 'Where are my parents?'

The screen glitches. The visuals aren't moving but the audio still comes through.

'Hello? Zoë?' her mum says. 'What's happening? I don't know if you'll hear this, but we love you. No matter what happens.'

'I can hear you ... I heard you. I love you too,' Zoë says, moving away from the screen and passing the phone back to Greta.

As Greta wraps things up with their parents, Zoë lets herself sink into the feeling. She can't remember the last time her mother said 'I love you' or validated how hard she'd been trying, and she wants to cement this moment in her mind.

She pinches the skin under her forearm, just to triple-check she's not dreaming, and her gaze catches the fading heartbeat tattoo on her wrist.

One preference to go.

Samira

Day 6: 6.11pm

Thousands of people mill around the stadium. Some are in extravagant costumes, while others have come from the beach in wet swimsuits and sundresses. The sound of the pre-show entertainment inside the stadium is scrambled with the screams of fans outside.

Samira and the Peachies huddle together by the stadium entrance. Samira catches a glimpse of her reflection in Kris's mirrored aviator sunglasses. Bold lips, long lashes, swimsuit, purple cape. She's borrowed Kris's wig — a striking red bob that cuts in at the chin — as well as Tilly's silver knee-high boots.

Cameras flash as the stretch limousines arrive. The fans strain against heavy barriers near a roped-off red-carpet area that leads to the media wall. There's no sign of Alotta Peach, but a trickle of media personalities and influencers in sparkly colourful outfits wait off camera until the photographers wave them forward for their five seconds in the spotlight.

'Look,' Samira says, showing the Peachies her general admission ticket. It's burnt orange with silver edging, while their VIP tickets are pastel peach with gold edging. 'The differences are obvious. No way is security letting me in with you.'

Tilly adjusts her crown, eyebrows narrowing in concentration. 'We can pull this off,' she says, inspecting the tickets. 'When you want something bad enough, anything is possible.'

Samira and the boys trade smirks.

'Is that an Alotta Peach lyric?' Samira asks, twirling her plastic sword and shield.

Kris snorts. 'Sounds familiar.' He strains to reach around his bulky robot costume to fix his loose shoelaces.

'No, it's a Tilly special,' Tilly says, dropping to one knee to help him.

'Sammy, you're the Warrior — you have to come with us,' Harry adds.

Tilly jumps to her feet. 'He's right. Look at you in that wig and those boots — the embodiment of a true Peachie.'

'Exactly.' Harry smiles so widely cracks form in his face paint. 'Let's do this. VIP is through Gate 1.'

Samira checks her ticket. 'Gate 6 for me.'

Tilly runs over the plan again. She'll meet Samira near the bathrooms at Gate 3 in fifteen minutes and will have one of the VIP ticket stubs to smuggle her in.

They squeeze hands, then part. Samira is alone again. The thundering noise from the music and crowd is overwhelming and she makes her way to Gate 6 in a daze, like she's stumbling through a fog.

Through the gate, along a walkway, past Gate 5, up some stairs, along another walkway, past Gate 4, weaving around people until she spots the Gate 3 sign. To the right of it are the bathrooms. She can't remember if she and Tilly agreed to meet in front of them or inside.

She goes inside and waits in the furthest corner of the bathroom, trying to be invisible as people come and go, which isn't the easiest act for someone carrying a plastic sword and shield. Head lowered, she leaves the bathroom and returns to the bustling walkway. She can't see Tilly in the swarming crowd, so heads back into the bathroom, past the line of girls, to shelter in the corner again.

She scrolls through her phone, willing a text message or notification to show up to numb her feeling of awkwardness. Nothing appears so she gives in and calls her mum, who answers on the second ring.

'Sammy! You're on speaker, darling.' Teta's voice cheers in the background. 'How is it?'

Samira turns her back on the waiting girls and leans against the wall. 'Things are good, Mum, just wanted to hear your voice,' she murmurs. 'I miss you.'

'I didn't think you'd have time,' Mum says, raising her voice as the thumping music inside the stadium kicks in even louder. 'What's all that noise?'

'I'm at a concert.'

'Is it someone famous? Get an autograph and take photos for me. You haven't posted any photos.'

'I know. I know.'

'So much mystery. Well, how's it all been? Perfect as planned? I bet everyone's loving it.'

'If you could let me get a word in ...' Samira glances up as a group of girls wearing rainbow bows on their heads parade into the bathroom. Still no Tilly. 'Mum, I think I need to tell you something.'

'Are you hurt? Talk to me.'

'No, I ... It's silly, really ...' Samira's voice crackles with emotion.

'Darling, what's happened? That's it, I'm coming to get you right now! I already have a suitcase packed.'

'Mum!' Samira can't help but smile. She hears Teta yelling out for answers in the background. 'I love you, both of you, but that is not happening. Besides, you hate driving at night.'

'I hate hearing my baby upset even more.'

'Listen to me — I'm alright. But I need to tell you the truth.'

'You always can.'

Samira pauses. 'Can you take me off speakerphone?' she asks. Then she confesses everything, barely drawing breath and sparing no details. The break-up on the platform only minutes before the train arrived. Meeting Tilly. Being pushed over by a stranger at the foam party. The exorcism. Being third wheel to Anoush and Dan. Overhearing the girls bitching about her. Running away to the train station. The widening rift in their friendship that eventually cracked wide open. Becoming the Warrior. Anoush forgetting her birthday. The lighthouse, the boat, the island. Zain wanting to get back together. The spontaneous hotel sleepover with Tilly. She even tells her mother how she'd convinced herself she was ready to lose her virginity to Zain, but is relieved she's waited after seeing him swoop from girl to girl all week.

As the words spill out, raw, unfiltered, Samira feels herself stand a little straighter. When she stops, she feels lighter from sharing the load.

She braces for an onslaught of questions, advice and judgment, but despite sounding stunned her mum absorbs it all and assures Samira she is proud of her for opening up.

'I'm sorry I didn't tell you any of this before,' Samira says. 'I didn't know how to say everything has fallen apart.'

'You say it like that, darling. You say: "I don't have the words yet but I need you." I never want you to feel this alone again. Never. Come to me, always.'

Samira wipes away a tear. 'I think you'd like the Peachies, Mum,' she says. 'They're good people.'

'They sound it. But I'm still coming to get you.'

'No, Mum. I want to finish this on my own. I need to.'

'I'm not sure …'

'I'll text you from the train tomorrow, okay? I'll be home so soon.'

The bathroom door bursts open. 'Sammy! There you are!' Tilly squeals, waving a torn VIP ticket. 'I got lost but I'm here to save you.'

Samira presses the phone a little closer to her ear. 'That's Tilly. She's great, huh? Everything is going to be okay, I promise.' She grins. 'And think of the upside: you won't have to meet Zain's mum after all.'

Her mum sighs. 'Oh, Sammy, you and your funny, busy brain. Call me if you need anything. I don't care what time it is. I love you.'

'Bye. Love love love you both.' Samira hangs up the phone and turns to Tilly. 'Hi.'

'Hey! All good?'

'I've never been better. Are we late?'

'Not at all.' Tilly passes the ripped ticket to Samira, then presses her stamped hand against hers. The red VIP imprint is smudged but passable. 'There's still another DJ and a singer to go before she's on.'

Holding hands, the girls run against the crowd through a maze of walkways, following the sound of the pulsing music. They reach Gate 1 and show their tickets to a bored-looking security guard, who ushers them through into the blackened stadium.

Glow-in-the-dark wands light up the space, and giant inflatable ice-cream cones, peaches and rainbows bounce around in the audience.

'You ready?' Tilly asks, gesturing to the long walk down the steps to the front of the mosh pit.

'Absolutely.'

'Wait!' Tilly fiddles with Samira's cape so it sits evenly on her shoulders. 'That's better. How's my crown?'

Samira leans in to adjust the angle. 'Fit for the Queen.'

Dahlia

'I'm more pancake than girl right now,' Dahlia says, dusting crumbs off her T-shirt. 'I've lost track of how many we've eaten.'

'Free pancakes three times a day adds up,' Kiko says with a groan, snatching another pancake from the paper plate wedged by their feet in the sand and smearing it through a tub of sugary syrup.

Florence gives a thumbs-up to the volunteers manning a tent on the sweeping lawn by the beach. 'Brinner is the best.'

'Brinner?' Kiko asks. 'What's that?'

'Breakfast for dinner,' Florence says, taking a bite of her pancake. 'Brinner.'

Dahlia laughs. 'I love anything free right now.' She pauses, noticing groups of people moving in one direction along the footpath and stretch of sand. Many are dressed up in costumes; others sing at full volume. 'Wonder where they're headed?'

'I bet it's that pop star's concert,' Florence says. 'There are billboards everywhere. Alana Peach or something.'

'*Alotta* Peach?' Kiko asks.

'Same, same.'

'Hang on, I won tickets to that,' Dahlia says, rifling through her tote. She pulls out a crumpled envelope with torn edges. 'Four of them.'

'Jelly-wrestling spoils!' Florence says. 'Although Hostel Bandit didn't want them so is that a bad sign?'

'Don't ask me,' Kiko says. 'I don't know her stuff.'

'Let's try to sell them,' Florence suggests. 'We can bump up the price and make some money.'

'Scalp them?' Kiko's jaw drops. 'No way.'

'We should go to the concert,' Dahlia says. 'It's free and we need to find *something* to do before Florence gets us arrested.' She checks the tickets again. 'The pre-show's already started. We better hurry up if we want to make it.'

She stands up and dusts sand off her legs, noticing Kiko and Florence swap surprised looks as she strides across the grass towards the footpath.

* * *

Thousands of people swarm towards the stadium gates. Dahlia checks their tickets. They want Gate 9. 'It must be further along,' Dahlia says, pointing ahead and around the corner. 'Let's go.'

Florence grins. 'Yes, boss.'

The girls pass food trucks, people selling merchandise and best friends taking selfies, but they can't find Gate 9.

Kiko stands on tippy-toes, straining to look in each direction. 'There's Gate 1. Gate 2. Gate 3. Gate 4 …' she recites.

Dahlia swears. 'Maybe it's in the other direction? I can't see Gates 5, 6, 7 or 8 either.'

'Let's find someone to ask?' Kiko suggests.

Florence yawns. 'Or go back to the hostel?'

Dahlia wishes Stevie was with them right now. She always claimed to have an internal compass, which she assured Dahlia would be of endless use when they worked overseas as au pairs.

She looks around and notices a long alleyway stretching along one side of the stadium. It's blocked off so there are no screaming fans, just the throbbing sound of music from inside.

'Let's try through here,' she says. 'Could be a shortcut to the other side.'

She limbos beneath the red tape roping off the area and starts off down the empty alleyway.

'Are we meant to be doing this?' Kiko calls out from behind her.

'*This* being trespassing?' Florence giggles. 'You bet and I'm here for it.'

'We're not trespassing,' Dahlia says. Then she notices the *Do Not Enter* and *Wrong Way, Go Back* signs. 'Well, maybe we are.'

'I like this side of you,' Florence says, skipping along beside Dahlia.

Kiko glances over her shoulder. 'I'm terrified of it. What's come over you, Dahlia? I thought Florence would be the one to get us in trouble, but it might be you.'

Florence laughs. 'Shotgun the biggest cell when we're tossed in jail.'

'There's no-one else around,' Dahlia says. 'We're fine.'

They walk on, past garbage bins, empty tables and chairs, and more warning signs.

Suddenly, a woman storms out of a stadium door and into the alleyway. She's wearing a full-length peach unitard, flowing peach wig and peach platform heels that could snap an ankle. Her bright red lips form a tight line as she presses one palm against the outside wall of the stadium, and the other against her hipbone. The girls watch as her hand moves to her chest and she inhales and exhales on repeat. She begins a vocal warm-up, but her voice cracks. She sighs, closes her eyes and reverts to taking long deep breaths.

'Is it her? Alotta Peach?' Florence whispers. 'We should go before she sees us.'

Kiko's eyes widen. 'I don't think she's okay.'

Dahlia is frozen. She can't look away from the pained expression etched across the singer's face. Dahlia sees herself in the other woman's distress and feels an ache of empathy. She's been lost in worry herself more times than she can remember.

Alotta's eyes snap open and she steps back when she notices them in the alleyway.

'Stage fright, anyone?' she jokes, offering them a tiny smile. But Dahlia can see the edges of her mouth quivering.

'I'm so sorry, Ms Peach,' she stammers. 'We'll … we'll get out of here and give you some space.'

'We got lost looking for Gate 9,' adds Florence. 'Any chance you could point us in the …' Her voice trails off as Kiko glares at her.

Alotta draws in a deep breath. 'Not sure, sorry.' She exhales another breath, then launches into a vocal run. It crackles at the start but then flows into a faultless stream of rising and falling notes. 'I get butterflies before every show.'

'But you're so successful,' Dahlia says. 'You perform all the time.'

Alotta nods. 'Means I feel like this *a lot*.'

'Do you do that thing where you picture everyone in the audience naked to calm down?' Florence asks.

That gets a laugh. 'Can't say I do.'

'Being a star must be exhausting,' Florence continues. 'Dahlia is famous too. She was front-page news.'

Dahlia's eyes widen. '*Florence*.'

Alotta laughs again. 'Sounds like we have a few things in common.'

'I guess I get nervous too.' Dahlia can feel her cheeks burning.

5 Ways To Escape An Awkward Moment
Shout 'What's that?' and run away

Collapse and wait for medics to bring a stretcher
Dig a hole and tunnel out of there
Cover eyes and wait for everyone to feel so
    awkward they leave
Hitch a ride with a UFO flying overhead

Alotta offers her a smile. 'Sounds human to me.'

A door behind Alotta swings open. 'You're up, Ms O'Connell,' a woman with a clipboard says.

'Kate's fine.'

The girls swap glances. *Kate.*

'Of course, Ms O'Connell ... I mean Kate! I've got three people yelling down this earpiece at me to get you back to hair and make-up for a touch-up.'

'I'll be there in a moment.' Alotta turns to the girls. 'You're learning all my secrets.' She adjusts her wig and adds, 'I guess you want a photo? Peachies always do.'

Dahlia blushes again, embarrassed by their free tickets. 'We don't want to hold you up.'

'There's plenty of time,' Alotta says. 'Plus, this is fun for me too, and what's the point of life if there's no fun?'

They huddle into a group and Alotta says, 'Say peach!' and snaps a selfie with Dahlia's phone.

Kiko grins. 'I'm going to frame it.'

'See you out there, girls,' Alotta says, and with a wave she disappears through the door.

'That was incredible,' Kiko says, grabbing Dahlia's hands and jumping up and down.

'Still want to go back to the hostel?' Dahlia asks.

Florence holds up her hands in fake defeat. 'Not a chance. I'm obsessed and her unitard was beyond.'

'You know what I remembered while Dahlia and *Kate* were becoming best friends?' Kiko asks. 'Stevie had *Meet a celebrity* on her list.'

'She did,' Dahlia says, and holds out her phone showing their selfie with Alotta. 'And there's our celebrity.'

Kiko smiles. 'Now, on a slightly related note … where the hell is Gate 9?'

Zoë

The line swells out from the stadium entrance, stretching along the fence and zigzagging down the street. Every few moments someone screams an Alotta Peach lyric into the air, which propels everyone to throw up their hands in a pulsing, rolling wave.

Zoë holds on to the back of Prakash's T-shirt, clinging tighter every time the crowd goes wild.

Beside them, Greta stands on her tippy-toes, peering around. 'I can't believe how many people are here. I don't even know her songs!'

Prakash laughs. 'None of us do.'

'Except for that one track that was used for a car ad,' Zoë says, adjusting the straps of Greta's wings. 'She's clearly a big deal.'

'And clearly I need to get out from under my rock more often,' Greta says, gesturing at the mass of fans.

Just ahead, Luca, Akito and Violet have edged closer to the front of the line and Darius is with them.

'Hey, what's the deal with that guy?' Greta asks. 'He looks older than me.'

Zoë grins. 'He must be old then.'

Greta giggles. 'I'm serious! Why's he here?'

'You're here!'

'Reluctantly,' Greta jokes, then adds, 'it's a bit creepy, right? What if he comes to this week year after year to party with everyone?'

'There's something off about him, hard agree,' Zoë says. 'But can you switch off your "protective older sister" setting for a few hours? I want a relaxed night.'

'But how did you even meet him?'

'Blame Akito!' Prakash jokes. 'He met him at the resort on day one and there's been drama ever since.'

'How much drama?' Greta asks.

'Switch it off, Greta,' Zoë says with a laugh. 'Let's have fun. As far as I'm concerned, Darius ceases to exist.'

Just then, they hear Luca yelling ahead of them at the front of the line.

Zoë and Greta exchange glances. 'What now?' Zoë murmurs as they push through the queue towards their cousin.

Violet's hands are on her hips. 'What do you mean they're not legit?' she snaps at the woman on the door.

'Our friend bought these tickets,' Luca says. 'Darius, tell her.'

Darius's face is ashen. 'I ... yeah, I did,' he says, taking a long drink from a bottle of water.

The woman cocks her head to one side. 'I'd be curious to know from where. These tickets aren't real.'

Violet swears. 'Like I've said a million times, *Tiffany*,' she scowls at the woman's name tag, 'Darius bought the tickets and—'

'Miss, please lower your voice,' Tiffany says. 'I can't let you in.' She turns to Darius. 'Sir, did you resell these scalped tickets to your friends?'

Violet gasps. 'What?'

Luca turns to Darius. 'These are from a scalper?'

'Nah, bro, I ... I can explain.'

Akito crosses his arms over his chest. 'Spit it out.'

'I thought they were legit,' Darius says. 'This happened a few years ago too and it was all a mix-up.'

Tiffany's lips harden into a thin line. 'If you could all step to the side while I get the manager down here to look at everyone's IDs and tickets that would be appreciated,' she says. 'They'll be all too happy to assist with this little *mix-up*.'

'We're not going anywhere,' Luca says, eyes blazing. 'We paid for these tickets fair and square.'

Zoë leans in to him. 'It doesn't sound like we did though,' she whispers. 'I think we should go.'

Luca scowls. 'No way. This concert will be everything.'

'You didn't even know who Alotta Peach was until earlier today.'

'We've done nothing wrong,' Violet says, chin jutted out. 'Just show her your ID, Darius.'

Tiffany flashes them all a dirty look and speaks into her walkie-talkie, asking for back-up at Gate 5. Their gate.

'Let's roll,' Darius mutters, elbowing Luca in the side to flag all the security people milling around the stadium. 'This isn't good. On the count of three, we run.'

'Why?' Violet asks. 'I hate running.'

'Are we in trouble?' Greta asks Zoë.

'Maybe,' Darius says. Three burly security guards lumber in their direction and he adds, 'Remember what I said before? One, two, three … run!'

Zoë's sandals rub against her heels as they all sprint through the crowd and out the stadium gates. The straps of her dress slide down her shoulders, but she doesn't stop running, following Darius down the street, past clubs and stretches of beach and games of night volleyball.

Darius leads them into a laneway decorated with fairylights and painted murals. He dumps his water bottle and wallet on the cobblestones, heaving and wheezing to catch his breath.

'You sold us dodgy tickets?' Violet accuses. 'What the hell?'

Darius doesn't reply.

'Answer me!'

'Don't be so uptight, it's never been a problem before,' he says with a shrug.

'Excuse me?' Violet snaps. 'Uptight?'

Zoë walks over. 'Enough of this — how old are you, Darius? Honestly.'

'Huh? I'm … your age.'

Zoë purses her lips. 'Yeah, right. Back at the stadium,

you said something about this happening "a few years ago".'

'Which suggests this isn't your first time at this week,' Greta adds.

Darius sighs. 'I might be a bit older. Who gives a shit? We're all here to party.' He sizes up Greta. 'Who the hell are you?'

'Don't talk to my sister like that, you walking red flag.' Zoë glares at him. 'Your parties are basically a daycare centre — I bet we're toddlers compared to you.'

'Zo, maybe let's all take a breath,' Prakash says.

'She's right, he's ancient!' Violet calls out from behind them, holding up Darius's ID. She's picked up his wallet from the ground. 'Look! And he gets even older next month.'

Darius steps closer. 'Joke's over, give it back.'

Violet looks at the ID again. 'And he lives at the resort!' she says, waving it around.

'You're kidding,' Prakash says.

Akito gasps. 'Wait, so that rooftop hot tub is yours, man? *Sweet*.'

'Not the point, Akito,' Zoë says, rolling her eyes.

Violet pulls a small bag filled with a few coloured pills out of Darius's wallet. 'Hey, what are these?'

'Violet …' Luca warns, swearing under his breath.

Darius's jaw has hardened. 'Give me my stuff,' he says, taking a step towards Violet. 'Now.'

'We want our money first,' Violet tells him.

He shrugs. 'I don't have it. Check for yourself.'

She leafs through his wallet, swears, and throws it at his feet. 'I can't believe I ever let you kiss me.'

'Whatever,' he says, stuffing his wallet into his jeans pocket. Without another word, he legs it down the laneway.

'Stay the hell away from us, bro!' Akito yells as Darius disappears into the night.

Zoë shakes her head. 'Ding dong, the creep is gone.'

'He made my skin crawl,' Greta says. 'We should report that guy.'

'We didn't get our money!' Violet groans. 'And you all saw the pills, right? He's dodgy.'

'Duh,' Zoë says.

'This is bullshit,' Akito says. 'How about that stolen couch and graffiti too?'

'It's suss as,' Luca says.

Violet purses her lips. 'I bet he owes money or something.'

'Shake it off, Violet,' Prakash says. 'You'll be living off telling this story for months.'

Zoë yawns. 'Can we go back to the resort? I'm exhausted.'

Greta raises an eyebrow. 'You mean back to where he lives?'

'We'll lock the doors,' Zoë says.

'And I'll be security,' Akito adds.

'More like Violet and Zoë will, man,' Prakash says with a grin. 'You two dragged him.'

'And now I'm drained and ready to go full sloth,' Zoë says. 'Someone get me a recliner.'

Violet twirls around to show off her fairy wings. 'But we look so adorable, Zo,' she whines. 'Let's go clubbing! I can't let the last person I kiss this week be him. Ew!'

'It's been a *day* though,' Zoë says. 'Although … maybe we could hit up the beach cinema?'

'I'm listening,' Prakash says.

Luca nods. 'We can get comfy in beanbags.'

'And eat all the pizza we want,' adds Zoë.

'And ice-cream,' chimes in Akito.

'You're all boring and suck for ganging up on me,' Violet says, then breaks into a grin. 'But there'll be boys there, so throw in lollies and you've got a deal.'

Samira

Day 6: 10.13pm

The band leave their instruments onstage and disappear into the wings. Tilly elbows Samira in the side as the lights fade to black and the crowd roars Alotta Peach's name, begging her to return for an encore.

Everyone in the stadium stomps their feet and thunders as one when gold confetti strips and balloons rain down. Samira stands on her tippy-toes, her fingertips grazing the falling balloons.

Moments later, lights flash red and a siren sounds. Samira looks up to see Alotta Peach raising a diamanté-covered microphone to her lips. She's high above the crowd, dressed as a peach and perched on a giant swing. Her birthmark, which runs beneath her eye and across her cheek to her right ear, is outlined with sequins.

The beat kicks in and Alotta's husky voice cuts through the noise.

'Our girl!' Tilly wails, gripping Kris's and Harry's arms. 'An encore! She's back! She's doing it!'

She's broken but strong
And she's dancing alone
But the monster is moving on

No more tears left to cry
She's awake for the first time
And the monster is moving on

'I don't know this song,' Tilly says, wiping away tears. 'This isn't the usual encore! Am I in heaven?'

Alotta waves as she flies above the crowd, never once falling out of tune.

The nights are still long
And she's holding on tight
But the monster is moving on

She'll fight for her life
She'll fight for her rights
And the monster is dead and gone

As the swing is lowered towards the screaming audience, some jostle to create space for it, while others surge forward to get closer.

Alotta gracefully slides onto the shoulders of two dancers, who carry her up the sweeping stairs onto the stage. She steps into a lone spotlight, one hand gripping the microphone. She lifts her other hand, calming the crowd in seconds. The music falls away and the stadium rings with the sound of her voice.

She's finally free
She tore down all the walls
And the monster is dead and gone

The lights go out. More confetti strips fall as the audience swells in a standing ovation. It's so powerful that Samira's cheeks hurt from screaming.

Finally, the spotlight reappears and Alotta steps into its circle and lifts the microphone to her lips.

'Hello again, my Peachies,' she begins.

The crowd rumbles with excitement. Someone screeches, 'We love you, Alotta!'

She blows a kiss in their direction and more cries echo through the stadium. Alotta lifts her hand again and waits for silence to fall.

'Before tonight's show, lightning bolts were rocketing inside my brain,' she says. 'My chest hurt. Stage fright can be palpable. But then something happened: I met a few beautiful humans in an alleyway. And afterwards, sitting in my dressing room and reflecting on what we'd spoken about, it was clear: I love *every* part of this ride — even the tough bits.' The crowd thunders but she raises her hand again. 'Especially the tough bits. They make me strong and they make me who I am. But most of all, I love everyone in this room!'

The crowd screams again as more gold confetti and balloons float down.

Tilly leans in closer to Samira. 'I adore her so much that I'm about to have a heart attack,' she hisses. 'Or wet my pants. Possibly at the same time.'

'Understandable,' Samira says with a grin, her gaze locked on the stage.

'I always want to give you more,' Alotta continues. 'So that last song? It's called "Monster" and it's not out for a few months, so that was a little surprise even for my stage manager.' She beams at someone in the wings. 'Sorry, I'll buy you dinner tomorrow!'

The audience laughs and Tilly clings to Samira. 'Yep, heart attack is imminent. I may also be having an out-of-body experience.'

'My Peachies,' Alotta says, 'I needed to share that song with you tonight. It couldn't wait another day. I need you to know you can level up, despite any voices in your head telling you you're not good enough. You can change your future, despite past mistakes. You can fall over and get up and try again, no matter what monsters try to scare you into believing you can't. You don't need anyone's approval except your own. I love you so much and you can live your way, baby!'

Dancers holding a sparkling rainbow parachute form a circle around Alotta and she disappears behind the shimmery material. It balloons in and out, and then the dancers let go and the parachute drops to the stage floor.

Alotta is revealed dressed in a gold catsuit. She growls and the familiar beat of 'Live Your Way' kicks in.

I nearly ran away
To start things over
Instead I'm gonna
Take what's mine

Live your way
Live your way
Live your way, sweet baby

Samira's fingers find her Alotta Peach bangle. Tears glisten in her eyes as the music soars and Alotta prowls around the stage.

There's a fire
Inside my soul
Getting up, getting out
Like I want
Live your way
Live your way
Live your way, sweet baby

Live your way
Live your way
Oh, oh, live your way, baby

Pyrotechnics sparkle at the end of the song and the stage falls into darkness. The audience begs for more, but this time the house lights go up. The show is over.

Samira and the Peachies huddle together as Tilly snaps photos, then Harry scoops up some of the confetti strips from the floor.

'Look,' he says, holding them out. 'There are lyrics printed on them!'

Tilly gasps. 'She's never done that before.'

'Iconic,' Kris says.

Samira crouches down to pick up a strip of sparkling gold next to her foot. She turns it over and reads the words *There's a fire inside my soul*, before slipping it into her pocket.

Day 7

Samira

Day 7: 12.11am

Samira lies on her bed in full costume and stares up at the ceiling. She's still buzzing from the concert. Beside her sits her packed suitcase and a ripped copy of Alotta's set list. She rolls onto her side to look at it again. The edges are covered in tape, some songs have been crossed off and new ones scribbled in. Alotta's handwriting scrawls across the corner of the page:

For Sammy the Warrior, who's free at last.

Keep showing the monsters who's boss.

Alotta xox

It's a gift from Tilly after her VIP meet-and-greet with Alotta, during which Alotta touched Tilly's shoulder for two seconds, her right hand for three seconds and her back for five seconds when the Peachies joined her for a photo.

Samira lingers on the phrase *free at last*, then places the set list on the bedside table. A small smile twitches her mouth every time she steals a glance at it.

Her phone buzzes. Tilly.

Sammy! Check my pulse tomoz? I think being in the presence of her greatness killed me

Samira laughs and flops back on the bed.

Unable to resist, she does a quick scroll through social media and sees Anoush and the group partying at Dan's earlier in the night. There's Zain and Mathieu lounging on oversized blow-up doughnuts in the pool, and Rashida posing in a tiny bikini while sipping from a coconut.

Samira sits up and keeps scrolling. On Anoush's feed, there's a group photo in front of a row of palm trees with a caption saying #squadgoals. On Claire's feed, she sees Claire has changed her profile picture to a shot of Anoush and Rashida kissing her cheeks. In another of Claire's photos, Mathieu, Zain and Rashida dancing is stamped with the header #myfriendsarebetterthanyourfriends.

It stings to admit it, but the longer Samira stares at the photos, the clearer it is that, other than Anoush, she doesn't truly know these people. Not beyond surface level. Not in a way she'd ever consider them real friends.

Suddenly, there's a loud shriek. 'Samira, you're here! You scared me!'

She looks up to see Anoush in the doorway, balancing awkwardly in heels.

'Omigod, do I look that bad?' Samira jokes with a weak smile.

Anoush teeters towards her. 'Nah, girl, I just wasn't expecting to see you tonight.'

'I could say the same about you.'

'I need sleep, like, so bad,' Anoush says. 'My body's going to be covered in bruises from falling over so much at the rollerskating rink.' She pauses, taking in Samira's look. 'What's with the boots and wig?'

'Alotta Peach concert, remember?' Samira points to the plastic sword and shield in the corner.

'Oh. You still went?'

Samira nods. 'Yeah.'

'It's a whole vibe, huh?'

'Kinda. It was pretty amazing,' Samira says, sitting up and pulling off the silver knee-high boots. 'The perfect way to end the trip.'

'You're leaving early? No!' Anoush perches on the corner of the bed. 'Because of Zain?'

'Because of lots of things. The new ticket's booked for tomorrow.' She glances at the time on her phone. 'Well, technically today, I guess.'

'Cancel it. We can all head back together as planned.'

'If there's anything I've learnt this week, it's that plans change,' Samira says. 'I'm ready to go. I don't want to be in this house any more.'

'I guess it's, like, been a long few days for you,' Anoush says. She hangs her head in her hands. 'Shit, I … Samira, I have to tell you something. It's been weighing on me.'

'Yeah?'

'Don't hate me, but I knew Zain wanted to break up,' she says in a rush.

Samira nods. 'I know.'

Anoush peeks through her fingers. 'Really? You do?' She swears under her breath. 'I'm so sorry I lied. The situation snowballed and I didn't know what to do.'

Samira swallows. She's been waiting for the right moment to face Anoush and this is it. 'So is that what happened with the bitching too? It snowballed?'

Anoush raises an eyebrow. 'What do you mean?'

'The other day ... I heard you all talking about me before Dan's party.'

'I ... I didn't say anything.'

'You said, or didn't say, enough.' Samira's voice grows stronger; she's no longer worried about the outcome or upsetting Anoush. '*Stalker*? *Clueless*? And let's not forget *she's not one of us*. I'm supposed to be cool with all that?'

'Samira, listen, I'm sorry ...' Anoush slides closer. 'You know what they're like — they love the drama. It means nothing.'

'Maybe not to you. It means something to me though. Imagine if you overheard them calling you tragic behind your back? You'd be so hurt.'

Anoush nods. 'I know. But I swear Rashida and Claire aren't so bad once you get to know them.'

'Well, I guess I *really* don't know them because they seem pretty horrible to me,' Samira says. 'The worst part isn't even that I heard *you* bitching about me too. It's that I thought we were friends, like, close friends. Turns out I was just an annoying assignment the teachers lumped you with.'

'Samira, no! That's not true. I'm sorry you heard all that. And I'm even sorrier I said what I did. It was awful. And we *were* friends. We are.'

She totters over to her open beauty bag on the chest of drawers and pulls out a handful of colourful nail polishes.

'What are you doing?' Samira asks.

Anoush looks at her with watery eyes. 'We planned a girls' pampering session and it never happened, so I'm painting your nails. Toes or fingers? Your choice.'

'It's fine. You're tipsy and I'm over it. I just want to go to sleep.'

'Please,' Anoush says, her voice trembling. She sits on the bed next to Samira. 'I can't have you leaving tomorrow without things being okay with us. I got lost in the drama, caught up with Dan. I screwed up.'

Samira bites her lip. 'The thing is, I'm glad Dan's been making you happy. You deserve that. He does make you happy, right? He's treating you well? Respectful?'

Anoush nods. 'And I love that you care about that for me.'

'Of course.'

'It's only a holiday thing, I guess — it's not like he's from our side of the country — but he's a good guy. We might even stay friends ... well, until he gets a cute girlfriend and my head explodes with jealousy.'

Samira laughs. 'Tick, tick, boom.'

'I'm sorry I haven't been around,' Anoush says, wiping her eyes with the back of her hand. 'It's, like, being here, away from our real lives, helped me to escape this year, you know? The final year of school's intense. Like, I still don't think I've come down from it. But I never wanted to be the girl who puts a guy before her friends.'

'Even if he's amazing?'

'Even then. And I know things are going to change soon with me moving away—'

'Don't stress,' Samira cuts in, her cheeks burning. 'I'm not under any illusion that we'll be hanging out. I'm not like the girls — I get it. I'm me, and that's never going to change.'

'What I was *going* to say is we can still catch up when I come home for holidays.'

'You'd want that?'

'Yeah. The two of us, away from the drama. And you're glorious just as you are.'

Samira smiles. 'Can I quote you on that?'

'It's a date,' Anoush says, fanning out the polishes on the bedspread. 'Now, can I paint your nails?'

Zoë

The sky shimmers pale pink as Zoë walks out onto the balcony. Prakash is stretched out in the hammock, eating watermelon and flicking through his phone.

'Morning, Zo. You're up and at it.'

'I couldn't sleep,' she says. 'How about you, early bird?'

'We crashed out after the cinema.' He passes her a slice of melon. 'Didn't need any more.'

'We'll be the first ones at the markets,' she says, taking a bite and sending juice dribbling over her chin. 'Greta and Luca are keen too.'

He waves her closer. 'Here, check this out.'

Zoë grins and clambers into the hammock with him. 'It's not more of Violet's videos, is it? I saw she got her wish and ended up at a club with Akito.'

He laughs. 'They did, big time, but that's not it. I got a reminder on my profile and this memory's sent me into a nostalgia vortex.'

She takes Prakash's phone for a better look. It's a photo of them from two years earlier, taken after their last day of work experience. She'd gone to the local hospital, he'd gone to a radio station. They're both beaming and Zoë clutches a piece of paper.

'We were such happy little dorks,' she says.

'Were?' Prakash cracks.

Zoë looks closer at the photo. The paper in her hand is a printout of the hospital's reference for her. She's read it so many times in the past year that it's committed to memory.

> Zoë Russo is a determined and engaged young
> woman who demonstrates maturity, intelligence
> and a passion for the medical field well beyond
> her years. Her natural talent, combined with
> her determination, will see her go far. We would
> welcome Zoë back to our unit anytime and
> recommend her for any further placements or
> additional study or internships.

Zoë had shadowed different doctors and nurses on their rounds of the hospital wards. She'd seen mothers feeding newborn babies, bones being set, temperatures being taken and comforting words being given. On the last day, she'd been granted one-on-one time with three doctors to ask them anything she wanted about working in their field. She'd fired so many excited questions at one doctor that she'd had to politely ask Zoë to leave her office because her shift was over.

'That week was incredible,' she says.

Prakash laughs. 'Maybe for you. I pressed the wrong button and killed the announcer's microphone on live radio.'

'Less than ideal.'

'I did like reading the news though,' he says in a formal newsreader voice, then cracks up. 'Although they weren't as impressed when I read the weather in a fake accent.'

'Correction: a terrible fake accent.'

He grins. 'It was only mostly terrible. Hey, remember when my parents and I busted you calling yourself Dr Russo in the mirror at my sixteenth?'

'No!' she says. Then, 'Yes. I scarred the poor Patels for life.'

'More like eternity.'

They break into laughter again.

Afterwards, they fall into silence until Zoë says in a quiet voice, 'P, I still can't believe I didn't get into Number One.'

'I know,' Prakash says, his arm folding around her shoulders. 'Me either. I know how badly you wanted it. Wanna talk?'

'And say what? It is what it is.'

They fall into silence again and watch the sun weave a tapestry of bright oranges and pinks across the sky.

Prakash breaks first. 'Well, one thing I *could* say is I'm convinced things will work out, even if it's not the way you expect.'

'I hope so,' Zoë says with a small smile. 'Still waiting to hear on Number Two. My last shot.'

'Nah, there are so many pathways, Zo. If you don't get the answer you want, there'll be another way.' His mouth breaks into a smirk. 'And worst-case scenario: we concoct an evil plan to smuggle you into a medical degree. You've already got the bad girl rep after your night in a cell.'

'Shut up,' she says, elbowing him.

'Here's my theory: some slick producer will make a movie about you, the famous doctor — and me, because I'll be the best-mate sidekick, of course. There'll be a big premiere and you'll take me as your plus-one, and some agent will see my raw potential, fall in love with my show reel and land me the role of a lifetime in Hollywood.'

Zoë passes him another slice of watermelon. 'You've got it all planned out.'

'I'm flexible,' he says with a wink. 'I'm open to directing a movie too. Oh, that reminds me …' He passes her his phone again. 'I cut together a little montage. It might be a while before we're all together again and turns out Violet going full paparazzi was good for something after all.'

Zoë laughs. 'The police photos better not be in here.'

'Tempting, but I wouldn't do you like that.'

'P?'

'Yeah?'

'This is all I wanted: my favourites, a hammock, a sunrise,' she says, gesturing to the sky blossoming with reds and pinks.

'Instead you got a sore head, family reunion and, as a bonus, a night in jail.'

'Hey, it was only a few hours. Oh, and don't forget my spill down the slide into the ball pit.'

Prakash grins. 'The lesson here is: be more specific the next time you say you want a week to remember,' he says, tweaking her nose. 'I'm going to miss this, Zo. Hanging with everyone.'

'I've never heard you admit that before.'

She rests her head on his shoulder as he presses play, and together they watch their week fly by in a mish-mash of colourful clips and photos.

Dahlia

Day 7: 7.49am

'I've done something,' Kiko says, pulling a folded piece of paper from her bag and passing it to Dahlia and Florence. 'Look.'

Florence swallows the rest of her pancake and snatches the paper.

Beside her, Dahlia tries to peek over her shoulder. 'What is it?' she asks.

'A revised list of everything we've done for Stevie,' Kiko says. She pulls a baseball cap out of her tote and spins it on her closed fist. 'Things this week, things before. It's a mix of her original list and our humble attempts to make her proud. I felt all inspired after the concert last night and put it together.'

Dahlia snaps off a blade of grass and twirls it around her finger. 'What about skydiving?'

'I did that years ago, remember?' Kiko replies. 'Won that voucher through the school fundraiser. Based on our financial limitations, I vote that it counts.'

'No argument here.' Florence pulls the paper closer. 'Learn the guitar? When did we do that?'

'I play a few chords, badly, and I've had some lessons,' Dahlia offers.

'But none of us have been to Fiji,' Florence adds. 'A trip there was definitely on her original list.'

'Shit, I forgot about Fiji,' Kiko says, rifling through her tote. 'And I don't have a pen to add to the list.'

'We'll remember,' assures Florence.

'She also wanted a tattoo,' Dahlia adds, her voice soft Kiko shudders. 'Needles.'

'Yeah.' Florence grins. 'We've already vetoed doing that.'

There's a long lull as they realise that the list isn't complete.

Then Dahlia clears her throat. 'Maybe we could go on a holiday to Fiji one day?'

'You mean fifty years from now, because that's how long I'll need to save up,' Florence says.

Dahlia laughs. 'Me too.'

'It would be amazing,' Kiko says, shaking her head with a wistful glimmer in her eyes.

'Right?' Dahlia plucks another blade of grass and twists it around the tip of her ring finger, winding it so tight the skin glows red. She stops herself. 'I can't believe this week is nearly over. If I go overseas—'

'When you go overseas,' Florence corrects her.

Dahlia smiles. 'When I go … I'm going to be so far away from you both and I'm scared we'll never see each other again.' She cringes. 'Who slipped me the truth serum on this trip?'

'Of course we'll see you,' Kiko says, placing her baseball cap on Dahlia's head. 'And you can always be honest with us.'

Florence breaks into a warm grin. 'We'll all be seventy years old and rocking bikinis in Fiji, remember?'

'Exactly,' Kiko says. 'You can't get rid of us that easy.'

'Good.' Dahlia laughs. 'Wouldn't want to.'

'There's that truth serum again.'

'No more reveals!' Dahlia says. 'Haven't I admitted enough?'

'This conversation reminds me we can add another thing to the list,' Kiko says. 'Radical honesty. Stevie was obsessed with the concept — no matter the consequences.'

Dahlia winces and pretends to hide beneath the cap. 'Nightmare.'

Kiko smirks. 'Here's some honesty: this week has been perfect.'

'Right,' Dahlia scoffs. 'We got robbed, nearly had a plane crash, my luggage *still* hasn't shown up, I lost Stevie's list—'

'We swam at midnight, kissed on a beach, survived a haunted house, Florence skinny-dipped, you danced on a podium and we met Alotta,' Kiko adds. She holds up her half-eaten pancake. 'Even this terrible overcooked piece of rubber is perfect to me.'

'We have done a lot of stuff,' Dahlia admits.

'That's why Stevie would be proud: she knows how much we hate doing anything that involves getting off our bums,' Florence says. 'Here's my radical honesty:

I have this urge to go for a walk by the water right now because it looks so beautiful. Maybe I don't hate doing stuff as much any more?' She shudders. 'Shit, am I earnest now?'

Dahlia laughs. 'Who *are* you, Florence?'

The girls link arms and, with the sun beating down on their shoulders, walk towards the foamy cobalt waves rolling in to shore.

Dahlia expected to feel contentment when they ticked more items off Stevie's list, but her mood falls flat. Out of instinct, her hand moves to her hair, winding the short pink strands around her fingers. She stares at the water, biting the inside of her cheek and feeling a year's worth of emotions churn through her. Her sunglasses hide it all.

'I miss her.' Kiko's cracked voice is quiet and small with grief. The paper dangles from her fingers. 'So, so much.'

There are no words that feel enough, so Dahlia laces her fingers through Kiko's.

Florence wipes away tears, staining her white T-shirt with mascara and lipstick. She steps in closer and they fall into a group hug.

Dahlia doesn't know how long they stand like that; a human pretzel of limbs. She gives the others an extra tight hug, then gently peels back, making sure they're all still connected.

'I don't think we'll ever stop missing her,' she whispers. 'I watch these videos of us sometimes and think why wouldn't we miss her? Stevie was wonderful.'

Florence sniffs. 'I bet there are people who met her once, had a whirlwind time, never caught her last name, don't even know what's happened, who *still* talk about her.'

'Exactly,' Dahlia says, her fingertips grazing the fine gold chain around her neck. 'She's the most missable person.'

Kiko nods. 'Trying to stop myself missing her makes it so much harder, like I'm fighting the most natural thing.'

'It's impossible,' Florence says, rubbing at the red and black smears on her T-shirt.

'So maybe we don't try to stop ourselves missing her?' Dahlia continues. 'It makes sense that we miss her.'

'It's a feeling that's here,' Kiko says, closed fist to her chest. 'Always.'

'It is.' Dahlia squeezes both the girls' hands. 'And I know I've been struggling this week — well, this year — but she was all of ours. I've been so lost in my own stuff I couldn't see past myself.' Her eyes fill with tears. 'I'm sorry I haven't been there for you too.'

Florence wraps an arm around her. 'Hey, you're missing a little part of your heart, like the rest of us,' she says.

Kiko flashes a weary smile. 'Stevie would love this though.'

'Us pining for her?' Dahlia asks.

'And snotting over our clothes,' Florence adds, tugging at her stained T-shirt.

'No, not that part ... well, maybe.' Kiko chuckles. 'But us all being together on this trip. The laughing, the crying, the dancing, the list. It's how she lived.'

'Stevie gave life her all,' Florence says, before snorting at herself. 'I sound like a soppy card that you buy in a gift shop!'

'It's true though,' Dahlia says. 'Even if she was running at fifty per cent, she was still more alive than most people on earth. If she was here right now ...'

She looks around. The toilet block is in one direction, the shuttle stop is in the other. A shuttle pulls in and a group of people wearing feather boas and crowns spill out of it.

'The shuttles are free, right?'

Kiko nods. 'Yeah.'

'Perfect. Any idea where they all go?'

'None,' Florence says.

'Shall we?' Dahlia asks.

'It's not quite skydiving or getting a tattoo, but let's do it,' Kiko says with a smile. 'But first, more free pancakes.'

Samira

Day 7: 8.11am

Time can't be stretched out any further so Samira says her goodbyes to the Peachies. Harry pecks her on the cheek and slips a handful of Alotta Peach confetti strips into her luggage. She and Kris share a misjudged hug that almost ends with a broken nose, then he insists she keep the red wig.

Tilly smiles a big bright smile, then hooks her arm through Samira's and whisks her across the front yard away from the others.

'Sammy, this has been some kind of magic,' she says.

'So you did place a hex on me,' Samira teases.

'I love my Peachies. We've been best friends forever and we've got another six months of following Alotta around. I couldn't do life without them. But I've never made a good friend besides them, especially not out of nowhere, you know?'

Samira fights back tears. She does know.

'We'll come visit,' Tilly adds. 'I promise.'

Samira has heard those words more times than she can count from the friends at her previous school, who inevitably stopped messaging and drifted back into their own lives. But there's something in the warm, open-hearted way Tilly looks at her that feels different this time.

Her stomach whirls and she dares herself to say it, her voice shaking a little. 'I'd love that. And I'll visit too. Maybe even save up enough money to meet you at an Alotta Peach show.'

'Yes, yes! Who else can I watch old movies in fluffy bathrobes with?'

'And devour fancy three-course meals and talk in front of portaloos with.'

'And eat spontaneous dumplings and hold midnight exorcisms that absolutely, definitely work.' Tilly bites her bottom lip. 'I know you want to finish the trip in your own way before leaving today, but are you sure you want to be alone? I can stalk Alotta in a shopping centre anytime.'

Samira laughs. 'And I'm sure you will. Thanks, but I need to do this final part by myself. Sounds weird, I know.'

'I like weird.'

She smiles at the familiar words. 'Me too.' She pulls Tilly in close. 'Last hug.'

'For now.'

Samira winces. 'I hate goodbyes. They suck every time.'

'This isn't a goodbye. It's an "I'll see you soon".'

'Then I'll see you soon. Thanks again for the sword and shield. And for everything.'

'The Warrior needs a sword and shield.' Tilly grins. 'And you deserve everything.'

Zoë

Day 7: 8.20am

The shuttle stop is flooded with people waiting for a free ride. They laze on the grass and pace the footpath running the length of the beach.

'Delays,' a man in a high-vis vest tells Zoë. 'There's a backlog from a jam on the highway. Shouldn't be too long.'

Zoë joins Prakash, Greta and Luca who are stretched out on a patch of lawn not far from the shuttle stop.

'What's up with the wait?' Prakash asks.

'Traffic jam,' Zoë says. 'There'll be one soon.'

'Or I could book us a ride?' Greta suggests.

'Yes!' Luca says as his phone bursts into life. 'Oh, wait up, it's Mum. Better take this.'

'Say hi to Aunty Elena!' Zoë calls out, while the others pull silly faces at him.

Luca shoos them away and wanders off, phone to ear, to stand by a large tree with a craggy trunk etched with love hearts and people's initials.

Zoë's phone buzzes. She looks down. There's an email notification on her home screen.

'It's Number Two,' she says. 'I can't bear to look.' She throws the phone at Prakash, who fumbles to catch it. 'I want to have a relaxed day at the markets.'

'Zo, do it,' he says, holding the phone out to her. 'Not looking won't change anything.'

She refuses to take it. 'It changes everything. Once I know, either way, nothing will feel the same. And if it's a no, I don't know what I'll do.'

'If it's a no, we'll be here with you. Whatever you need.'

'Prakash is right,' Greta says. 'But what if it's a yes?'

Zoë groans. 'Fine! You two look, although you'll probably need a password for the portal.' She buries her face between her knees and pulls her arms around her. 'Tell me when the pain's over.'

There's a long, tense pause but then she hears Greta gasp. She looks up.

'Zo, there isn't a portal ...' Prakash stammers.

'What do you mean?' Zoë's eyes widen. 'It says it in the email?'

Chest pounding, she snatches the phone from him. She only manages to read the first two sentences before her eyes are wet with tears. Her sniffs transform into heaving sobs and she flops back onto the grass, burying her face in the crook of her elbow.

'You okay?' Prakash asks. 'Zo?'

'I ... I don't know what to say,' she gurgles, struggling to catch her breath.

Greta reaches for her hand. 'You read it properly, right?'

'Am I hallucinating?' Zoë asks. Her voice is almost a squeak. 'Is it a dream?'

Prakash breaks into a grin. 'Nope. The doctor is in!' He punches the air, scoops her up into his arms and swings her around. 'You did it!'

'Read it again,' Greta urges.

Zoë exhales, hands shaking, barely feeling connected to her body.

Dear Zoë,

It is with great pleasure that I write to inform you that you have received early acceptance into our faculty of Medicine.

You have been given this opportunity in recognition of your personal and academic achievements.

For more than 125 years, students have entered our institution and left prepared for success in their field.

We attach a booklet with this email for you to review and familiarise yourself with the campus and its many facilities. A welcome package with further details will be mailed out within the next week.

While we encourage you to take your time to consider your options, we do request confirmation of your intent to enrol within fourteen days.

In the meantime, if you have any queries, please don't hesitate to contact us.

We look forward to welcoming you.

With very best wishes,
Margaret R. Wessen
Admissions Committee Director
Faculty of Medicine and Health

Zoë sinks back onto the grass, letting a feeling of calm spread over her.

Moments later, Luca sits down beside her. 'I couldn't get Mum off the phone. It was all "Luca, let me tell you about this potato soup I made", and "Luca, which vacuum cleaner should I buy?" Do you ever draw breath, Elena?'

The others trade looks, trying not to grin.

'It's my hair, isn't it? You bullies rushed me out the door and I didn't get to put gel through it,' Luca says, as they break into laughter. 'What's going on? What did I miss?'

Dahlia

Day 7: 8.35am

Dahlia catches up with Florence, who's pretending to steal a look at the shuttle stop timetable.

'Don't you dare cheat!' Dahlia says with a laugh, clamping her palms over Florence's eyes. 'We have to keep the destination a secret.'

Florence struggles to break free, giggling and breathless, as Kiko steers the girls away from the street.

'Dahlia's right, we need some mystery,' Kiko says, swatting at Florence with a half-eaten pancake. 'It's what—'

'Stevie would do,' Florence adds with a cheeky grin, squealing with laughter as Kiko lunges at her. 'Except the truth is if Stevie was here, she'd blow up at you two for killing my fun.'

'Nah,' Dahlia says, 'she would've wrestled you onto the pavement in five seconds.'

She tries to catch her breath as she looks around. Instead, she gasps. There's a girl with cat-eye glasses being piggybacked around on the grass by a guy with a familiar beaming white smile.

'What's up?' Florence asks, escaping Kiko's grip again.

'Isn't that the girl who fainted?' Dahlia replies, pointing. 'Zoë? It is, I know it is.'

She never thought she'd see Zoë again and wonders if crossing paths here, on this day, means something. She fights the urge to shy away and walks over.

Zoë grins when she recognises her. 'This girl!' she says, clambering off the boy's back and waving at her confused-looking friends. Dahlia notices that Violet, the girl who was with Zoë when she collapsed, isn't there. 'This girl and her friends were amazing to me that night I fainted.'

'It was nothing,' Dahlia says, taking off the baseball cap and gripping it tightly between her palms. 'I ... I'm Dahlia, by the way.'

'Hi. Love the hair.'

Dahlia blushes. 'Thanks. So you're okay now?'

The other girl in Zoë's group steps closer. 'Zo, what is she talking about?'

Zoë rolls her eyes. 'Just a little fall, Greta. It's nothing.'

'Was that the same night you spent in jail?' Greta asks. 'Because it's getting hard to keep up.'

'I'm sorry, *what*?' Florence asks. 'You were in jail?'

'Greta!' Zoë laughs. 'No, I ... well, yes, for a little bit. I'm not proud of it.'

'I think you are, Tiny Sloth,' says another guy. 'Admit it.'

'Not as proud as we are of her getting into Medicine,' says the guy with the bright smile. 'She just found out.'

'Prakash, quiet,' Zoë murmurs, elbowing him in the side.

Dahlia shakes her head, impressed. 'Congratulations!'

'Zoë, I feel like we can add about three new things to our list after meeting you,' Kiko says.

'You don't have a tattoo, do you?' Florence asks. 'Because that would be handy.'

'I had a temporary one if that helps?' Zoë replies with a shrug.

Kiko wrinkles her nose. 'Not quite list-worthy.'

'What *is* this list?' Zoë asks.

'It's a long story, but we had a friend, a truly spectacular friend, and—' Dahlia breaks off as she sees a shuttle bus headed in their direction. 'Hey, look! It's here!'

Everyone rushes into a messy winding line at the stop, but the shuttle drives past. A few people boo when the attendant explains it was full and there'll be another one soon.

Greta groans. 'The last two shuttles were crammed with people too.'

'Looks like time's on our side,' says Zoë, turning to Dahlia. 'Now, tell us about this list.'

Samira

Day 7: 8.59am

Samira's handbag thumps against her hip as she strides towards the shuttle stop, suitcase in tow. The red wig flaps under one armpit, and she holds the plastic sword and shield under the other. She struggles under the weight of it all, trying to catch her breath without losing speed.

She arrives at the stop moments after the shuttle pulls away. She checks the board. There's another in five minutes so she sits on the bench and pulls out her phone.

Tilly has messaged.

Miss you already! xx

There's a group selfie of the Peachies blowing her kisses, standing on the front lawn where she left them. She snaps a quick photo of herself waving and sends it to Tilly, then slips her phone into her handbag.

The next shuttle is packed and loud.

'Just you?' the driver asks.

'And a suitcase.'

He looks over his shoulder. 'Get on,' he grunts, then calls to the passengers. 'Alright, you lot, move towards the back, we've got one more to fit.'

Samira's shoulders hunch over as she shrinks in on herself. 'I'll wait.'

The driver mutters something unintelligible and gestures for her to hop onto the shuttle. Samira obeys, dragging her suitcase and dress-up gear with her, and slides onto the seat upfront that's been cleared.

A girl sitting on the opposite side of the aisle looks over. Strands of butterscotch hair frame her face. 'Nice sword and shield,' she tells Samira without a hint of sarcasm.

'Um, thanks.'

The girl edges closer. 'I have at least eighty-nine questions about this situation.'

A girl in a baseball cap in the seat behind her groans. 'Florence, leave her alone.'

'It's fine, really,' Samira says. 'I wore them to the Alotta Peach concert ... you know, the singer? She's probably not your thing.'

'We know Alotta!' Florence says. 'Dahlia here is basically best friends with her.'

The girl in the baseball cap shakes her head. 'As if.'

Another girl with a blunt black bob sniggers.

'Facts are facts,' Florence says. 'Ooh, is that an Alotta Peach bangle too? I saw them everywhere last night.' She points to Samira's wrist. 'What does yours say?'

'How many questions are we up to now?' Samira jokes, extending her arm. 'It says *Live your way, baby*.'

The girls swap looks.

'That's very Stevie,' Florence says to her friends. She turns back to Samira, her voice lowering to a whisper.

'Hey, you seem cool … Do you … well, do you know where you're going?'

'In life? Not at all.'

Florence cracks up. 'No, I mean … literally,' she splutters.

Dahlia shoots Samira an apologetic smile.

Florence collects herself and adds, 'As in, do you know where this shuttle goes?'

'Oh.' Samira blushes. 'The next stop is one of the beaches, I think, and then it goes to—'

'Florence!' pipes up the girl with the bob. 'We're meant to keep it a secret.'

'Sorry,' Samira says. 'I didn't mean to—'

'It's all good,' Dahlia assures her. 'Florence, we made a deal. Whatever will be …'

'Fine!' Florence moans, before leaning towards Samira again. 'Back to my questions then. Easy one: what's your name?'

'Samira.'

'I'm Florence.' She gestures to the sword and shield. 'So are you off to a fight?'

'With a plastic sword? No.' Samira giggles. 'This is … it's my everyday sword.'

Florence points to the red wig. 'And that is magnificent.' She gasps. 'Wait! Are you one of those Alotta Peach super-fans?'

'A Peachie? Not really. An honorary one maybe. But I know a few.'

Florence's friends pinch her arm to catch her attention, but she wriggles out of their grasp and turns back to Samira. 'You know, I hope you enjoy the place you're going to on this shuttle that you're not allowed to tell me about.' She pauses, grinning. 'And jog my memory — where might that place be?'

'Stop asking!' the girl in the baseball cap says. 'It's for Stevie, remember? She'd want the mystery.'

'I know, I know.'

'Hope you enjoy wherever you end up,' Samira tells Florence, pretending to zip up her lips.

'I usually do.'

Samira smiles at that.

She settles into the corner of her seat, energised after joking with the girls, and takes in the view. Stretches of blue water and sand flash past, strips of restaurants, cafes and nightclubs, the main first-aid tent, a skate park.

Her stomach flips with excitement. *Enjoy the place you're going.*

The Johansen Nature Reserve. The original group ticket she booked isn't until later in the week and the company doesn't offer refunds. So after the Alotta Peach concert the previous night, Samira shuffled around her limited savings and bought herself a single pass to the reserve, followed by a buffet meal with the tour group.

A commotion erupts at the back of the shuttle. A girl with cat-eye glasses stands up, finger jammed on the buzzer, and calls out that she needs to get off. She looks vaguely familiar, but Samira can't place her. She notices the girl's group protesting, and Florence and her friends seem invested too.

'I'll pull up here on the left, but you better make it quick, kid,' the driver calls out, glaring in the rear-view mirror. 'This isn't an official stop.'

'Thank you, thank you, thank you!'

'Zoë, stay with us,' another girl, slightly older, says. 'Please, Zo!'

It couldn't be. Samira sneaks another glance. *Zoë*. The girl who fell down the slide at the foam party.

Samira shakes her head, trying not to laugh out loud at the coincidence. That was the day she saw Zain with the redhead. The day she met Tilly and the Peachies. The day everything changed.

'Greta, stop worrying,' Zoë says. 'I've got to do something and it's my only chance. I'll meet you all at the markets.'

Florence celebrates the discovery of another one of the shuttle stops, while her friends roll their eyes in annoyance.

Greta stands and follows Zoë down the aisle. 'Then I'm coming with you.'

'Fine,' Zoë says, reaching for the overhead rail as she struggles to keep her balance. 'But I'm doing what I need to do, no matter what you say. No drama. Deal?'

'What's happening, Zo?' a boy calls from the back seat. He looks familiar too and Samira wonders if he's the friend from the foam party slide.

'And how long will you be?' another guy asks. 'We're meant to be celebrating your genius self.'

'I'll be as quick as I can,' Zoë says as the shuttle pulls over to the side of the road. 'We'll get an express there afterwards.'

'After *what*?' Greta asks.

'You'll see.' Zoë turns back to the others. 'Love you, Luca! Back soon, P!'

Samira notices Zoë waves goodbye to Florence and her friends too. 'This is me helping you finish your list for Stevie,' she tells them, before jumping off the final step and onto the road.

'What does *that* mean? For Stevie?' Florence asks her friends, who both look a little stunned. She turns and waves through the window. 'Bye, Zoë! Can't wait 'til you're our doctor one day!'

The bus pulls away again and Samira puts on her headphones and props herself against the window. Outside, the flickers of blue water are transforming into the green of the lush mountainside. She gets out her phone and scrolls through her playlists, pursing her lips as she realises how many of them are for other people.

Chilled Vibes (Mat's Faves)
Rashida House Party
Zain Love Songs XOXO
Play This One Tonight — Claire

Other people's interests. Other people's requests. Other people's favourite songs.

She scrolls on, then pauses and scrolls back. Her finger lingers over *Zain Workout Jams*. She deletes it and swipes again. *Songs That Remind Me Of Us* — gone. *Zain Birthday Toonz* — deleted.

She swipes until her music library is empty.

She sits with the feeling for a while, then creates a new playlist: *My Favourite Songs*.

Zoë

Day 7: 9.21am

The backs of Zoë's thighs stick to the chair's torn vinyl and she swipes at a droplet of sweat lingering on her brow. It's impossible to ignore the buzzing sound so she dares to look around the room. An older man is getting song lyrics etched into his bicep.

'Are you of age?' asks the woman with the silver fringe from Zoë's first visit.

She holds up her ID. 'Yes.'

After reuniting with Greta, the early acceptance into Medicine, running into Dahlia again and learning about the Too Late List, and driving past the first-aid tent, it feels right to Zoë to be back here. Only the faintest outline of the temporary tattoo remains on her wrist and she misses its bold, jagged lines. She wants the heartbeat, a tiny reminder of what she wants more than anything in the world, to be permanent.

'Any alcohol in the last twenty-four hours?' asks the tattoo artist.

'None.'

The woman raises an eyebrow. 'In this week?'

Zoë shrugs. 'It's true. I went too hard too early.'

Greta stifles a laugh. 'That's putting it lightly.'

'What about skin sensitivities?' asks the tattoo artist. 'I'll need to disinfect the area.'

'All good. I'm good. Let's do this,' Zoë says, but she can't help wincing as the woman disinfects the skin on the inside of her left wrist. 'That's cold.' She swallows. 'Wait!'

The tattoo artist pulls back.

'This will sound bizarre but I think I need to know your name. This moment feels important and I like details.'

'It's Blair,' the woman says with a grin.

'Okay.' Zoë exhales. '*Blair*. One heartbeat, please.'

Blair turns to Greta. 'Sure you don't want the two-for-one deal? We can fit you in.'

'Not a chance,' Greta says, hopping off the chair to look at the designs on the wall.

'Hey Greta,' Zoë murmurs, holding out her right hand, 'can you come back?'

Her older sister returns to the seat and takes Zoë's hand. 'Of course.'

'My hand's so sweaty.'

Blair places the tiny tattoo stencil on Zoë's left wrist. 'Happy with it?'

Zoë wrinkles her nose. 'Maybe a little closer to my hand?'

Blair shifts it.

'Perfect,' Zoë says. The heartbeat is just for her, and

this way it'll be hidden beneath her bangles, cuffs and watches. 'Thanks.'

'Your design is small so this won't take long,' Blair says, 'but you're going to feel some sensations. Anything from slight stinging, burning, even annoying vibrations to the dragging of a needle across the skin.'

Zoë's stuck on the word *burning*. 'Okay.'

'Some people find it hell on earth, others find it peaceful. But mostly it'll feel like an odd scratching pain.' Blair leans in. 'You ready?'

Zoë squeezes Greta's hand again. She squeezes it back.

'Yep,' she says.

The buzzing and sting of the needle hit simultaneously. Zoë grips Greta's hand tightly, too tightly, as she adjusts to the feeling. The sharp, scratching sting soon settles into a repetitive warm sensation and Zoë relaxes a little. She's too nervous to look down, so she keeps her gaze fixed on Blair.

'And done!' Blair announces just as Zoë's getting used to it.

'Already?' she asks, taking a peek. The skin is reddened, but the tattoo is flawless.

'Aftercare is easy with a tattoo of this size, but it's still important.' Blair passes her a pamphlet. 'It's all in there. Follow the advice and you'll be sweet.'

'Thanks,' Zoë says, watching as Blair wipes down the tattoo with something that stings her nostrils, then places a small bandage over it. 'This is it, right?'

Blair grins. 'Forever and ever. Hang out as long as you want, otherwise you're free to go.'

'Thanks, Blair.'

'You did it, Zo, I can't believe it,' Greta says, stunned.

Zoë leans back in the chair, fingers outlining the bandage. She's traced the heartbeat pattern for days and now it's hers.

While Greta combs through a jewellery stand, Zoë checks her phone. The screen is lit up with notifications from their group chat.

where are you???

Hey losers, anyone seen Zoë and Greta?

Who's Greta??

omg, Akito, keep up

Come soon! P and I have run out of things to talk about

lmao!!

are you back in jail, Zoë?

bet she's in jail again

hahaha

Zoë glances at the bandage on her wrist, then types:

Got a tattoo!

There's a pause. Then the messages flood in.

Yeahhhh and I'm second in line to the throne

did you get it while IN jail?

Violet, where's your tattoo? lol

Akito!

no way this is true

Show us then

Did you really get one?
as if
Ohhhhh and congrats Zo! Luca told us!
Congrats, Dr Russo
Proud of you, doc!!!
I think I need a physical
ew!!
you're my hero
OK BUT ZO DIDN'T DENY BEING IN JAIL
she's def in jail
totally
what did you do this time???!

The banter continues in a flurry of messages that pile up faster than Zoë can read them.

Greta walks over holding two pairs of earrings. One set is silver and plain, the other is sparkly and bright. 'Thoughts?' she asks.

'They're pretty, but you don't even have your ears pierced.'

Greta inspects the sparkly set. 'But what if I did?'

Zoë's jaw drops. 'As in, get them pierced right now? *You*?'

'I was always too chicken, but what am I waiting for?'

'Then you should.' Zoë extends her hand. 'Got a spare one of these for you.'

'Thanks,' she says. 'Zo, this week has turned out to be ...'

'I know.' Zoë smiles. 'To think I almost missed it. Having you here has been ... Well ...'

'Annoying?' Greta asks.

'Incredible.'

Greta blushes. 'Blair didn't inject you with something, did she?'

'I'm as surprised as you. Turns out I really like hanging with you, big sis.'

'The feeling's mutual. Obviously.' Greta wraps her arm around Zoë's shoulders. 'Now call Blair over to pierce my ears before I talk myself out of it,' she adds, already gripping Zoë's hand so hard her nails dig in.

'Does Mrs Pepper's lemon tree need pruning?' Zoë whispers. 'I can whisk you out of here no questions asked and at least my hand will still be in one piece.'

Greta softens her grip. 'No Mrs Pepper needed,' she says. 'I'm ready. I want this.'

'So, just quickly, I realised something good about my Number Two preference,' Zoë says as Blair comes towards them. 'It's only a forty-five-minute drive away from you. We can catch up some weekends, if you want.'

'That's the best news ever,' Greta says with a smile.

'And by the way, everyone thinks I'm in jail so let's maybe go along with that? It'll give the cousins something to talk about.'

Greta breaks into a fit of giggles, setting Zoë off, and they double over with laughter that rings through the tattoo parlour.

Dahlia

Day 7: 10.07am

Dahlia glances across the aisle at Samira. She's still settled against the window with her headphones in and her wig, sword and shield propped next to her. She doesn't budge when most of the passengers pile off at the markets; her fingers continue tapping her thigh to a rhythm only she can hear.

Florence waves at Zoë's friends through the window as the shuttle pulls away. 'I can't believe we'll never know what Zoë did for Stevie,' she groans. 'We should have swapped numbers.'

'It's life though, right?' Kiko replies. 'We can't know everything.'

'And you rarely get closure,' Dahlia adds.

Florence rolls her eyes. 'Stuff that! I want to know where Zoë went. What did she do? I can't live like this.'

The shuttle hums along the road. They've left the beaches behind; instead they're surrounded by towering green trees.

'My guess is Zoë's confessing her love to someone she's known for a day,' Kiko says with a grin. 'Her one true love.'

'No way,' Dahlia says, then laughs. 'Oh! Imagine if she's gone all vigilante and is tracking down the Hostel Bandit for us.'

'Or losing her virginity,' whispers Florence. 'Can you imagine?'

'*Florence*,' Kiko says with a groan.

'I'm kidding! We all know it wasn't on Stevie's Too Late List.' She winks. 'I'd wonder if Zoë's gone jelly-wrestling, but someone on this shuttle's already covered that.'

'Don't forget hot-dog-eating and podium-dancing,' Kiko chimes in.

Dahlia snorts. 'Are you two ever going to let me live that down?'

'All signs point to no, Bubblegum,' Florence says.

'Omigod, are you talking about the dance comp at the beach the other night?' It's Samira. Her headphones hang around her neck.

Dahlia blushes. 'Why?'

'Sorry to interrupt, but was that you up there?'

'Ah yeah, it was!' Florence cheers, whipping off the baseball cap and ruffling Dahlia's hair. 'Our tiny dancer.'

'Guilty,' Dahlia says.

'As charged,' Kiko adds.

'You were amazing!' Samira says with a warm smile. 'I saw it on the news. You were, like, so carefree.'

'It wasn't my most dignified night.'

'She's a legend,' Florence says, pinching Dahlia's cheek. 'Famous now!'

Dahlia rolls her eyes. 'Not this again.'

'I've had a weird week, like a total rollercoaster, and seeing you dance ...' Samira pauses as she presses the buzzer to stop. 'Well, my friend Tilly and I loved it. I saw it on my birthday and—'

'Hey, happy birthday!' says Kiko.

'Thanks.' The shuttle pulls over and Samira slides her suitcase and gear along the seat, then stands and slings her handbag over her shoulder. She gestures out the window to a sign: *Johansen Nature Reserve*. 'Anyway, this is my stop. Guess the secret's out. Horse-riding and ziplining.'

'That's bad-ass.' Florence turns to Kiko. 'Can we?'

Kiko laughs. 'We have twelve dollars! No chance. But it's definitely list-worthy.'

Samira cocks her head to one side. 'What list?'

The driver clears his throat. 'Are you getting off or staying on? We're already running behind schedule.'

'Getting off!' Samira turns to the others. 'Enjoy wherever you end up.'

'Thank you for adding to the list!' Florence says.

'Happy to help.' She gives them a confused smile, then slips on her headphones and gets off the bus, giving the girls a salute through the glass.

Dahlia's foot hits something in the aisle. 'Samira dropped her wig!'

The shuttle door is already shut so she presses her nose to the window and waves the wig around.

'Careful with that thing,' Kiko says, ducking out of the way.

Samira glances up and spots Dahlia with the wig. Her mouth opens in surprise, before she collects herself. 'You keep it!' they hear her shout. 'It's yours!'

Florence stands up in her seat and punches the air. 'Yesssss!' The shuttle driver glares at her in the rear-view mirror. She takes the wig from Dahlia and slips it on. 'I wish she'd left that sword and shield behind too.'

She takes out her phone and snaps a few selfies of herself wearing the wig.

The three of them fall into comfortable silence as the shuttle drives on, stopping at empty stop after empty stop.

'Now what should we do?' Kiko eventually asks. 'Any ideas?'

'This is our last full day here,' Dahlia says. 'Shouldn't it be something incredible?'

'It kind of is already, right?'

As Florence draws swirls with her finger on the window, something catches her eye outside. She kneels on the seat and looks closer.

'What's up?' Dahlia asks.

'You know how earlier in the week I was into those two guys Matt and Seiji—'

'*Mitch* and Seiji?'

'Whatever,' she says, twirling strands of the red wig around her finger. 'Yes, them. They were cute, huh? Although Steve from the mixer was gorgeous and so funny, which made him even hotter. I wonder what he's doing today?'

'Focus, Florence!' Kiko says. 'What's up? Did you see Mitch and Seiji out the window?'

'No, but I *think* we're almost at that theme park.'

'WonderWorld?' Dahlia swears. 'This shuttle must do a full loop. We've been on it for over an hour and we haven't done anything!'

'Well, we did see that girl Zoë,' Kiko offers. 'And thanks to our list for Stevie she's now doing *something* amazing.'

'Something we'll never find out about,' Florence complains, but then gestures to the wig. 'And we got this beauty from Samira, the mysterious girl with the headphones. And Dahlia, you inspired her! Plus, I think we can cross horse-riding and ziplining off our list in her honour.'

'Agree, but what do *we* do now?' Dahlia asks, leaning back in her seat. 'Jump another shuttle? Investigate if there's any last-minute free activities? A beach party?'

'I don't know about you two, but I need a break,' Florence admits, throwing her hands up. 'Living your best life is gruelling. I'm not cut out for it!'

Kiko gives a sheepish smile. 'I could use some downtime. We've done so much.'

Dahlia claps. 'Yes! *Yes!* Let the record state *I* was the last one standing. Me!'

'I'll deny it to my death,' Florence says with a smirk, but she takes off the red wig and places it on Dahlia's head. 'For you, oh worthy one, in lieu of a crown.'

Dahlia straightens it and sticks out her tongue. 'I accept! But I hear your cries for mercy. From now on, nothing but naps and pool time.'

'Keep talking, that's the stuff,' Kiko says, hiding a yawn behind her palm.

Florence nods. 'Our girl Stevie's going to have to be proud of us doing sweet nothing.'

Dahlia laughs. 'Florence, Stevie *is* so proud of you. And Kiko too. I know it.'

Florence murmurs, 'Hope so,' as she straightens the lightning bolt brooch on her tote.

* * *

The girls leave the shuttle back where they started, and wander up a hilltop overlooking the ocean. Trees tower over a park bench with a perfect view.

Florence flops back onto the grass behind the bench and gazes up at the moody grey clouds, while Kiko kicks off her sandals and stretches into downward-dog position beside her.

Dahlia takes the bench and watches the sea, choppy and inky blue. Out of habit, she reaches for her phone. Her fingers trace their usual path and she finds herself looking at an old photo from two and a half years ago, one nobody else has seen.

Stevie is wedged into her childhood cubbyhouse because she wanted a hiding place to try smoking a cigarette. Her knees are bent up to her chin and her head is ducked low to avoid touching the ceiling. She'd convinced her older cousin to hook her up with a packet, and kept it hidden for months until this day. In the photo, there's a stubbed-out, barely touched cigarette on the cubbyhouse floor. Stevie and Dahlia had both hated it, and had walked to the shops immediately afterwards to buy ice-creams to get rid of the taste. Stevie dared Dahlia to take the cigarette home with her as a souvenir, but she'd declined.

Dahlia puts her phone down and stares out at the open sea, lost in its expanse. She suddenly feels like the smallest being in the world.

Moments later, a whale breaks the ocean's surface, its glistening charcoal body seeming suspended as its spout releases a spray of water, air and vapour. As it thunders down into the big deep blue, Dahlia is frozen, too captivated to make a sound.

The whale's mammoth tail resurfaces, fanning out momentarily, before crashing back into the ocean's depths. It doesn't resurface.

Dahlia turns to the others, jaw dropped.

Florence is spread-eagled on the grass, earphones in, humming an Alotta Peach song.

Kiko is in tree pose, eyes closed.

They didn't see it.

Dahlia shakes her head in disbelief. No photo, no evidence, no witnesses. She knows that eventually the memory's edges will fade and she'll wonder if it ever happened at all.

Samira

Day 7: 12.23pm

The horse veers to the right again, ignoring Samira's protests. When she attempts to bring it back to the middle of the track, it stops to chew on some overgrown bushes. Samira digs in her left heel and pulls on the reins. The horse grunts.

Samira swears under her breath; she doesn't remember horse-riding being this frustrating.

She tries again, but the horse lurches deeper into the bushes.

'Help, please!' she shouts. The rest of the tour group have plodded ahead, unaware she's left behind. 'Someone!'

The leader of the group, Peta, hears her call and trots back to Samira's side.

'She's stubborn, our Dot,' Peta says. 'But she's got a heart of gold.' She clicks her tongue and steers Dot onto the path, unfazed when the horse snorts and attempts to pull away. She looks over at Samira. 'Ready to keep moving?'

'Sure,' Samira fibs. 'How much longer until we're at the zipline base?'

'Just around this trail and across the grassland until we're higher up the mountain.'

Samira exhales, imagining her and Dot galloping through a lush green pasture. 'Walk,' she commands the horse and they start along the steep trail.

A few metres in, Dot surges sideways again, burying her face in another bush.

'Peta ...'

'Don't give up, honey.'

Samira uses her heels to steer Dot back to the path. 'We've got this, girl,' she mutters, jaw hardening with determination. 'We're finishing this.'

Once they hit the grassland, Dot picks up the pace. Samira's knuckles whiten on the reins as they pass rows of trees that are dwarfed by the looming mountains. The wind whistles through her long hair as she takes in the sweeping views. Everything feels clearer here. The air. The stretch of cloudy sky. Even her mind. There's a peacefulness. A freedom. She draws in a deep breath, wishing she could bottle the feeling and take it home.

When they arrive at the ziplining base, the others are sitting around waiting, already wearing their harnesses and helmets.

Samira climbs down from Dot, thighs aching, and strokes the horse's face. 'Good girl, Dot,' she whispers. 'You did great.'

Samira drags on her harness and clips on her helmet, wincing as the strap pinches her skin. Her palms are sore from gripping the reins.

She and Peta join the group at the first line of the ziplining course. The cable seems to stretch forever. She squints, trying to glimpse the landing platform at the other end, but it's a speck in the distance.

Her stomach churns as she imagines holding onto the bar, stepping off the platform, flying through the air high above everything. She tells herself to enjoy the sweeping views and don't look down.

She looks down.

Far below she sees trees, grass, dirt and boulders. She never liked the flying fox at the playground, so she wonders why she was so keen to sign up to ziplining. Like everything earlier in the year, it seemed like a brilliant idea at the time.

'This is an easy line to get everyone started,' Peta says without a hint of sarcasm. 'A warm-up.'

Samira swallows and pulls her harness, like the others are doing, to check it's tight enough. In this moment, it seems like the flimsiest safety equipment in the world.

Peta walks over and tugs on Samira's harness, giving her a sharp nod of approval. 'You're good.'

While the others chat, Samira steps closer to the railing. She forces herself to look up and out instead of down. This time, she focuses on the swollen clouds straining across the ashy sky. Her fingers find her bangle and she imagines Tilly and the Peachies hanging out in their courtyard in full costume, Alotta Peach blaring as they reminisce about meeting their hero. She thinks of her mum and Teta waiting for her at home.

She wonders what Anoush and Zain are doing, before realising that she doesn't need to know. She pictures her future, an empty slate, ready to be filled with whatever she wants.

'Who's up first?' Peta's voice cuts through the daydream.

There's a long silence, then Samira's volunteering before she's even grasped the words coming out of her mouth. Yet her feet remain cemented to the platform.

Peta calls her over to test the harness again. 'It's perfectly safe, honey,' she says, one hand on Samira's shoulder. 'There's no way you can fall, so technically you don't even need to hold on.'

'I can't let go!' Samira says. 'Not a chance.'

'It's an option.' Peta winks. 'Enjoy being on top of the world. There's nothing like it. Now, it's time.'

Samira's stomach churns. She keeps her chin up and shuffles forward to the edge of the platform. Her fingers fold around the bar, knuckles whitening.

The rest of the group cheer and clap, urging her on.

Samira takes in the sweeping green mountainside and hint of ocean far away in the distance. Her grip tightens on the bar, then, fighting her natural instincts, she leaps from the platform. A shriek of joy erupts from the depths of her stomach.

Time freezes as she glides above the treetops, her ponytail whipping behind her and her feet dangling below. She leans back, palms burning, mouth stretching into a grin so wide her cheeks hurt.

As she sinks into the harness and flies towards the landing platform, an overpowering pull to do the unthinkable returns. She doesn't fight it.

She takes a deep breath, lets go of the bar and hollers into the wind.

Dahlia

Day 7: 4.21pm

Kiko's and Dahlia's wet skin glistens as they stretch out on their towels by the pool. Kiko sits up, then pulls a small purse from her tote. She places it in front of Dahlia, who's on her stomach, pulling at a loose thread at the corner of her towel.

'What's this?' Dahlia asks, turning the purse over.

'Just look.'

Inside, there's a handful of Polaroid photos.

'From Stevie's camera?' Dahlia asks, heart racing.

Kiko nods. 'My pictures though.'

'I haven't seen you take any. I didn't even realise you'd brought it.'

'I don't like wasting the film, so I save it for special moments. Otherwise it's tucked under my pillow.'

Dahlia holds up the top photo. Florence is sitting on Dahlia's shoulders in the pool. The sun beams brightly in the corner of the picture, the water shimmers, their arms stretch out wide and they're laughing so hard their eyes are clamped shut.

Dahlia giggles. 'We look possessed. Especially me.'

'Look,' Kiko says, pointing, 'Florence still has sauce stains on her shoulder from the plane ride from hell.'

'And I think I was relieved to be alive,' Dahlia says with a wry grin. 'What a start to the week.'

She turns over to the next photo. It's of her. The nape of her neck, the curve of her back, the arch of her body draped in Kiko's sheer white T-shirt as she runs her fingers through wet sand.

She glances at Kiko, who averts her eyes and plays with the zip on the purse. Neither of them say a word.

In the next photo, Kiko and Dahlia are entwined on the couch at the hostel, each reading a book from the free street library on the corner. Dahlia's head rests in Kiko's lap, while Kiko's fingertips run through her pink hair. Florence must have fished the camera out of Kiko's bag and taken the photo when they weren't looking.

Dahlia swallows. 'Kiko, I, um …' Her voice falters and she can't finish the sentence.

'I know. Me too.' Kiko gestures at the photo of them on the couch. 'Would you like to keep it? I mean, only if you want.'

Dahlia sits up, knees pressed to her chest. 'Is that okay?' she asks, shivering a little. 'I do love it.'

'Yes, I'm sure,' Kiko says, wrapping her towel around Dahlia's shoulders. 'Always have been when it comes to you.' She blushes. 'Sorry, cheese alert.'

They laugh.

'It's okay, it's great,' Dahlia says and bites her bottom lip. She wonders if this is how the edge of love feels. 'It's just … everything is nearly over. It's terrifying.'

'Or everything's just beginning,' Kiko says. 'Let's not do goodbyes before we have to. You're going to be the best au pair.'

Dahlia breaks into a smile. 'Debatable. I don't even know if I like kids and I can barely look after myself. Why did I ever think it was a good idea?'

They crack up laughing again.

'Although, I know one thing for sure,' Dahlia adds. 'You're going to tear up the programming world.'

'That's my plan,' Kiko says with a grin.

Dahlia sighs. 'All my shit aside, I want to go overseas. I just wish it wasn't a whole ocean away.'

Another list pops into her head.

5 Things To Say To Kiko If I Wasn't So Scared
I'll miss you
I'll miss you
I'll miss you
I'll miss you
I'll miss you

Dahlia leans closer and brushes their lips together. The words slip out in a whisper. 'I'm going to miss you so much. But let's pretend I didn't say that.'

'As if,' Kiko murmurs, pulling her even closer. 'I'll never forget you said that.'

Soft folk music plays as Dahlia dawdles through the hostel's empty common area, fingertips tracking the edges of the photo in her pocket. She passes the corkboard and notices her newspaper clipping has vanished beneath a pile of outdated flyers for free meditation sessions and guitar tutors. After a quick look around to ensure she's alone, she rips the clipping from the board and folds it around the photo of her and Kiko.

As she walks past reception towards the stairs to their room, someone calls out in a deep voice. Dahlia looks up. A guy with long thin braids is leaning towards her over the front desk.

'You one of the girls in Room 22?' he asks. 'Got some luggage here.'

Dahlia's heart flutters. 'You do?'

The man pulls a red backpack from behind the desk. 'This it?'

She squeals, overcome with relief. 'Thank you!' she says, rushing to collect it. 'Thank you, thank you!'

'Need a hand getting it up the stairs?'

'No, no, I'll be fine,' she says, lugging it into the empty common room.

She sits on a beanbag, lays the backpack flat before her and unzips it. On top is her make-up bag. She opens it. Nestled between lipglosses and mascaras is a Polaroid photo of her and Stevie from Kiko's camera. They're hugging and sporting matching pink overalls.

She turns the photo over to soak in Stevie's scribbled handwriting on the back.

Love you! Sx

Heart racing, Dahlia sets the photo aside with the newspaper clipping and photo of her and Kiko, then continues leafing through the backpack. Her bikinis. Her sundresses. Her sandals. Her books. Her toiletries bag. Her lucky shell. Her pencil case. Her favourite pen. Her journal.

She sinks back into the beanbag, a foot tucked up beneath her, and turns to one of the journal's unmarked pages. Her fingers play with her hair and she nibbles on the end of her pen, before writing four words in bold lettering on the first line.

Do It Now List.

Thank you for reading *Can't Say it Went to Plan*.

If, like Dahlia, you would like some extra support, you can get in touch with one of these wonderful organisations:

Beyond Blue: beyondblue.org.au
headspace: headspace.org.au
Kids Helpline: kidshelpline.com.au
Relationships Australia: relationships.org.au

ACKNOWLEDGMENTS

As always, creating a book takes a village.

A huge thank you to the marvellous HarperCollins dream team: Lisa Berryman, Cristina Cappelluto, Eve Tonelli, Nicola O'Shea, Michelle Weisz, Yvonne Sewankambo, Kady Gray, Pam Dunne, Amy Fox, Holly Ovenden and the HarperCollins Design Studio. Years on and I'm still amazed by your professionalism and passion for stories, design and creativity.

To JT, you've been there from the beginning and this wild ride would be impossible without your support. Living with a writer isn't for the faint-hearted and I'm so grateful to share a life of creativity and storytelling with you.

Darling Sienna, my little outside heart: your imagination, sparkle and affection for books fill me up every day. I love how you see the world.

And to my family, especially my parents and sister, thank you for everything: the pep talks, the cheerleading, the babysitting, the lot of it.

Oh, and how I adore my kindred spirits, whether we're catching up over a tea, a glass of wine or a flurry of messages in the dark. What we share is a kind of magic and I cherish it so much.

Special mention to the people who championed with me and the Australian book community to raise funds for bushfire relief in 2020, especially Lesley-Anne Houghton, Sara Tacey's book club and the real Kate O'Connell, whose generosity and friendship meant the world during a difficult time.

Last but not least, thank you to my beautiful readers for joining me on another adventure. This story is, as always, for you.

Gabrielle Tozer is an award-winning author and freelance writer based in regional New South Wales. She has published six books, including the young adult novels *Remind Me How This Ends*, *Faking It* and *The Intern*, which won the 2015 State Library of Victoria's Gold Inky Award.

Her first picture book, *Peas and Quiet* (illustrated by Sue deGennaro), was published in 2017, as was her young adult short story 'The Feeling From Over Here' (featured in *Begin, End, Begin: A #LoveOzYA Anthology*). Gabrielle's debut children's novel, *Melody Trumpet*, hit shelves in 2019.

Can't Say it Went to Plan is her latest young adult novel, and she is currently working on her next project. Gabrielle loves sharing her passion for storytelling and creativity with readers and aspiring writers, and has appeared at numerous events including the Sydney Writers' Festival, the Somerset Festival of Literature and the Children's Book Council of Australia's national conference.

Say hello: gabrielletozer.com

Also by
GABRIELLE TOZER